Out
OF THE
ASHES

RC BOLDT

DEDICATION

Matty,
You'll never be able to understand how grateful I am to
you for showing me what true love is all about. While I
was definitely no phoenix, you certainly pulled me from
the "ashes".
P.S. I still love you more.

A,
You are—and will always be—my favorite girl in the
whole, wide world. Never change—except for that whole
temper tantrum thing. That, I'm totally okay with being
86'd. Otherwise, you're golden.
I love you "more than the world *and* the universe".

To our fallen warriors and veterans,
May you know your sacrifices are not forgotten nor taken
lightly. You will forever be heroes in our hearts.

PROLOGUE ONE

Initial News Report

"Al Alam News has received reports of explosions in an area known to be an ISIS stronghold in the Helmand Province. These militants have declared they are holding a United States Special Forces officer captive and demand eight hundred million dollars in exchange for him. We have reached out, but US officials have declined to comment."

Six months later

"We at BBC News have just been made aware of some breaking news. In a press release from the United States government, it was confirmed that a Special Forces unit was ambushed in the Helmand Province of Afghanistan, leaving no survivors. US officials are dismissing the reports from ISIS claiming they have a Special Forces officer captive. Families of the fallen have been notified."

One year, ten months, and seven days after capture

"We're interrupting this broadcast for breaking news. The United States government has confirmed reports that a member of the United States Special Forces has been found alive. He was one of five soldiers declared dead when their helicopter was shot down during a mission. The name of the

individual has not been released, but they have confirmed he is now in a hospital at Landstuhl, Germany, due to be transported stateside."

* * *

**Walter Reed National Military Medical Center
Bethesda, Maryland**

Hendy

Two months later

I could hear the voices at the doorway of my hospital room, and while I recognized both, one of them stood out.

One of them caught me off guard.

That same voice elicited anticipation from within me. I'd never gotten serious about any woman, but she was one I thought might have potential, the only one I could see myself getting serious with.

Katie was a nurse I'd met while visiting another SEAL in the hospital, and we had hooked up anytime I returned stateside. For whatever reason, she hadn't been a hit-it-and-quit-it for me, and we'd kept in touch via email and sometimes Skype—whenever I was graced with a decent internet signal on my deployment.

"How is he?"

"He's…doing better." The hesitation was clear from Nurse Ratched's tone. That woman earned her nickname. Her bedside manner was non-existent—not to mention, she could give the Navy medics a run for their money when it came to the "I start an IV by shoving a needle in your arm and then dig around to find a vein" thing.

"They've been working me nonstop, and I just now got a chance to come see him." Katie sounds nervous.

I'd be lying through my teeth if I said I wasn't nervous as shit for her to see me.

"He's been awake for a short time, but he might still be a bit groggy," Nurse Ratched warns. What she doesn't realize—or doesn't care to notice—is the fact I rarely press the button that automatically dispenses pain medication via my PCA pump. After hearing "Pain is just weakness leaving the body" over and over from the start of BUD/S training—Basic Underwater Demolition/SEAL training— and throughout my career as a SEAL, it's engrained in me.

Not to mention, feeling pain means I'm not dead, and I have to admit I'm still shocked I made it out alive.

The tentative footsteps entering the hospital room draw my attention from where a muted *Jeopardy* plays on the television. Katie comes into view; her blond hair pulled back in a clip, she's clad in plain scrubs. Luckily for her, the door to the room is to my right, so she's greeted by the unmarred side of my face.

Unlike the left side. *Much* unlike the left.

Drawing to a stop at the foot of my bed, she offers a gentle smile. "Hey, handsome."

I attempt a slight smile—at least as much of one as I can offer. The scarring and muscle damage in my left cheek creates more of a lopsided grin now. When I turn toward her—allowing her a full view—I see it.

The revulsion.

The horror.

The disappointment.

It's all written there on her face. It's in those widened, hazel eyes.

"So, uh…" she falters, stammering as if we're acquaintances and not two people who've gotten to know one another—intimately, if nothing else. "How are you feeling?" She winces as she realizes how lame her question is.

But I answer just the same. "I've had better days."

Her laughter sounds stilted. "I can imagine." Her eyes dart to the left side of my face before jerking away, as if she's looked directly at the midday sun. Wincing. Painfully.

"It's good to see you, Katie." My tone is far too polite.

She needs to go. I know this, and so does she. Obviously, she was only into me for my looks, and I should've known better. After all, I *was* the manwhore who slept my way through quite a few single women before all this happened.

I never had any complaints—all of them knew the score. A SEAL. A guy who'd deploy to some random part of the world no sane person wants to visit. A guy who chose his country over himself. A guy who killed sometimes as much as he saved.

For those reasons, I was also a guy who didn't do attachments—a fun guy. I'd never slept with a woman who turned into a "bunny boiler" or flipped out on me in some equally psychotic way. We always parted on good terms, amicably, thanks to the charm instilled in me long ago, courtesy of my mother.

But it isn't until this moment that I realize how vain and callous I'd been. Shallow. Because at times like this, people need support—need to be appreciated and loved for more than their looks.

Life is totally giving me a big fat *fuck you* right now.

That much is certain.

"Yeah, it's…great to see you home." She clasps her hands together; her expression so overly bright it's painful. "And doing so well, too." Her energetic tone grates on me.

"Well"—I blow out an exaggerated breath—"I'm actually pretty beat, so I think I'm going to rest."

It's an easy out. I know it, and she knows it. I'm giving her the reprieve she's searching for, so she doesn't have to look at the damage. More specifically, she doesn't have to look at the left side of my face.

Relief washes over her features before she stifles it. She might have been quick but not quick enough.

"Oh, of course." Her words come hastily, almost frantic. "I'll let you rest."

I close my eyes, partly to shut her out. "Take care, Katie." *Goodbye, Katie. Have a nice life.*

"Bye, Hendy," she says softly before her footsteps fade away.

Only then do I open my eyes. Training my gaze on the television, I press the button to increase the volume slightly.

"Who is Rembrandt?" I murmur.

And I continue doing so—rambling off answers and answer attempts—until exhaustion finally overtakes me. All the while, in the back of my mind, it's confirmed; it's a done deal. The damage to my face is far too extensive for anyone to see past it. I was right—I wasn't completely off-base when I first caught sight of my reflection in the mirror.

My face is the sight of horrors, and no one will be able to see past it.

Not even me.

PROLOGUE TWO

Hendy

Two and a half months later

CNN, critics' discussion at "The Round Table":

"First of all, it's absolutely unheard of for them to hold anyone alive. This same group televises beheadings!"

"On top of that, many question how this individual could have mistakenly been presumed and *then* declared dead when, in fact, he was alive, held captive, and tortured by the enemy."

"There were only charred remains."

"That doesn't matter! He was declared dead! Can you imagine what the family members have gone through?"

I flip the channel, turning it back to *Jeopardy*, my favorite game show. It's one of the many things I missed when I was in bumfuck hell.

"What are capillaries?" I murmur beneath my breath.

"What is *The Odyssey*?"

"What is cacao?"

"What is 'When it rains, it pours'?"

By all rights, if I were on the show right now, I should have quite the impressive cache of, well, *cash* to my name.

Life would be fucking sweet if I were on *Jeopardy* and winning.

Instead, I'm laid up in this goddamn hospital bed like a weak ass—a fucked-up version of Frankenstein.

The approaching sound of swishing fabric catches my attention. Turning toward the interruption, I watch as Dr. Emerson enters my room. The lead on my medical team, she's in her mid-forties and quite the looker.

Oh, and happily married.

Yeah, I'd asked. Afghanistan may have taken the lives of some of the best guys I've ever known, but it sure as shit didn't take away my sense of humor—or my horny tendencies. Hell, some days, that's all that gets me through. Not that I'm delusional enough to think any woman would give me the time of day with the way I look now. Before all this, women flocked to me. I sound like a dick saying that, but it's the truth.

Now, though, they run in the opposite direction. There's no shock and awe here; it's just horror.

"How's the pain today, Hendy?" She's one of the few docs who heeds my request and calls me by my nickname.

"Barely feel a thing. More like a paper cut, really."

Her lips quirk as she marks notes on my chart. Likely jotting down something like, *Patient is still a smartass.*

She and I have a code, though. When I say it hurts like a paper cut, she knows what I mean; I'm downplaying it because I hate the pain meds handed out like candy at the hospital. If I'm honest, the pain is often so bad it feels as though a million fire ants are crawling over my skin, eating me alive—creating the sensation that my skin is ablaze—especially in the areas of my skin grafts.

Dr. Emerson swears these sensations are normal and

simply the nerve endings—it's natural. It might be *natural,* but it doesn't make it any less fucking painful.

After developing an infection, I had to undergo hyperbaric oxygen treatment to help increase my blood's circulation and oxygen to assist in the healing process. Finally, after multiple treatments, my skin grafts began to heal properly.

"I need to check your wounds. Specifically"—she nods toward the left side of my face—"this one right here. Want to ensure you're healing as expected to stay on schedule with your release." She offers a kind smile.

Every time it's checked, I wince visibly—inwardly, too—because I'm reminded of just how fucked up my appearance is now. I've been left with such a vivid reminder of my time with those fuckers who tortured me for shits and giggles. Those who would carve my flesh until I didn't feel anything—until I was numb from the pain—only to send someone in to rub salve on my wounds to heal me.

Once a thin layer of new skin covered my wounds, they would begin the torture all over again. Asking the same damn questions—ones I didn't have the answers for, as well as ones I couldn't answer. I still have the occasional dream—nightmare, really—with that shitty interpreter's voice on a loop.

"Tell us about your father."

"Why were you sent here?"

"Who were you trying to find?"

"What did your father tell you?"

Every single time I refused to answer, as we'd been trained to do, I'd internally scream out in frustration. Because my father was dead—he'd died before I was even born—and I had no idea why they kept asking me about him. At my refusal, the torture would escalate.

Dr. Emerson, now examining my back, murmurs, "Looking good."

"Don't forget to check out my back, too," I quip, implying she's checking out my ass. I smirk when I hear her soft snicker. She's also one of the few doctors treating me with a sense of humor.

The super soft cotton pants—donated by one of the foundations started by a former SEAL himself, Heath Mitchum—are a saving grace. He donates modified hospital clothing to combat-wounded patients. They slide around a bit without a firm elastic waistband, but it prevents any irritation on healing wounds, so I'm sure I've flashed Dr. Emerson some crack.

She continues her examination in silence before finishing with a pat on my shoulder. I shift back to a sitting position as Dr. Emerson brings a chair next to my bed and takes a seat. I can tell by the look in her eyes and her sober expression that I'm not going to be a fan of whatever she's about to say.

We've been over this a dozen times. She's worried about me—about my emotional and mental health, as well as my physical recovery.

"We need to discuss your options for continuing your care." Leaning forward slightly, she pleads with her brown eyes. "Please." She pauses, her lips rolling inward before she does it. Puts the nail in the coffin—cuts off all arguments from me.

"Do it for the friends you lost."

CHAPTER ONE

Hendy

Fernandina Beach, Florida
One Month Later

"Dude! You totally double dipped."

I shoot a hard glare at Foster Kavanaugh, one of my best friends. However, right now, I'm grossed out by him sticking his chip in the bowl of homemade salsa—twice.

He smirks like the cocky bastard he is. "What's worse is that you don't know where my mouth's been recently." Popping the salsa-laden chip into his mouth, he crunches, eyeing me smugly.

Darting a glance over into the kitchen, I catch sight of his fiancée, Noelle Davis, and my eyes return to his. "Pretty sure I have an idea." A thought hits me. Raising an eyebrow, I taunt, "Guess I can say that I've had my lips on your woman, now can't I?"

His expression darkens, eyes turning flinty. "Don't even go there."

I shrug. "You're the one who started it." Then, pushing the envelope because, hey, it's what I do, I add nonchalantly,

"Plus, you couldn't really blame her if she chose me over you. I mean look at me." Waving a hand, I gesture to my face and body. "I'm hot as shit." And I'm full of it, too, which Fos and I are both fully aware of.

"Oh, I'm looking at you all right." Foster's tone is low, lethal, and he gives me a death stare.

Grinning manically, I flash my eyes wide at him. "You missed me giving you shit. Admit it, Fos."

Squinting at me dangerously, he mutters, "Not about my woman," before scooping another chip in the salsa.

"Kavanaugh, be nice to your friend," Noelle calls out as she approaches with a platter full of what looks to be slices of mozzarella, prosciutto, and crackers.

"I'm letting him eat our food. That's pretty damn nice," he grumbles, but his eyes have lost that dangerous appearance. They're now heated with affection for the blonde placing the platter on the coffee table before us.

And I don't miss how he tracks her movements, glossing over her ass and lingering there.

When he turns to face me again, he catches me watching him, and I give him a shit-eating grin. I lower my voice but not enough to prevent Noelle from hearing. "Do you always eye fuck the hell out of her when she bends over?"

Before he can respond, Noelle chimes in. "Pretty much." She walks back toward the kitchen, tossing a saucy wink over her shoulder. "And that ain't all he does when I ben—"

"Davis," Foster warns, but his stern tone is at odds with the lightness in his eyes, and the corners of his lips tip up slightly. "Language."

Her laughter trails off as she leaves us in the living room, watching ESPN, and I focus on my friend again.

"She's good for you."

It's like I'm looking at a different version of Foster Kavanaugh. Sure, he's still the same shit-talking, tough, intimidating dude, but something else has replaced the darkness that has always lingered behind his eyes.

Happiness. Contentment. Love.

All because of the blonde in the kitchen.

Never in a million years would I have expected this, and I'm not only glad but relieved he appears to have put his demons to rest and returned to the land of the living.

Tipping his beer to his lips, he takes a swig, his eyes still trained on the two college football teams playing on the large, flat-screen television. "Word is you're trying to find a better doc for pain management."

Unsure of where he's going with this, my answer's brief. "Yep."

"Got someone in mind for you."

"Really?" Since when does Fos have his finger on the pulse of physicians?

His whiskey-colored gaze lands on me. "Raine's been singing the praises of this chiropractor in town. Turns out the doc is also a licensed naturopath, as well."

With the casual mention of Raine, who's married to Mac, a former SEAL buddy of ours, he shifts slightly, propping his left arm along the back of the leather couch. "Could help you get off that toxic shit they prescribe."

We've talked about the nasty meds they've prescribed me—and insist on me taking. I've steered clear of the antidepressants, but when the pain gets to be too much, especially at night when I know I need to rest, I'll admit that I've succumbed and taken one or two of the pain meds on occasion.

I always end up regretting it. Not because I don't feel manly—well, maybe a little—but more so because I hate the way that shit makes me feel. Loopy. Not in complete control. Just…*off*.

Eyeing Fos skeptically, I cock an eyebrow. "And you'd take Raine's recommendation if you were me?"

"Absolutely."

His immediate answer surprises me. I know that Raine is known as a bit of a "witch doctor", of sorts, among my friends. Hell, once when I was back here for a visit and went surfing, I felt the onset of an earache. She put some oil of oregano or some shit in my ear and cured me within a few hours.

It doesn't mean I'm not skeptical about going to this doctor, though. But nothing else has worked, and the VA has agreed to let me see someone outside their network of doctors. I've just been putting that shit off.

"I'll consider it." I uncap my bottle of water, drinking to assuage my thirst. I'm dry-mouthed at the idea of someone new looking me over and seeing my damaged body… watching as their expression morphs into utter repulsion.

"Made you an appointment."

My head jerks around to stare at Foster who merely shrugs.

"Figured you might put it off, so I helped you out." Tipping his head toward the dining room table and gesturing to the thin, stapled stack of papers, he adds, "Got you the new patient info packet to fill out, so you'll be all ready to roll."

"Great," I grumble, wishing I had a beer in my hand instead of this damn bottle of water. But even I know alcohol encourages inflammation, and I need all the extra help I can get at this point.

Tipping the bottle back, I drain it, ready to get another one. Maybe I can pretend it's an ice-cold beer.

"You have an appointment Tuesday morning at nine. Kane will drive you."

My hand clenches the plastic bottle, the loud crinkling sound resonating throughout the house as it's crushed beneath my grip.

Friends. Damn interfering fuckers.

CHAPTER TWO

Presley

B*e a chiropractor*, they said. *It'll be fun*, they promised. Yeah, except for one, tiny side effect when you're adjusting someone's spine.

"Sorry, Presley."

This apology comes from sweet little Mrs. Sommers. The woman's pushing eighty and fit as can be, which she attributes to her love of Pilates and daily prune smoothies.

I'll repeat that for you. Prune smoothies. Every. Morning. So that apology should now be clearer.

"I just don't know where all this gas is coming from," she expresses in surprise. The same way she says it every time she comes in for her weekly adjustment. "Do you really think it might have something to do with my smoothies?" she asks me—again. The way she always does.

Every. Single. Week.

"You're darn tootin.'" I grin, helping her up from the adjusting table.

But I can't be upset with her. She's just too adorable and sweet as pie. Not to mention, she makes these pralines at Christmas that are to die for. So, for that, I overlook her flatulence.

Again.

Being a chiropractor and naturopathic doctor in Fernandina Beach is more than rewarding. I get to help people achieve optimal health, not be as dependent on pharmaceuticals, and when they see the results—feel and look better—that's what makes me the happiest. Helping others.

"See you next week, Mrs. Sommers." I wave as she heads down the hallway to my receptionist waiting to take her payment. As soon as the older woman is out of sight, I grab one of the issues of *Chiropractic Wellness Magazine* and fan it around the room to dissipate the odor.

"Damn prune smoothies," I mutter under my breath before setting the magazine down beside the small computer monitor. I quickly input my notes on the electronic file before heading to the other room to see my next patient.

And I'm not going to lie. I'm praying this next patient hasn't also jumped on the prune smoothie bandwagon.

* * *

Kicking off my shoes as soon as I get in the door of my house, I breathe a sigh of relief and set my small briefcase and keys down on the far corner of my dining room table. The same dining room table my fiancé, Dylan, had been so adamant I purchase because we'd end up "having many large family dinners there."

Fast forward to three years after the purchase of said table.

Clue: Number of large family dinners we've had at this table.

Answer: What is zero?

Padding over the hardwood floors to grab an apple from the fridge, I slide onto a dining room chair and pull out the thick, burgeoning file from my briefcase. Clara, my receptionist, had finished scanning the documents and uploading them to our electronic filing system, but I much prefer the tangible paperwork in my hands. I hadn't made it all the way through Mr. Hendrixson's file today—not only because of its size, but also because it had become so difficult to pore over the contents.

I will soon be responsible for treating a former Navy SEAL. While that might sound kind of thrilling to the average person, the real kicker is this isn't just *any* Navy SEAL. I'll be treating the SEAL pronounced dead along with his fellow men when they went missing after an attack while on a mission in Afghanistan.

Except for the spoiler alert of sorts—he wasn't actually dead. He'd dragged his fellow brothers-in-arms, who had been either critically wounded or killed in the ambush, managing to hide their bodies so they wouldn't be found and mutilated to celebrate and broadcast on their own terrorist version of YouTube. He'd managed to evade the enemy for days before finally being captured.

But that's not the worst part. He was held captive and tortured for over a year.

While I know for a fact these documents don't contain everything that happened to Cristiano Hendrixson, or "Hendy," as is deemed his nickname, due to confidentiality and classification of top-secret information, what's in this file is enough to make even the most callous-hearted person sit up and take notice.

On top of that, the VA is killing me. *Killing*. Me. And not softly or with a ballad, like The Fugees' song. Nope.

With our new president completing such an intense overhaul of the Veteran's Administration and subsequent care, things have changed, and our government's health-care system designed for veterans is passing the buck in an attempt to "get the job done." Those under the VA's care who are not responding to their current treatment are now eligible for referrals outside their network of doctors... with Uncle Sam readily footing the bill.

This is how Cristiano Hendrixson's care has fallen into my hands. I'll treat him for the next six months, at which time I'll be required to submit a full assessment to the VA—including all physical, emotional, and psychological aspects.

When I finish reading through my new patient's file, I find myself sitting, dazed, staring down at the photocopied picture of his military ID. My index finger traces over his face, my heart aching for this man I've yet to meet, aching for all he's been through and the extent of the injuries he's sustained.

The documents show that the majority of his doctors never thought "outside the box," not to mention the obvious lack of concern for their patient. He hasn't experienced much relief with his back, and my fingers itch to get my hands on him. I would bet all my savings his spine resembles that of a coiled snake and is completely unaligned, which could lead to much of the pain he's been experiencing.

"Cristiano Hendrixson..." I find myself murmuring his name under my breath, my eyes still trained on his identification photo. "I'm going to do everything I can to get you back to normal," I whisper, tracing a finger over his photo. "I promise you that."

* * *

I pore over his file and X-rays again in my office while I wait for my new patient to arrive. For a Tuesday, it sure as hell has felt more like a Monday. Much of that is because I'm equally anticipating and dreading my meeting with Cristiano Hendrixson.

Anticipating it because I know I can help him. Dreading it because, well, I'm not entirely certain he's truly on board with me treating him. That point was driven home, even more, when Clara informed me that his friend had picked up his new patient paperwork.

And I get it. People usually dismiss me once they discover I'm a chiropractor. When I also disclose I'm a naturopathic doctor, that's when the barely concealed smirks appear.

Most people think I'm a joke, like a witch doctor of sorts. Like I cackle while stirring a boiling cauldron and sprinkling in the hair from a bison or tossing in a rabbit's foot. Granted, my heterochromia—two different colored eyes—freaks some people out right off the bat. But I swear I'm not a witch. If I were, I'd have cast a spell long ago to give me bigger boobs.

Because, you know, that's a top priority when you're a B cup.

Hell, even my parents think I'm a bit of a witch doctor. Having two successful cardiologists as parents, I'm certain the moment I told them I wanted to go to medical school and then a chiropractic college, they experienced some crazy arrhythmia and thought they were about to stroke out from the news. Either way, to say they weren't pleased is an understatement.

"Are you sure you don't want to practice real medicine, honey?"

That question. I heard that all through medical school, the moment I graduated with my license to practice naturopathy, and even after I finished chiropractic school.

It doesn't matter that I treat two of the most exclusive athletes in the area—the running back and quarterback of the local NFL team in Jacksonville. Sure, we attended the University of Florida together, but they weren't believers in chiropractic treatment until injuries and ailments started lingering.

Those first adjustments I made to their spine made them believers. And now, I'm their go-to chiropractor when they're here. Sure, they've tried to get me to travel with them—and I nearly fainted at the insanely exorbitant amount they offered to pay me—but I'd always wanted to be my own boss and have my own practice locally.

Again, my parents nearly stroked out when they discovered I turned that deal down.

"Clara has your new *pat*ient all set in exam room two."

My head snaps up to find Lucia, my best friend and massage therapist, standing in my office doorway. A smile stretches my friend's lips, her gorgeous, tanned skin glowing as always.

Her Colombian accent is my favorite thing about her, reminding me of the actress, Sofía Vergara. It's still thick and just plain adorable—the way she accents certain words, parts of words, or separates the syllables of words as she speaks.

She's been such a godsend by sharing the rent for this office. She has half of it set up for her massage therapy while the other half is for my practice where I adjust patients and consult with them regarding ways to eliminate their dependency on pharmaceuticals.

"That man," she says in a hushed whisper, darting a quick glance toward the hallway. "His body is like a *jung*le gym I want to climb on."

I shake my head at her reference of Mr. Hendrixson, scooping up his file as I walk over to Lucia. As I'd perused the contents last night, the copy of his standard, no-nonsense military photo ID made it evident he had been one hell of a handsome guy. Now, though, after gaining knowledge of his extensive injuries, I find myself wondering what I will find when I walk into that room.

Lucia doesn't budge from her perch in my doorway. Flashing her an odd look, I ask, "Are you planning to let me see my new patient?"

"I'm serious, *Pres*ley," she hisses. "That man is *im*pressively built." Then, her expression turns uncharacteristically somber and she whispers, "But you need to pre*pare* yourself for his face."

"*Lucia*," I respond in a much more hushed whisper of warning.

She shakes her head. "Trust me, when I tell you *that* man"—she tosses a thumb in the direction of the exam room down the hall—"*still* exudes testosterone and crazy pheromones." Lucia steps aside to let me pass but snags my arm at the last minute, leaning in close.

"Guard your *la*dy parts well with *him*." She punctuates this with a firm nod.

Chuckling softly, I head toward exam room two where Mr. Hendrixson awaits. Knocking softly on the door to announce my arrival, I quickly enter and greet my new patient who is—

Oh, holy shit.

CHAPTER THREE

Hendy

I haven't been waiting long in this room in the chiropractor's office, and I'm already fighting the urge to flee. Like a fucking pansy ass.

"You've got this," I whisper to myself, tugging the brim of my ball cap lower over my eyes. "Maybe she won't totally freak out at the sight of you."

Ha. That's fucking hilarious. Not only am I resorting to whispering to myself like some mental patient, but I'm also delusional as shit.

My eyes take in the space as I sit in one of the available chairs placed against the wall on either side of the room. Of course, I choose the chair which places my left side facing away from the room's entrance.

What I assume to be a chiropractic adjustment table is in the center, and a few feet away is a small desk with a computer atop it and a small desk chair neatly pushed in beneath it. Framed awards and diplomas are on the east-facing wall while the other walls include a display of the entire spine—nerves and muscles affected when misalignment occurs.

I'm here because nothing else has improved the

discomfort in my back. And although I'm no physician, I can assume from the X-rays the receptionist placed on the illuminator that my spine is messed up damn bad. From those views, it resembles the letter S, and even I know that's not a good thing.

The door opens, drawing me from my amateur assessment of my spinal column, and suddenly, I'm face to face with my new doctor.

And I realize how fucked I am.

This woman—she's not at all what I expected. Not for the first time since I've returned "from the dead," I wish like hell I was the old Hendy. Because the old Hendy would've turned on the charm like no other, made her laugh freely, wooed the pants—nice, slim-fitting gray pants that look finer than fine—off her and fucked her so good she'd forget her own name.

And would only remember mine.

Yeah, that would be pretty sweet but no dice. Not now.

She falters as she enters, and for a quick moment, I wonder if maybe she's taken by my looks—at least, the right side of my face. I can still pass as decent looking when someone focuses on that side only.

The other side, however, is a totally different story.

I'm still fit because, at this rate, it's the one thing I've got going for me. And women usually dig the whole tall, dark, and handsome thing. Since I'm well over six feet tall and darker skinned, thanks to my father's Latino ancestry, ladies have always flocked to me.

I should say they had always flocked to me. With an emphasis on had, past tense. Now, though, it's touch and go. With more emphasis on the *go*.

"Hello, Mr. Hendrixson. I'm Dr. Presley Cole, but my

patients normally call me Presley." As soon as she reaches out, I grasp her smaller, petite hand with my larger one, engulfing it in size, and I'm simultaneously blasted with the force of her smile.

The crazy thing is I find myself not wanting to release her hand. Like a fucking creeper.

Jesus. Maybe I really do need to get out of the house more like Dr. Givens, the psychiatrist I've been seeing, has been preaching—er, *telling* me. Because I've never been the guy who holds someone's handshake longer than is socially acceptable.

Great first impression, dude. Just fucking great.

Offering her a smile in return, I force myself to release her hand when her fingers loosen.

And damn if I don't feel bereft afterward; as if her touch alone had made me feel a little less empty and lot more human.

Sweet Jesus. **Clue**: A bellyacher, whiner, sissy, or wimp.

The answer to that would normally be "What is a wuss?" but in this case, the answer is far more specific.

Who is Hendy?

CHAPTER FOUR

Presley

My initial reaction is to look for cameras because I was certainly not expecting this—*him*. I must be getting *Punk'd*. Or I'm being featured in some sort of *Candid Camera* skit because this man is unbelievably alluring—by his looks alone.

His firm, solid muscles are evident beneath the soft, cotton T-shirt, which emphasizes his pectorals and stretches across each of his large biceps. The dark khaki cargo shorts do nothing to hide his muscled thighs. He's tall—I recall his file listing him at six-foot-four. His skin is darker, and based on his first name of Cristiano, I'm assuming he has Latino ancestry.

But the moment he raises his head, drawing his downcast eyes up to meet mine, he sends me reeling. The wariness in his gaze is more than apparent, and I can't help but notice he's chosen the chair that would place his right side toward me instead of the more scarred left.

His ball cap's seen better days. Part of the brim is worn and frayed, and I can tell it isn't because he bought it that way. When his large hand rises, long fingers grasp the brim of his ball cap and pull it down as if he's trying to disguise his face more and not allow me an unencumbered view of his face—and it tugs at my heart.

From what I can see of the short hair at the nape of his neck, it's almost black in color, and his jawline is strong and square with a nose that's far from straight. But that's not what holds my attention. It's his eyes, which remind me of smooth, dark chocolate, that appear to hold so much depth.

I've always believed that eyes are the gateway to the soul, and in this instance, it seems so incredibly true. Because Mr. Hendrixson's eyes hold a myriad of emotions brimming at the surface—pain, anxiety, and…embarrassment.

Mentally shaking off the slight stupor brought on by my new patient, I reach out a hand, greeting him.

"Hello, Mr. Hendrixson. I'm Dr. Presley Cole, but my patients call me Presley." As soon as he reaches out and his large hand grasps mine, I find myself a bit dazed by the force of his smile.

My God, his smile. Lucia would be *Ay, Dios mío*'ing from here to kingdom come if she were here to witness this. It's just…*wow.*

"Nice to meet you." His grin is slightly lopsided yet somehow endearing, the left side of it not lifting as much as the other, likely due to the scar tissue.

Returning his smile, I regretfully release his hand, slide his file onto the desk, and take a seat.

"I've gone over your file, and I figure you'd prefer to cut to the chase since you're here because your recovery wasn't progressing as intended or desired. I see you've been prescribed quite a few different pharmaceuticals. How have they been working for you?"

His stare darts over to take in one of the framed diplomas on the wall. Not meeting my eyes, he says, "They're working well enough, ma'am."

I count to ten silently, bracing my palms on my pant-clad legs. "Mr. Hendrix—"

"Hendy," he interjects, his brown eyes meeting mine before tacking on the ever polite, "ma'am."

"Hendy," I repeat. "Can I be frank with you?"

His lips quirk up at the corners. "I thought you were Presley."

Ah, we've got a joker on our hands, do we? "Nice try deflecting." Pinning him with my stare, I continue. "Let me guess. You're not taking them except for maybe the"—I turn, flipping to the page in his file where I'd marked the list of prescriptions he's currently on—"hydrocodone when the pain gets to be too much and you need rest?"

His lips flatten into a straight line as if he's upset that I called him out. Or maybe it's that he's one of those He-Man types who figures admitting pain shows weakness. Those are the worst.

"Possibly."

That's a yes in my book.

Folding my hands, I offer, "What would you say to me guiding you through the process of weaning you off those medications?" Glancing over, I note his current temperature, height, weight, and blood pressure readings recorded by Clara. "And instead, put you on cleaner, herbal options?"

There's that lip quirk again. "I'd say there wouldn't necessarily be any weaning involved."

"You haven't been taking them at all? None of the antidepressants?"

His jaw clenches slightly. "No, ma'am."

"Would you be opposed to trying some natural, herbal options?"

"I'm not depressed, ma'am."

Baby steps, Presley. Baby steps. "Okay. How about an anti-inflammatory enzyme? No fillers or chemicals and nothing that disrupts your body's chemistry or messes with your brain."

He holds my eyes for a beat before nodding slowly. "I'd be okay with that."

"Good. They're not as toxic overall, especially for your kidneys and liver. Now"—turning to wake up my computer, I move the mouse to log in—"I'm going to ask you to remove your shirt and ball cap for me. Put on the gown and leave it open to the back so I can do the non-invasive thermography scan of your entire spine." Gesturing to his hat, I clarify, "The reason I need you to remove that as well is because I'd also like to feel around to see how out of alignment your upper vertebrae are."

My words are met with silence as I get the program set up. Turning to face him, I notice he appears nervous.

"It's non-invasive," I repeat. "I'll be using this"—I show him the thermal scanner with the rolling wheels which are placed on each side of the vertebra—"along your spine, and it tells me the amount of stress each vertebra is experiencing and what we're dealing with from the start."

I shift attention to his X-rays displayed on the light box, pointing at certain areas. "While you do have a slight curvature here, it's not something I can't work with. It is correctable. And your spine looks good, considering all the impact I'm sure it's endured in such an active career as yours.

"I'll step outside while you remove your shirt—"

Exhaling loudly, he rises from his chair. "That's not necessary. I know I'm not the first guy you've treated nor the first you'll see shirtless but…" He trails off, a heavy cloud of hesitance in his tone. "Well, you'd better brace yourself for the freak show ahead."

After tugging off his ball cap and setting it on the now vacant seat, he reaches for the hem of his T-shirt and quickly removes it, dropping it to join his hat on the chair.

My stomach sinks, lungs feeling as though they're collapsing—as all the air is sucked from the room.

Oh, dear God in heaven.

CHAPTER FIVE

Hendy

The silence is the worst. Without meeting her eyes, I gingerly situate myself on the exam table. Waiting for her to begin, I pray she hurries the fuck up so I can put my shirt and hat back on.

Look at me; I'm a fucking pansy—like Linus with his blanket. Because my shirt and hat serve as my security blanket of sorts. I don't like exposing anyone to my fucked-up body.

"Mr. Hendri—"

"Hendy." My tone is short, and instantly, I feel like an ass. It's not her fault I look like this. "Ma'am."

"Hendy." Her tone is gentle, understanding. "Your file says you don't have any pain in the areas on your back where the wounds have healed, but I want you to tell me if you experience any pain or discomfort. You shouldn't, as I'll be touching each section briefly, but please tell me if you do."

"Yes, ma'am."

She begins, and I hear the faint clicking of the ther-mography scanner as it recordsreadings for each section of my spine. Her voice is comforting as she continues. "So, tell me. How are you really dealing with everything?"

Huffing out a laugh, I twist my lips in a humorless grin. "Honest, no-shit answer?"

"Honest, no-shit answer."

"Some days are decent. Others, not so much."

"Can you tell me what makes the decent days differ from the bad ones? Is there anything outright that makes it different?"

Presley's voice is solid gold. This woman has gone into the right profession because it has a comforting quality and instantly puts me at ease—even when, in this case, I feel the furthest from that.

Blowing out a breath, I subdue my tone, and it's quieter than normal. "I fucking hate my face and back. Hate that I make people cringe in horror. Hell, I can't blame them because it makes *me* cringe in horror.

"Most of all, I hate that I feel the need to wear a ball cap to hide when I go out in public. Because of the stares…the gawking." I pause. "And the questions."

"Questions?"

Blowing out a long breath, I roll my lips inward before answering. "Some people are assholes. They want to know what it was like to be tortured, to be declared dead. Others are different—they mean well—and want to shake my hand and thank me for my service. But I want to be able to go out in public and not have anyone stop me. I want to move past it but…"

"But it's hard when so many things—people—aren't letting you," she finishes softly.

My muscles relax infinitesimally at the understanding in her tone. "Exactly." Then after a pause, I add, "And what you see right now doesn't help."

"I can understand why you hate it because of what it might represent to you. Is that right?"

"Yes, ma'am."

"You don't have to call me ma'am, Hendy. We're going to be working together for the next six months." I hear the smile in her voice before she changes the subject. "Do you enjoy sports?"

"Love playing pretty much any sport. But I enjoy running more than anything."

"But lately, you've been unable to do much of that?"

"I went for a run on the beach one day." My body tenses, recalling the memory. "Not thinking, I took off my shirt because it was getting hot. I tucked it into the waistband of my shorts, and, uh, that was short lived." Trying to play it off, I add, "Guess Halloween came early for some kids on Fernandina Beach."

She falls silent for a moment. "I have a lame chiropractic joke for you."

A smile tugs at the corners of my lips. More and more, I get the feeling that being treated by Presley Cole is going to be like no other experience I've had.

"Okay, hit me."

"What did the chiropractor say to the one guy about to get into a bar brawl?"

Furrowing my brows, I think for a moment but come up empty. "I don't know. What?"

"Don't worry, man. I've got your back."

A small laugh bursts forth at Presley's joke. She's quirky, no doubt about it, but adorable as hell.

Finally, she moves away, taps the computer's keyboard, and then swivels her chair to face me.

"If you'd like to look at this scan with me, I can explain

the readings."

Shifting, I move toward her; she glances my way, and her eyes drift over my chest and down to my abs. I catch the appreciation in her eyes before she quickly wipes her expression clean.

That, right there, is what I relish, what I miss. Women's appreciation of my body. Even if most of me is scarred to hell and back, at least I've still got my chest and abs, which are not nearly as marred with scars as the other areas.

Oh, and my dick. That sucker's still very much intact.

Gazing at her profile while she records something in my file, I note her light brown hair, the subtle blond highlights, her straight nose, and a pair of lips just full enough to have me thinking things I have no business contemplating at a moment like this.

She's slim and fit, but her ass could easily fit in my hands. Totally fuckable. Damn, it's been far too long since I've gotten laid. Longer than ever before. I can almost picture it now. Stripping the sexy doctor of her clothes and shoving her legs apart as I fuck her on that chiropractic table, hearing her moan my name, clenching all around my cock as I thrust dee—

Fuck. Adjusting in my seat while willing my hard-on to deflate, I catch sight of it.

On her left hand, adorning her slim ring finger, is a fucking diamond ring.

She's engaged.

I don't mess with women spoken for in any way. Serious boyfriend, fiancé, or husband means I don't get near them with a ten-foot pole.

Normally, once I realize a woman's taken, I brush it off and don't give it a second thought. But there's something about her, something different about Presley Cole. She's not easily fazed, nor did she shriek in fear and disgust at seeing my house-of-horrors appearance.

I sure as hell hope this dude's good enough for her because I can already tell she's one hell of a class act.

Throughout the first adjustment of my spine—with each exhibit of her quirkiness in the exaggerated fist pumps and exclamations of *"Yesssss"* after only what she deems a good, deep adjustment of my vertebrae—along with the initial supplements she gives me, I find myself doing something I never did before. Something I sure as hell didn't expect.

I find myself looking forward to my next doctor's appointment.

"Apply ice to those areas I mentioned, and if you see a strange number on your caller ID later tonight, it's just me." She smiles up at me as we walk down the hallway to the front desk. "I like to call my patients to check and see how their initial adjustment went."

Grinning down at her, I swear I detect a faint flicker of something in her eyes, but it's gone before I can think more of it. "Does that mean I can call you if I need you, Presley?"

"Noooo, but you can call meeee." Lucia's accented voice is full of flirtation. Smiling up at me, she winks before her eyes dart over my shoulder briefly. "Just don't bring back that big, *bur*ly man with the strange accent, okay?"

"Now, darlin'." Kane steps up, his Southern Texas drawl thicker than ever, sounding amused. "You know you love my accent."

He's come to pick me up and take me home, courtesy of Foster Kavanaugh. That fucker knew he was smart to send someone to escort me to this appointment. To ensure

I would show up.

Not that I'll ever admit to him I likely wouldn't have, had Kane not been assigned to *Hendy babysitting duty.*

Leaning his thick forearms along the counter of the front desk, Kane fixes his megawatt smile on the saucy Colombian massage therapist. "Don't you know that Southern men are sweeter than all the rest?"

Lucia waves a hand dismissively, but I don't miss the way her eyes drift over him in quick appreciation. Kane's built—and that's saying something coming from me since SEALs don't normally like to admit anything about other Special Forces guys. But Kane Windham, a former Green Beret, is built like a brick house—tall, sturdy, and muscular as hell.

He's also damn formidable looking if you don't know him. I have no doubt he's intimidated many a guy—and many terrorists—with his mug, whereas the ladies and his friends are more familiar with his easy smile and copious Southern charm.

"Don't you go trying to sweet talk me, *bud*dy."

I lay a hand on his shoulder. "Well, sounds to me like that's our cue to head on home." Winking at Lucia, I say, "Until next time, ma'am."

My eyes dart over to Presley and I nod. "I'll see you at my next appointment." Taking a moment for her kind, easy smile to settle over me, I turn to exit the office with Kane trailing after me.

Of course, he can't resist getting in the last word. "Adiós, my Colombian beauty!"

As the door falls closed behind us, we can hear Lucia muttering something in Spanish as Kane hits the key fob for his truck to unlock it.

Walking around to the passenger side door, he offers, "Need me to give you a boost, old man?"

Flipping him the bird, I open the door and gingerly seat myself, already feeling some achiness in my back from my adjustment. Presley warned me it would occur as my muscles protested their proper alignment.

"Need help getting buckled in, son?" Kane's aquamarine eyes are alight with humor.

Tugging the seat belt across my chest and securing it, I shoot him a glare, but it lacks contempt. "That's enough. *Son.*"

Shit talking is our forte—it's a common ingredient among all us Special Forces guys. It's how we got through shitty deployments and missions that sucked ass.

"So…" Kane starts, pulling out of the parking lot and onto the road to head back to our place. "You think I have a chance with her?"

Tossing him a sharp look, I furrow my eyebrows. "Hell, no. She's engaged."

And my answer is greeted with silence. Not only is this unusual for Kane, but it also lasts far too long.

And that's when it hits me. *Shit.* Presley's adjustment of my spine must have knocked me for a loop because I normally wouldn't be this off my game.

Kane pulls the truck to a stop in our driveway, turns off the ignition, and directs his gaze to me, fixing that shit-eating grin on me. "I don't recall Lucia being engaged, darlin'."

Fuck me.

Attempting to school my expression and tone, I shrug. "My bad. Thought you meant Presley."

His grin widens. "Uh-huh."

Shifting to exit the truck, I roll my eyes at him. The

worst part is he's my damn roommate, as well.

As we walk up the steps to the beach home on stilts, Kane starts whistling a familiar tune.

Elvis Presley's "Can't Help Falling In Love".

CHAPTER SIX

Presley

Sorry. Can't make it. Too much work.

An audible sigh escapes my lips when I read the text message that just came in, and I set my phone on the bar in disappointment. I was waiting for my fiancé in the local microbrewery pub in the historic downtown area of Fernandina Beach. I've already ordered their raspberry ale waiting on Dylan, so I figure I might as well stay and finish it.

Internally, I scoff. *Nothing's more pathetic than a woman sitting alone at a bar, drinking after her fiancé stands her up.* Nothing.

Before I can get too involved in my pity party, a deep timbre sounds behind me.

"Now, what's a sweet lady like you doing alone in a place like this?"

Turning in surprise, I find my eyes come to rest on a familiar man, ball cap tugged low over his eyes and casting a shadow over his face. Noticing that he's garnering numerous looks from other nearby patrons, I wonder if he's used to this. My heart hurts for him to see people stare at him in such an obvious manner.

On the flip side of that, though, is the rapt attention he's receiving from women, and I can't say I blame them. The man is seriously built, and I think most women would lust over a set of massively broad shoulders like his along with his tapered waist. He's powerful looking with a more-than-impressive physique. Regardless of the scarring on one side of his face, one can't deny the chiseled, square jawline. And those lips of his are nicer than what most men are graced with.

Not to mention, the feeling I get when he watches me with such intensity is… It's both unnerving and thrilling.

And shit. That was terribly inappropriate. *He's my patient—and I'm engaged…to Dylan.*

"Mind if I join you?"

"Help yourself." With a smile, I gesture toward the empty high-top barstools on either side of me. I watch as he chooses the seat beside the wall, placing his back to it while also positioning himself so that his left side won't be exposed to the view of others.

He makes a slight grimace. "One of my 'assignments' is to go out in public at least once a week."

I'm thrilled to hear he's actively trying to assimilate, based on the advice of the therapist he's been seeing. It's critical to his recovery, even if painful.

As he slides onto the stool, his movements are far more fluid than when he'd first come to my office a few weeks ago. When he asks the bartender for a beer, I peer over at him.

"I certainly hope you're limiting yourself to one drink, Mr. Hendri—*Hendy*," I correct myself. My raised eyebrows and telling gaze are meant to remind him of my previous warnings regarding alcohol. As the bartender slides the pint in front of him, I can't help but think about the increased swelling and inhibited healing held in that glass.

He raises his frosty beer glass. "First and only. Scout's honor."

Smirking, I swivel back around to face the bar. "Were you ever a Boy Scout?"

He lets loose a laugh, and the sound of it skates across my skin, warming me. "No, ma'am." Pausing for a beat, he forms his lips into a pout, giving me a look of playful dismay. "You think so poorly of me that you think I'd disregard my doctor's orders and have more than one drink?" Shaking his head, he adds a dramatic, "I'm wounded."

Raising an eyebrow, I tip my head to the side. "Oh, really?"

"Indeed, I am." His smile is wide, and that slightly lopsided effect is far too endearing. "Just for that, I have to insist I keep you company while you wait for…" His eyes focus on me with a sudden intensity that warms me through to my center before darting over my shoulder as if looking for someone. He lets his words trail off, hanging there expectantly for me to finish the sentence for him.

Turning my attention to my beer, I take a sip of the smooth brew, stalling. Stifling a sigh and setting my beer back down in front of me, I focus on it, and my index finger traces a path on the frosty glass. "No one now."

He's silent for so long that I toss a glance at him curiously. I find his attention on his own beverage as if lost in thought.

"My fiancé," I offer, not knowing why I feel compelled to explain, "got held up at work and couldn't make it."

Warm, dark brown eyes find mine. "Well, surely he won't mind me watching out for his beautiful fiancée then."

As if an afterthought, he adds, "Kane got held up unexpect-edly at work, too, so you're in good company."

We fall silent for a moment before I notice Hendy catch the attention of one of the bartenders, whose name tag identifies him as Ryan, just starting his shift.

"Hey, Ryan." He reaches out to shake the young bar-tender's hand. Ryan, at first, appears to falter when he catches sight of the part of Hendy's face beneath the ball cap before reciprocating the handshake with a smile.

"I'm Hendy, and this here is Presley." Ryan nods his hello to me before Hendy goes on, making quick small talk with the young bartender, and I witness the smooth, easy way he distracts Ryan by way of charming him with such a friendly attitude. "You wouldn't mind changing this particular TV"—he motions to the one on the wall above us—"over to *Jeopardy* until the game starts on ESPN, would you?"

Ryan glances around as if to verify patrons aren't visi-bly interested in the show on that particular mounted tele-vision before nodding. Reaching beneath the bar for a re-mote control, he points it at the television, flipping through channels until finding the game show.

"Thanks, man." He nods at Ryan.

Jeopardy. Hendy just asked for the channel to be changed to *Jeopardy*.

My nerd parts are squealing right now. *He asked for Jeopardy!* Because honestly, that's like foreplay for a geek. And Dylan *never* likes to watch it with me.

I can't help but stare—gawk, really—at Hendy. Without turning toward me, he keeps his eyes trained on the television.

As Alex Trebek goes through the brief introductions of

the contestants, he speaks. "You're staring."

"I'm…surprised."

"Why's that?" He tosses a quick glance in my direction.

"*Jeopardy* is my favorite show." Wow. I sound like an idiot. But really, I'm just…stunned.

"What is Dante's *Inferno*?" he murmurs, eyes still glued to the television screen. Then with another quick glance my way, he says, "I'm a fan of trivia." He lifts one shoulder in a half-shrug. "I like random facts." Then, "What is The Stamp Act?"

Mentally shaking off my daze, I steer my eyes toward the screen, and a moment later, Hendy and I both murmur in unison, "What are the Himalayas?"

Darting a glance over at him, I notice his lips tip upward in amusement although his eyes still focus on the show. The lightness in his demeanor is evident, and I allow myself a moment to take in the sight, feeling pride that maybe—just maybe—I had something to do with him feeling better these past two and a half weeks.

"What is *Seabiscuit*?"

Damn. I should've gotten that one.

Jerking my eyes away from the handsome man beside me who I'm discovering is full of surprises, I'm joined by a deep male voice when I answer next.

"What is Zimbabwe?"

* * *

"Then he tried to tell me he was attempting to broaden his horizons by cooking chorizo soup and that it had absolutely *nothing* to do with Lucia."

Hendy breaks off with another one of his deep, husky

33

laughs that are not only infectious but also make me smile wider by default. He's been entertaining me with stories about his friends—mostly Kane since they've become roommates—all while watching the college football game being broadcast tonight.

Now that the game has ended and Ryan slides our bills across the bar top, I'm startled when I check my phone and see how late it is. It dawns on me that Dylan hasn't called or sent a text message—sadly, I'm not surprised.

"You okay?"

Turning to Hendy, I find him watching me in an unnerving way, but there's also concern there.

"I'm good. Just didn't realize how late it was getting." I wince. "Sorry you got stuck babysitting your doctor."

There's a quick flash of something in his eyes—desire maybe—before it's gone, and he offers me an easy grin. "Clue: Spending time with a beautiful, crazy smart woman in a pub on a Thursday."

Tipping my head to the side, I offer, teasingly, "What is a horribly boring night?"

He makes a disappointed sound before leaning in closer, close enough to allow me to admire his long, dark eyelashes beneath the brim of his ball cap and for the scent of his masculine cologne to drift over me.

"Correct answer is: What is one of the most fun nights I've had in far too long?"

CHAPTER SEVEN

Hendy

We both sit frozen, my stare locking onto her lips. They look unimaginably soft, but it's her eyes that continue to mesmerize me. Like she can peer inside, like she notices what I keep locked deep within, that she can—

Rrrrrrrrr!

Jolting from the loud vibration of her cell phone on the lacquered bar top, Presley jerks away. She grabs her phone like it's a lifeline as the screen lights up with the name *Dylan*, signifying an incoming text message.

She scans the message, and I can't help but notice it's a generic text saying good night and he'd talk to her the following day. And a part of me feels a little…jealous.

Shit.

Seriously, man. Get it together. You shouldn't be getting close to another guy's woman.

But I'm not getting close. I'm having a fun conversation with a woman who happens to also be my doctor. A woman who's helped me tremendously in such a short period. A woman who is incredibly smart and beautiful. A woman who doesn't cringe in horror when she looks at me—who doesn't appear to register the presence of my scars. A woman who's a trivia nerd like me.

Damn if that last one doesn't give me some warm fucking fuzzies. I may have been with more than my allotted share of women who had an ass ton of space between the ears, but make no mistake…nothing turns me on more than a woman who's smart as a whip. And yeah, I got a semi during *Jeopardy*, hearing her softly spoken answers each time Alex read a clue. I'm a sicko, I know. But shit, she's got beauty, brains, and not to mention, she's incredibly kind. This Dylan guy had better realize how good he has it.

She reaches for her purse, reacting a split second too late to me slipping money to Ryan to pay our tabs.

"Wait! You can't—"

I cut her off with a look of faux sternness. "You didn't have to humor me and watch the game with me." A college football game that consisted of two small schools, no less, but it served as an excuse to get out of the house for a bit. While I hate having to hide behind my ball cap, it doesn't mean I want to become a damn recluse. "Or share a meal with me."

"It was my pleasure. But at least let me take care of the tip." Opening her wallet, she tries to produce her share.

Before she can pluck any bills from it, I lay my hand over hers.

She doesn't immediately look up to meet my eyes; instead, she appears transfixed by the sight of our hands together, and at the contrast in coloring, my darker, tanned skin to her fairer skin. It's then my mind veers off like the old Hendy.

To the fucking gutter. Because I imagine linking my fingers through hers while I fuck her against the wall, counter, bed—*wherever*—all the while whispering in her ear the *other* naughty things I plan to do to her.

Except she's taken. I need to remember that. And I sure as shit am not delusional enough to think anyone could love someone who looks the way I do. Least of all, someone as beautiful and sweet as Presley Cole.

Mentally shaking off my thoughts and removing my hand from hers, I wink. "Consider it my treat," I add softly, "for putting up with me these past few weeks."

What I get in return is an overly bright smile laced with a tinge of panic. She has such an unnerving way of seeing through me that I hope she didn't see through to my inappropriate thoughts from seconds ago.

"It's been a pleasure, Hendy."

Slipping off the barstool, I wait for her to grab her purse. Presley and I wave at Ryan, thanking him again as we exit and step out into the typical Florida still-humid-as-hell-even-though-it's-evening weather.

"Where are you parked?"

It's dark, and although Fernandina Beach, especially the downtown area, is much like Mayberry where the worst crime that occurs is shoplifting a pack of chewing gum, I need to see her safely to her car. Lord knows I gave my mother more than her share of gray hairs as a hell-raiser back in the day, but there's no denying she raised me to be a gentleman.

"Just over there." Presley gestures to the small parking lot nearby, a mere four yards away from where we stand. She pauses on the sidewalk, appearing nervous, and her eyes flit to me before darting away.

"Thanks again for tonight." I watch as she regains her composure, returning to doctor mode before meeting my gaze. "I'll see you for your adjustment tomorrow." Then she turns to step off the sidewalk, intent on crossing the street.

Without me.

Running a hand down my face with a silent groan, I quickly cross the street, following her. Approaching where she's standing at her car, I call out her name as her vehicle's lights flash twice when she unlocks it with her key fob.

"Presley." Drawing to a stop a foot away from her, I get this strange tightness in my chest at the fact she's leaving me to head home. Stupid as hell, but there's no denying it. There's just something about her.

But she belongs to—is engaged to marry—someone else. *Knock it off, man.*

Yet when she peers up at me with those eyes—one blue and one green—I could get lost in their depths. Reaching for the door handle, I offer a smile and open the car door for her.

"Get in. I want to make sure you leave here safe and sound."

At my words, I see something flicker in her eyes. And I know, at this moment, if she says anything remotely sweet to me right now, there's a good chance it'll send me crossing that line. And I can't have that. I've got a reverse case of Florence Nightingale syndrome. That's got to be it. Which is why I add my next words.

"Gotta get you home safe so you can see your man."

Fuck. It leaves a nasty taste in my mouth to utter that shit. Reminds me of getting the damn desert sand in my mouth when we were out in the middle of nowhere on a mission. That shit makes you want to spit, clean out your damn mouth, and rid yourself of that grittiness.

Her expression is shuttered, smile stiff, and her voice

subdued. "Thanks again."

Closing the door after she's safely inside and buckled up, I offer a quick nod, tugging the brim of my ball cap lower as I turn to make my way to my truck, which is parked along the curb near the bar. I don't look back—no quick glance—because the disappointment that the night has to end makes me feel bad enough.

But of all people, I should know best that all good things must come to an end.

CHAPTER EIGHT

Presley

"You're a sadist in disguise, aren't you?" Hendy groans as I assist him in a stretching technique for his IT band—or iliotibial band, which is connective tissue crucial to stabilizing the knee during running—he's been having some issues with.

"You're the one who decided to push your limits and run on the beach when the sand wasn't packed," I shoot back, slowly pressing his right leg toward his chest and trying my best to ignore his groans.

Trying being the keyword. Because those sounds send prickles of awareness running through my body, encouraging my mind in a direction it shouldn't go—especially when the individual is a patient. It's like I have a little Lucia on each shoulder, instead of a little devil and angel, whispering in her accent, "*I*magine him making those noises in bed. That man will make you *crazy* in the best way."

"I need you to take it easy for the next few days." Giving him a stern look when his lips part, I watch as he clamps them shut. "Otherwise, this will inhibit healing."

"Yes, ma'am." The way he says that simple phrase does something to me. Then he softens his tone. "Answer: Just what the doctor ordered."

Curiously eyeing him, I shake my head, not knowing where he's going with this. He grins wide, and it's smiles like this one—wide, unabashed, and bright—that take my breath.

"What is us catching some lunch later?" Even though it's supposed to be a statement, *Jeopardy*-style, he phrases it as a question.

Needing to put distance between us, I offer an apologetic smile as I move back and head to the computer to update the notes on his file. "You're my patient, mister. And"—I playfully wiggle the fingers of my left hand, trying to keep my tone light—"I'm engaged."

Something shifts in his expression before I turn my attention back to the computer.

"I know this, but your stomach was growling so loudly while you were torturing me a minute ago."

My face heats with embarrassment. "Sorry about that."

He laughs as I finish typing my notes. "Not a problem. Just looking out for your stomach, ma'am. Figure it's the least I can do—offer to bring you a salad from The Circle…"

Moving the mouse to click and save the updated notes on his file, I turn. "You do realize you don't need to feed me in exchange for treatment, right?" Holding his gaze, I continue, "This is my job; it's what I do. I enjoy helping people."

"You wouldn't want me to come back with the gorgonzola walnut salad then?" He gives me a knowing look.

"How do you know that's the salad—"

"That you would order from there?" I nod, and he grins. "Because I pay attention to things that matter." Rising from the table, he heads to the door of the small room. With a hand on the doorknob, he pauses without turning around.

"I'll drop by at eleven thirty when you're ready to close for lunch."

Before I can respond or protest, he's gone, closing the door quietly behind him. Leaving me with his words on replay in my mind.

Because I pay attention to things that matter.

And I refuse to admit the impact those words have on me.

* * *

"Your *de*licious patient is here for you."

I swear, when it comes to Hendy, Lucia's Colombian accent grows even thicker. Turning from my analysis of a thermography scan from a new patient, I see her standing in my office doorway and nearly groan at the look she's giving me.

"He's bringing you lunch *but*"—she glances toward the hallway before lowering her voice with a mischievous look—"you need to *pro*mise to tell me if he gives you more than salad."

"Lucia!" I hiss.

"Promise it's only salad, ladies."

Shit. Covering my face with my hands, I'm mortified to hear Hendy's deep voice, amusement lacing his tone.

Braving a glance toward the doorway, I see him grinning at me while Lucia gives him a full once-over.

"What size shoe do you wear?"

He looks at her oddly. "Twelve, why?"

Lucia gives me one of those "See? Told you so" looks. Luckily, my starving stomach interrupts.

"Let's get you fed." He steps into my office, toting the

bag of food. His body slides into the chair at the small table off to the side of my office while I pointedly ignore Lucia's eyebrow wiggling.

Moving my rolling desk chair toward the table, I let out a long sigh.

"Tough morning?"

"Yes. I have a patient whose insurance company is refusing our request and documentation for additional visits, and this person *really* needs it." Stabbing the lettuce with my fork, I add, "The joys of dealing with health insurance companies," before taking a large bite of my delicious salad. God, this is so freaking good.

Our conversation is easy, flowing flawlessly as we discuss his progress and how much easier and painlessly he's moving physically. He's noticing improvement, and it sends a fierce sense of pride running through me to hear this.

Once we've finished our lunch, I lean back in my chair, folding my hands over my stomach. I've got that feeling after eating something so delicious and filling that I'm food-drunk. Like a stupor of satisfaction. "That was so good." Turning to him, I smile. "Thank you."

"My pleasure." If I didn't know better, I'd swear his voice just dipped an octave to something low and sexy.

"So, tell me honestly," I begin, letting my eyes rest upon him. "How are you adjusting to everything?"

He studies me for a beat before looking away, peering up at one of my framed certifications on the wall. "What exactly are you asking?"

I don't like the fact that he won't look at me—don't want him to feel any ounce of embarrassment with me.

"I'm asking how you're doing with…everything emotionally. I know you're seeing Dr. Givens." This psychiatrist has quite a reputation for helping veterans through their transition to civilian life, especially those who battle PTSD.

Finally, he answers, his tone softer than normal, more pensive.

"I honestly don't know some days...because I have so many nagging questions." Raising his arms, he rests his hands on his ball cap, still staring sightlessly at the wall. "I wonder why? Why they did what they did? Why they kept me for so long—why they kept me alive? None of it makes any sense. Still." He pauses, voice lowering to barely a whisper. "Why did I survive and my guys didn't?" His jaw clenches tightly. "Good men died that night, and I lived. Why?"

Snorting derisively, he moves his hands to toy with the plastic straw in his cup. "I wonder if I'm ever going to meet anyone who's crazy enough to want this." Hendy gestures roughly to himself. "If there's anyone out there who will be able to see past it all."

His dark eyes meet mine, and the pain in the depths spears me. Lips twist up in what I've come to recognize as his trademark lopsided smile. "But obviously, I've been given a second chance, right? And I, of all people, can attest to life being too short to waste."

"Hey." Impulsively reaching out, I grasp his hand, giving it a reassuring squeeze. "Any woman would be lucky to be with you."

His dark brown gaze rests on me, studying me for a moment. "You think so?"

"I know so."

"*Pres*leyyyyy!" We both jump as Lucia's voice breaks the moment. "The *de*liveryman is here."

With a smile, I stand and push my chair over to my

desk area. Lucia knew I was waiting for the delivery of supplements since they'd accidentally messed up our prior order.

"Thanks again for lunch. Oh!" I reach for my desk drawer where my purse is stowed. "I owe you—"

"Presley." The way he says my name stops me in my tracks, and I turn back to him. "It's my treat." His eyes are soft and contemplative. "Clue: Having lunch with my doctor."

Wrinkling my brow, I shake my head.

"What is the best Thursday afternoon I've had yet?"

With a wink, he's gone, leaving me standing in my office, his words wrapping tightly around me like a cocoon. His sentiment slips deep within me with an intensely overwhelming effect.

And a part of me—a far bigger part than I'd like to admit—wishes he didn't have to go.

CHAPTER NINE

Hendy

"Saw you walking out with a bag of food from The Circle at around lunchtime today."

Rolling my eyes, I pad over the hardwood floor into the kitchen where Kane's preparing dinner. "You spying on me now?"

My roommate gives me his trademark grin. "Now, darlin', those are merely my impressive powers of observation."

Opening the fridge, I grab an apple and lean against the end of the counter where Kane's standing.

"What are you making?" Taking a large bite from the apple, I watch him mince some garlic.

"Sudado de pollo." Without looking up, he begins to dice bell peppers.

I can't restrain the grin spreading across my face, especially at the sound of Kane saying the dish's name with his thick Southern accent. At first, when Foster insisted I move to Fernandina Beach and told me he'd found me a place to live—and a roommate, no less—I wasn't sure what to think. But I'd lucked out because Kane Windham is a pretty cool guy.

Not that I'm planning to tell him that or anything.

I note his extreme concentration on his task. "Su-what?"

"It's basically a Colombian-style chicken stew." He finishes chopping the peppers and glances over at me with a sigh. "Go ahead and get it fucking over with."

Taking another bite of the apple, I chew, eyeing him. Swallowing, I mask my expression to be one of innocence. "I wasn't going to say anything."

His piercing blue eyes grow squinty for a moment. Then he nods, redirecting his attention to chopping an onion.

"Am I to assume your famous brownies didn't do the job of wooing her properly?"

Kane's broad shoulders drop slightly, continuing to carefully chop on the large wooden cutting board. "Nope."

"Huh." Kane's famous homemade brownies—for which he has a secret recipe—are damn delicious and totally worth the extra miles I need to tack on my morning run.

With a frustrated sound, he abruptly stops chopping the onions. Pausing to turn his face, he lifts his arm and wipes his tears on his shirtsleeve. "I gave her my damn seafood gumbo, too. And still, nothing." Leaning a hip against the counter, he gazes down at the floor.

"Don't go getting all maudlin on me, buddy. I get the feeling she's a tough nut to crack."

His gaze lifts to meet mine, studying me for a moment. "How are you doing?"

Caught off guard by the sudden change of topic, I don't immediately answer. "With?"

Kane waves his hand toward me. "With you. With everything. With trying to rejoin the ranks of the undead."

Noticing that Kane hasn't used his usual plethora of *darlins* or other terms of endearments that tend to spill from his lips—regardless of whether he's speaking to males or females—unease rolls through me. Because the absence of those terms serves as an alert to the serious tone of the conversation.

I raise an eyebrow. "The undead?"

He matches my expression. "It's accurate, don't you think? For someone declared—"

"I got it," I cut him off, taking a bite of my apple and turning my eyes away.

"Look, man, I get it. It's not like I've known you for long, but I'm also no stranger to seeing and enduring some terrible shit out there. I'm not saying I know exactly what you went through, but I know it took a while to get over what happened to *me*."

Folding his arms across his chest, the strength of his stare is unnerving. "You never go without a shirt or a hat, man. Never. And it's fucking Florida."

Huffing out a laugh, I try to play it off. "What are you saying? You jonesing for my body? My pretty face?"

Kane doesn't even crack a smile. "You need to come to terms with your appearance. Don't be ashamed of that shit, Hendy. Those are fucking battle scars. Trophies. A testament that you endured some crazy shit and lived to tell about it."

Looking away, he stares sightlessly at the oven. "Not everyone can say they came back from the dead." Turning to me again, he keeps his tone firm as if to brook no argument. "You *need* to own it. You rose from the ashes. Like the damn phoenix. Don't get me wrong. I get hiding beneath the ball cap because people can be insensitive as fuck. But this attitude…" He juts out his chin toward me. "This mentality that you're a freak show and have nothing to offer—it isn't healthy."

Eyes narrowing, I clench my jaw so hard it's a wonder I don't crack any molars. "You done?"

Our gazes clash for a long beat. Finally, his lips curve, and he softens his expression into the fun-loving, charming Kane I've come to know. Hooking his thick arm around my shoulders, he tugs me toward him, wrapping me in his arms.

"Bring it in, darlin'. Hug it out."

Jesus. Kane is massive, and if I didn't know better, I'd accuse him of being on steroids, but I know he's on the up-and-up. He works hard to stay in shape and keep his body as well-honed as it was during his days serving as a Green Beret.

I'm not exactly a scrawny guy, but he could easily serve as a taller version of John Cena. I'm a bit taller and leaner but still manage to stay in shape. It's been a bitch, at times, to continue to push myself to maintain a fit physique—especially throughout my recovery.

He hugs me tightly, lightly slapping a hand on my back. I go along with it because Kane's a hugger. Affectionate, fun, lighthearted.

Up until the moment he starts swaying us from side to side and humming, "I've Had The Time Of My Life" from *Dirty Dancing*.

Wrenching from his hold, I glare, but honestly, it's without much heat. "Not cool." I'm not really pissed. Yeah, he might get under my skin, but anyone with an ounce of sense can recognize he's a good person. Genuine. Not that Foster would hire anyone less than legit to work for his security consulting company.

Kane's shit-eating grin is wide. "Aw, darlin', don't be like that." Raising his eyebrows pointedly, he adds, "Not everyone's lucky enough to get me to break out my Swayze on them."

Rolling my eyes, I wave toward the remaining ingredients on the counter. "What can I help you with?"

The mood lightened, we work on preparing the dish—one of us sautéing while the other adds the remainder of the ingredients to a large pot.

But in the back of my mind, his words echo.

You should own it. You rose from the ashes.

CHAPTER TEN

Presley

'm so turned on that I'd swear heat is radiating from my body as his lips trail down my stomach. My surprise is warranted since Dylan *never* does this. He's usually more of a get-right-down-to-business kind of guy. And he's not a big fan of oral sex. Receiving it, yes—giving it, no.

Not to mention, the naughty things he's whispered in the dark silence of my bedroom. He's vocalizing what I've always wanted—words I've always fantasized about him saying. Things I've asked for that he's turned his nose up at and made me feel like a freak of nature for suggesting. Like something was wrong with me for wanting dirty talk.

Right now, however, it's as if he's experienced a complete change of heart; like he knows what I need—and want.

"Your sweet pussy's all mine, Presley."

Those words—let alone combined with the other deliciously wicked words he's been whispering—nearly send me over the edge right from the start. And the way he says my name, it rolls off his tongue sounding sexy, different, unique...*desired*.

His hands push my legs farther apart, lips latching onto my clit while he simultaneously slides one thick finger inside me. My body arches off the bed as pleasure floods through me. My arousal drenches his finger, and when he adds a second, there's no mistaking my soft moan echoing throughout the quiet bedroom.

Whatever brought out this version of Dylan... I hope he never retreats.

As he continues to glide his fingers in and out of me while his tongue and lips toy with my clit, I feel the signs of my fast-approaching orgasm. My hands move down to his head between my spread legs. As my fingers thread through the soft strands of his short hair, finding purchase, I tighten my grasp. His groan reverberates through me, pushing me closer to the edge. When he adds a third finger, pumping inside me and sending me over the precipice, he growls, "Look at me."

The moment I open my eyes, gazing down at him as he sucks my clit hard, still pumping his fingers in and out rapidly, I cry out, my inner walls clenching as my orgasm hits me hard.

I cry out in the dark bedroom, my body moving of its own accord, riding his fingers and coating him with my release. But it's for more than one reason.

I cry out from the pleasure he's given me. Yet within that cry are notes of surprise. Shock. Dismay. Guilt. Embarrassment.

I had an erotic dream—to the extent I orgasmed...by fantasy alone.

Guilt because the eyes I'd looked down into didn't belong to Dylan.

They had belonged to Hendy.

* * *

"Well, now. I must say someone looks *migh*ty satisfied this morning."

Doing my best to ignore Lucia's appraisal as I enter our building, I greet Clara as I pass her on the way to my office.

Setting my items down and placing my purse in my bottom desk drawer, I internally groan when I catch sight of Lucia standing in my doorway. With a sigh, I turn only to find her pressing her hands together in a praying pose, eyes closed.

"Please, Lord Almighty. Tell me that *Dy*lan finally rocked my chica's world. Pleeeeaaaassee."

At my silence, Lucia peeks at me with one eye. "No?"

I don't immediately answer, letting a beat of silence pass first. "No."

Lucia's crestfallen expression would be amusing—if it pertained to a different topic. Her shoulders droop, and disappointment lines her features. "Should have known *bet*ter than to expect a *mir*acle," she mutters under her breath.

"Lucia." There's no mistaking the warning in my tone. Lucia has never been a fan of Dylan's, but she's kept it well under wraps. Lately, however, she's been more vocal.

She tosses up her hands. "Ay, Dios mío! I simply want my friend to have hot sex!"

My eyebrows raise with a pointed look. "Because you, yourself, have hot sex?"

Squinting at me, she purses her lips. "Not. The. Point."

Barely resisting the urge to roll my eyes, I slide past her and set off to check in with my receptionist before we begin to see patients for the day. But before I make it two steps down the hall, Lucia's soft spoken words reach my ears.

"I think something *de*licious happened with you and that *man*."

Her words instantly bring an onslaught of heat to my face, and I'm grateful I'm not facing her. Because I know very well if I were, she'd see everything.

I don't dare dissect what happened; can't face what—*who*—woke me up this morning.

That the man in my bed while my fantasy played out was most certainly not my fiancé.

* * *

"How's the pain?"

I'm desperately avoiding eye contact because I swear the moment my eyes met Hendy's when I entered the adjusting room, I felt as though he knew everything. That he could tell what I had imagined earlier this morning when I was alone in my bedroom.

That he knew I had ridden his fingers—had soaked them with my release.

Oh my God. I need to get it together. *Act professionally, Presley*. But it's no use. It's like my lady parts are raising their hands—if they had hands, that is—and yelling out, "Hollaaaaa!" like the rapper Missy Elliott.

O-kay. Wow. That was just weird. Mentally shaking it off, I plead silently for a do-over for the day. I'm calling mulligan.

"The pain is nearly insignificant." His voice draws me back from my admittedly crazy inner dialogue. I notice his tone has a hint of surprise woven through it as if he hadn't really expected such impressive results.

Which, after everything the man's been through, I can't blame him.

"Great," I say, hearing his movements as he removes his ball cap before placing it in the other vacant chair. While recording notes in his file on the computer, I mentally prepare myself for his adjustment because it will mean touching him, although not at all in the way he "touched" me earlier.

Mentally slapping myself, I clear my throat. Rising from the chair, I move over to where he's sitting on the table.

"Lie face down."

When he makes no move to do so, my eyes dart up from where I'd been focusing on his left shoulder to finally meet his warm, deep brown gaze.

"Any reason you're avoiding looking at me?" His inquiry is soft-spoken, gentle, his eyes questioning.

"No, I—"

"Presley." The way he says my name, the way it rolls off his tongue, jars something from the recesses of my memory. He spoke it in my dream; he said my name in the same manner, in that same deep, dark, seductive tone. I don't think he even realizes how sexy it sounds.

"If something's wrong, if I've made you feel uncomfortable in some way, please tell—"

This time, I interrupt. "No." His eyes focus on me with great intensity. "You haven't done anything at all. I'm having an odd morning and still trying to get past a really…" I falter for a beat, glancing off to the side as I try to find the right words. "Odd dream."

Jesus, I shouldn't have admitted that. Totally unprofessional. But surely, he'll think I'm implying one of those eerily frightening dreams. The ones that don't make sense but are so bizarre they leave you reeling.

As soon as my eyes return to his, I know I'm screwed. Because at that moment, I watch as something flickers in his dark eyes. Intent, heat, and...*desire*. Just as quickly as I catch sight of it, though, it's gone.

And it leaves me feeling conflicted. While I'm grateful he's not calling me out on anything and not making me feel more inappropriate than I already do, part of me feels slightly bereft he didn't say anything.

That part of me—that part needs to take a hike. Because never in a million years have I ever considered cheating. Ever. And I'm not about to start now. Not mentally, emotionally, or physically.

Once Hendy finally lowers himself to lie face down on the table, I let out a tiny sigh of relief that he's decided to let the moment pass. Still, there's something I can't deny.

This tall, charming man who carries around more pain than anyone should have to deal with in a lifetime has awakened something within me.

And that just won't do.

CHAPTER ELEVEN

Hendy

Clue: Other phrases for an erection.

Answer: What is hard-on, full salute, and stiffy?

What is *me*, now that I've realized my doctor—who happens to be smart as hell, sexy, and beautiful—basically told me that she had a hot fucking dream?

About me.

I know women well enough to read them damn accurately. I knew something was up the moment she entered the small room. The way she avoided meeting my gaze. She didn't realize her eyes would dart over me and pause briefly on my crotch. It was brief, but I caught it.

It took every fucking ounce of willpower to ensure I didn't get a hard-on then and there. Undoubtedly, that would have sent things into a tailspin of a shit show. But I knew it when she hesitated over her words and the way her eyes flitted away to avoid meeting my gaze. An *odd dream. Odd* because she'd dreamed of me. Not only that, but she dreamed of me fucking her or something equally as hot, I'm sure. That much was clear by the flush that spread across her cheeks.

I had to remind myself—yet again—that she's taken. She belongs to someone else. I *never* poach on another man's woman.

No matter how much, for the first time ever, I want to. No matter how much of a pull I feel whenever I'm near her.

Once she's adjusted my back and I've turned over for her to work more on my neck, I've managed to get myself under control.

"Have you been keeping up with *Jeopardy*'s Teachers Tournament?" Raising my eyes to meet hers, I find her face upside down. She leans over me a bit to stretch my neck before she swiftly turns my head, realigning the vertebrae while I lie on the table.

"Definitely." Her lips turn up at the corners, and she turns my head to the other side, preparing to make another adjustment. "I'm going to miss tonight's episode, though, which is a bummer."

"Why's that?"

"I have a Chamber of Commerce awards banquet to attend." She finishes adjusting me and backs away as I sit up, sliding off the table to stand.

Reaching for my ball cap, I tug it on, pulling it low. "Banquet, huh? Sounds like a big deal."

Typing in her notes regarding my adjustment, she smiles, facing the computer. "They're naming the winners of the local 'Best of the Best' voted in Fernandina Beach. I'm going to receive the award for best chiropractor." Saving the information, she clicks on something, and the monitor displays the screen saver. Then she turns to face me.

"That's awesome! Congratulations, Presley."

She flushes from my praise, murmuring her thanks before opening the door for us to exit. I'm her final patient for the morning before they close for lunch.

Walking down the hallway, we continue chatting as we make our way to the front desk. "I have to wear a fancy dress and heels, so it's going to be more torturous than anything else. But it's exciting. And an honor."

My eyes take her in, imagining her in a cocktail dress and—

Fuck. I shouldn't imagine her in anything. I have no damn business going there.

"*Pres*ley. I have some bad news for you," Lucia interrupts my self-recriminations. As Presley and I draw to a stop at the front desk, she continues, "*Dy*lan called and said he couldn't make it to the *ban*quet tonight."

Disappointment flickers across Presley's features, and she lets out a long sigh. "Great. That means I have to fly solo."

"Maybe *some*one can help you?" Lucia eyes me expectantly, totally obvious. This woman doesn't have a subtle bone in her body.

"You need a plus one?" I look over at Presley.

Her smile is forced. "No. Thanks, though. It's fine." One slim shoulder lifts. "Dylan might be able to make it after all." Checking the time on her watch, she excuses herself. "I'm going to catch up on some paperwork. See you on Tuesday, Hendy."

"Take care." I watch as she disappears back down the hallway to her office, and a realization hits me. I watched a woman walk away from me—an extremely attractive woman—and didn't check out her ass. Because I'm more concerned about her…feelings.

Shit. I'm suddenly worried about a woman's emotions to the point that I refrain from checking out her firm, luscious ass. Wearily dragging a hand along my jaw, I let out a silent groan, tugging my ball cap lower. Maybe I need to take up knitting and shit, too, while I'm at it because I'm clearly going soft.

"Tormented, eh?" Lucia's voice draws me from my inner turmoil.

My eyes meet hers, and there's no denying the amusement in her gaze. With a short laugh, I shake my head. "You're trouble. You know that, gorgeous?"

Her smile widens. "That's what I'm here for."

Saying goodbye while sliding on my sunglasses, I head out to my truck. As soon as I press the key fob to unlock the doors, I feel it. Something I haven't felt in a long time—not since I was in the damn desert of Afghanistan.

Eyes.

Watching me.

I immediately scan my surroundings once again. The small parking lot for Presley's practice and all the cars belonging to her and her staff—none unaccounted for, nothing out of place. Taking in the wide strip of landscaping separating her business from the small row of shops next door, I still can't pinpoint anything out of the ordinary.

An outdoor patio of the quaint tea shop has a handful of patrons enjoying the sunny weather. My eyes drift along the remaining shops, finding nothing out of place, but something brings my attention back to the tea shop's patio. Nothing but women, ranging from their late twenties to late sixties, are sitting and chatting over tea and sandwiches.

One woman is alone, reading on an e-reader and casually sipping her tea. Nothing stands out about her, aside from the fact she's alone, yet something brings my eyes back to rest on her. She raises her head, and even with the sunglasses covering her eyes, I can feel her gaze, her appraisal, before her attention returns to the device in her hand.

Shaking my head, I mutter to myself derisively, "Shake it off. Just because a woman checked you out doesn't mean anything else."

As I drive home, that lone woman stays in the back of my mind. If my days as a SEAL reinforced one thing, it was trusting my sixth sense.

It was never wrong.

In this case, though, I don't know what the hell to make of it.

CHAPTER TWELVE

Presley

" **B**ut, Dylan, you know how important this is," I protest, sliding the key in the lock to open my front door. My cell phone is pressed against my ear as I enter and lock the door behind me.

"I know, and I'm sorry, but I can't make it because this account is huge and—"

"You've known about this for a while." My tone is sharp, and strains of anger break through. "I told you about it and even had your secretary put it on your calendar as an additional reminder."

He lets out a long sigh as if I'm a small child he's growing impatient with. "It's only an awards banquet, Presley. It's not as if you need me there. And I thought you'd understand since you know I'm trying to make partner so we can have a bigger income and do more for the wedding."

But I don't care about any of that if you're never going to be around!

Tossing my keys on the counter, I attempt a deep, calming breath. "I have to get ready. We'll talk when I see you next." I pause when he doesn't respond. "I love you." My voice sounds far away, tiny, and there's an internal voice screaming at me with doubt, questioning whether that sentiment is true.

"Love you, too. Gotta run." Before I can say anything else, he's disconnected, and I'm left staring down at the cell phone in my hand with one nagging thought running through my mind.

It says volumes when your patient—your sweet, handsome, charming patient—is more excited and congratulatory about your achievement than your own fiancé.

Shaking it off, I head toward my bedroom and connecting bathroom to prepare for the banquet. With the knowledge I would be receiving an award, I'd planned to look my best. Dress to the nines so Dylan was proud to have me on his arm. Maybe even make him pay attention to me again. Things had been different for the past few months. Distant. Sure, I knew he was busting his ass at work, but it didn't mean I didn't miss him. Miss the way we used to be.

I shower quickly and apply more makeup than I've worn in years. Taking extra care with my hair as well, I curl it into loose waves. Carefully pulling on the red cocktail dress I'd purchased especially for the occasion, I falter briefly, wondering if I'll look okay.

And again, I wish Dylan were coming with me. He'd acted like this award wasn't a big deal. But having the entire community vote your business practice as the best—that's huge in my book. Knowing I'd helped that many people and they think so highly of me.

"Get over it, Presley." I stare at myself in the mirror, smoothing down the satiny material of my dress. "At least you get to dress up all girly for once, right?"

I have to admit, I look…*pretty* tonight. The dress's one shoulder strap complements my body and makes my already-mediocre-at-best bust line look larger. The hemline hits just above my knees and accentuates my slim waist. This look certainly contrasts with my everyday appearance at the office.

I pull a small, silver wristlet from the back of my closet and transfer what I need for the evening from my purse when my phone vibrates. Checking to see who has sent me a text message, I sense my heartbeat picking up at the thought of Dylan texting me to say he's on his way. Only for it to plummet when I see Lucia's name.

Still flying solo, chica?

Quickly, I type out a brief affirmative response before tucking my phone inside the wristlet and zipping it up. Sitting on the edge of my bed, I slide my feet into the strappy silver heels I know I'll regret and feel guilty for wearing. I stay on my patients' cases about wearing them—especially daily—educating them about the ill effects on the spine. But tonight is clearly an exception for me.

After fastening the straps, I rise, walking over to my floor-length mirror. The reflection shows me exactly why women wear these torturous shoes. Because they do amazing things for my legs.

Not that I have anyone to impress or to *wow* tonight.

Once I lock the door behind me, I carefully hold the railing and descend the stairs to the driveway, where I slip into my car and buckle up. On the drive over to the resort where the awards banquet's being held, I give myself a pep talk.

"You're a grown woman. You can accept an award by yourself. It's no biggie."

And the entire drive to the resort, I fail at believing anything I say.

CHAPTER THIRTEEN

Hendy

"That was a terrible call!"

Kane protests at one of the mounted televisions displaying a college football game with his team, University of Texas. Roman "Doc" Watts, former SEAL sniper who also works for Foster, sits with Kane and me on the large outdoor patio of Surfside Bar and Grill.

Surfside is one of my favorite restaurants, with an unobstructed view of the Atlantic Ocean directly across the street. That and they have numerous televisions around the perimeter for prime sports watching.

"Thought Fos was joining us?"

My gaze rests on Doc, who grins. His green eyes sparkle as he clearly enjoys offering up the answer. "He had to cancel since he got caught up dress shopping with Noelle."

The hand bringing my beer to my lips pauses as I stare at him. "Say what?"

"Dress shopping, darlin'," Kane chimes in without drawing his attention from the game. "Noelle surprised him by going so far as to schedule him leaving the office early with her to get his help in picking out a wedding dress. Said she didn't want it to turn into an all-day event with the other ladies, and since he had good taste in other things he'd bought her before—"

"Meaning *those* things," Doc interjects with a mischievous grin.

"I somehow can't picture Fos in a dress shop…" Trailing off, I curl my lips into a smile as I imagine my tough, former SEAL buddy helping his fiancée choose a wedding dress.

We all chuckle, but just as my lips part to speak again, the air shifts abruptly and I get that same feeling I had the day I left Presley's office. Like eyes are on me. Tugging at the brim of my ball cap, I catch Doc's gaze and watch as awareness hits the former SEAL sniper. It comforts me that I'm not alone in this feeling.

But it's *also* discomforting to know I'm not the only one to pick up on it.

"You feel it, too?" I ask Doc quietly.

Kane, still watching the college football game, doesn't miss a beat. "You mean the chick with the dark brown hair, sitting alone at the small bar, sipping her drink? Figured she was checking out Hendy and drooling over him as all the women do."

Casually darting a glance over to the smaller bar a few yards away from where we're seated, I catalog the details. Her posture and the way she keeps her sunglasses on even though an awning provides shade to those sitting directly at the bar. The way she doesn't appear to encourage conversation like most others or get the insider info from the locals on the best restaurants and must-see sights are also telling.

She looks similar to the woman I noticed on the patio of the tea shop the day I left Presley's office, but with her large, wide-brimmed woven straw hat and oversized sunglasses, it's difficult to determine if it's the same person.

"I don't get the nefarious vibe, though." Doc's remark draws my attention back to him, his eyes resting on me now. "Do you?"

Shaking my head slowly, I answer, "No, I don't."

"*What*? He broke the plane!" Kane bellows at the television so abruptly it causes a few patrons nearby to turn in alarm.

Doc and I exchange an amused look as Kane realizes his gaffe, flashing an apologetic smile at the four older women. "Sorry to disturb you, lovely ladies, and your meal. I tend to get a little worked up when my team plays."

Of course, Kane's thick, Southern drawl and charming smile immediately smooths things over. This guy is a snake charmer, I swear.

With a smirk, I tap on the keypad of my phone and send Foster a quick text message.

Did you find one yet?

I get a response right away.

Foster: Never realized there were so many different types of wedding dresses.

I can imagine Fos running a hand through his close-cropped hair, overwhelmed by it all.

Foster: She picked one out, though. Simple and perfect like she wanted. And man…

His words trail off, and it's now that I feel that tiny seed of yearning. For that. For that feeling. For that scenario.

For what he's found.

Quickly, I type out a response.

Can't say I'm shocked. Anything Noelle wears looks great on her.

And of course, in typical Foster Kavanaugh fashion, his

response is simple. I can almost hear the smug, prideful tone.

Foster: Damn straight.

"So, what are your thoughts on helping out?" Doc's question draws my attention from the text.

He's asking whether I'm going to help at TriShield Protection, Foster's security consulting firm, while Fos and Noelle elope to the island of Barbados where they'll also spend their honeymoon. Even though everyone's given them grief about it, neither of them wanted much fuss and decided to elope.

"Yeah, darlin'." Kane finally drags his eyes off the TV, only because it's gone to a commercial. "You were the initial investor, after all."

My head whips around to stare at him. "How the hell—"

"Do I know that?" Kane grins smugly. "I may not be a former SEAL, but Green Berets aren't slouches in the intelligence department either, darlin'."

Leaning back in my chair casually, I level a stare at my roommate. "So then you also know that, although I was the initial investor, I also—"

"Got your initial investment back within the first year of TriShield Protection opening for business?" Kane leans back, imitating my posture. "Yep."

Doc lets out a low chuckle, muttering, "The joys that go hand in hand when you work with former Special Ops guys."

"Getting back to the original question." Kane leans his forearms on the table, aquamarine gaze fixed on me. "Are you cool with helping out while Noelle and Fos are away?"

I nod. "I had planned on it."

"I, for one, am wounded I wasn't asked to be in charge."

Kane's lips form a pout as he runs a hand down his broad chest. His accent grows thicker, which means he's about to lay the bullshit on pretty heavy. "This fine, Southern Texan Green Beret could handle that duty blindfolded with my hands tied behind my back."

"But you would've darlin'd everyone to death," Doc and I say in unison before darting a half-surprised glance at one another and then dismiss it with an amused look.

"I'm sure Fos would like to come back and find he still has just as many clients, not less," Doc remarks with a smirk.

"Plus, I'm not asking for a paycheck." I cock an eyebrow at Kane, half-joking.

I'm not asking for a paycheck, even though I know Fos will give me a hard time and try to force me to take the pay. Thanks to wise investments, not to mention my benefits from my medical retirement from the Navy, I'm well-situated financially.

Kane discreetly flips me the bird while lifting his beer to his lips.

My cell phone vibrates, notifying me of another incoming text message. Assuming it's Fos again, I'm surprised to see an unknown number, and it takes me a moment to realize who it's from.

You need to arrive at the Magnolia Ballroom at the Plantation Resort no later than seven IF you don't want her to fly solo for her awards night.

As soon as I finish reading that message, another one comes in, and this one has my lips curving into a smile.

Wear something impressive. And not a ball cap. You need to look muy guapo—handsome.

Lucia. Lovely, meddling Lucia.

Rising from my chair, I toss money down to cover my part.

"Got somewhere to be?" Doc asks.

With a cocky smile spreading across my face, I answer, "Indeed, I do," before I say goodbye.

Walking across the large patio of Surfside, I notice the woman in the hat who'd been sitting at the bar is no longer there, and at the forefront of my mind is the undeniable surge of both excitement and panic running through my veins at the prospect of making an appearance at Presley's award ceremony. Panic for the obvious—having to bare my face and give others an unencumbered view of my scars. Excitement at being the man to swoop in and save Presley's evening and be her plus one.

Hell, maybe I can still be a hero after all.

* * *

This was a bad fucking idea. And the image staring back at me in the bathroom mirror is glaring proof.

Kane's reaction when he gets home drives that point home.

"Wooo-eeee! What do we have here?" Leaning against the doorway of the bathroom, he takes in the sight of me with a grin. "Now darlin', you'd better be prepared to turn many a head looking like that." He waves a hand, encompassing my attire. "Hell, I might even be tempted right now. Feel like getting with another Texas boy, darlin'?"

Rolling my eyes in response, I shove back from the bathroom vanity and step toward him to exit. As he shifts to the side, allowing me to slip past him, his tone sounds forlorn.

"Wait. Does that mean no? Well, hell. The melancholy'll set in like no other."

Roommates. I'll never know how I got stuck with one like this. Damn former Green Beret.

"Have fun and use protection, now," Kane drawls as I gather my keys and wallet. I hesitate when I grab my hat—or "cover," as it's referred to in military terms—knowing it's against regulations to wear my cover inside an establishment...which means I won't have anything to hide behind at the banquet.

Anxiety squeezes my chest like an unforgiving fist, considering the prospect of people recognizing me from all the news frenzy months ago. Of the intrusive questions. But worse than that, their pitying looks when they see my face, close-up.

"Hey." Kane's voice drags me from my conflicted thoughts. Once my eyes meet him, I find him focused intently on me. "You got this, man." His large hand lands on my shoulder in a show of solidarity.

Nodding, I say, "Thanks," before turning and heading toward the door. Just as I'm pulling it closed behind me, I hear Kane mutter, "Go rescue your woman and show her what's what."

During the entire drive to the resort, I ponder Kane's words, and there's no mistaking two things.

The idea of Presley being my woman is far more appealing than I could have ever expected.

And second, I've never wished—yearned—for a woman to be mine.

Until now.

CHAPTER FOURTEEN

Presley

"Dr. Cole! You look stunning this evening!"

Upon entering the ballroom where the awards ceremony is being held, I'm immediately pulled into a gentle embrace by the Chamber of Commerce Chairman's wife.

"Thank you, Mrs. Donnelly. You look gorgeous, as well." And she does. The older woman, whom I'd estimate is in her mid-fifties, is wearing a gold dress that flatters her figure, and her hair is perfectly coifed.

Mrs. Donnelly glances past me before her questioning gaze settles on me, brows slightly furrowed with concern. "Your beau? Is he not coming?"

Great. I'd hoped not to have to address this. But she was the one who dealt with all the RSVPs, so...

Inhaling a fortifying breath, I respond carefully; the sudden hush falling over the crowd of attendees doesn't immediately register. "No, ma'am. He couldn't make it, so I—"

"So I volunteered to attend in his absence."

That voice—that deep, husky voice is familiar. Which means I shouldn't be surprised the moment I turn around to face him. I also shouldn't feel a sense of comfort, of calm, settle over me by his mere presence. Nor should my heart beat wildly.

I shouldn't feel any of that. But I do. Because he came here for *me*. To support *me*.

The moment I take in the sight before me… Oh, wow… I can barely form words to express my thoughts. Because the sight is simply *incredible*.

Hendy's in his white Navy uniform with all his ribbons and medals on display. Hat tucked under his arm, he's standing before me looking so unbelievably handsome. But that's not what makes my chest tighten and my stomach lurch. It's that I detect his anxiety, the way he's unable to hide behind that ball cap like he normally does. That he came here tonight for me, aware of the risk he would be recognized and questioned—with the knowledge he'd be stared at.

Knowing all this, I'm assaulted with emotions. Because he's doing this—sacrificing his comfort—for me and expecting absolutely nothing in return.

"Hendy." I smile up at him, uncaring that my voice is breathier than normal. I attribute that to the extent of his handsomeness. Even adorned with his normal ball cap, he attracts the attention of women. Without it, without any shadowing of his face, even with his scarred left side on display, he's already garnering attention from other women. Yet his focus remains solely on me.

"Ma'am." He gives me a slight nod, with wary hesitance in his features, as if he's afraid I'll turn him away.

When I take one step toward him, he offers me the crook of his elbow. Sliding my arm through it, I smile up at him and lean in close enough for only him to hear.

"Thank you." And I hope with all that I am my tone

conveys how much I appreciate him doing this for me, how heartfelt those words are.

His dark brown eyes shimmer with a unique intensity. "Anytime."

His response isn't particularly unique or special, but he says it as if he's silently tacking on something at the end.

Anytime. *For you.*

* * *

"You are an absolute doll to appear and escort poor little Dr. Cole tonight, Hendy."

If this woman uses that gushy, patronizing tone one more time, I'm going to be hard-pressed not to accidentally-on-purpose spill my drink in her lap. The wife of the Chamber's Treasurer slipped into the chair on my right at the large round table when the seat on the other side of Hendy, who's beside me, was taken by another local business owner.

Not to mention, this wife—whose name I promptly forgot because she didn't even introduce herself—reached in front of me, holding her hand out to announce her name to Hendy. As it is, it's taking every ounce of resistance to keep from giving her a swift palm-shove to the face every time she leans around me to speak to him. And in the process, giving Hendy a view of her ample, surgically enhanced breasts.

God, I sound bitter. Itty bitty titty committee here is apparently having a pity party. Seating for one, of course.

"Oh, but it's Dr. Cole who's the doll. She's the one gracious enough to allow me to accompany her." Hendy shifts his large body, thigh brushing against mine before his fingers give a quick squeeze to my knee hidden beneath the tablecloth. He's trying to comfort me as if to tell me that he knows she's petty.

"Plus"—he turns to me, hand sliding off my knee, and I instantly feel the loss—"it's the least I can do since she's helped me in my recovery."

"Ah, yes. They left you pretty bad off, didn't they?" This comes from the owner of one of the local surf apparel shops, Mr. Semmes, who's sitting beside Hendy.

I tense, knowing this conversation can easily veer into territory that neither Hendy nor I want it to go in, but he handles it with ease, chuckling lightly.

"Clearly, I have more than my share of injuries, but nothing as bad as that poor Camaro you have. How's the work coming along on that, by the way?"

And promptly, the conversation veers to Mr. Semmes and his oft-talked-about classic Camaro he'd recently purchased. He's in the process of restoring it by popping out numerous dents and resurfacing before he repaints it.

The remainder of the evening progresses in the same manner, with Hendy singing my praises and redirecting conversation when it veers too close for comfort, making me feel like I have a "plus one" who wants to be there *with* me and *for* me. Who is proud *of* me.

And the moment my name is called during the awards ceremony, Hendy is the one who stands, offering his hand to help me rise from my seat. Giving it a comforting squeeze, he holds a warmth in his eyes that heats me through and through.

Leaning in quickly, he speaks as his husky voice deepens. "Congratulations, Presley. Knock 'em dead." With a wink, he releases my hand, and as I turn to make my way to the stage at the front of the room, I feel his heated gaze on me the entire time.

Accepting the award and offering my thanks in a brief but heartfelt speech, I can't resist meeting Hendy's gaze across the room. Within those eyes are emotions that make me feel conflicted. Because I've not witnessed these emotions from Dylan in far too long.

Heat. Affection.

But it's the last one, shining so brightly from his eyes and etched upon his handsome face, that causes warmth to spread through me and to make my stomach give that little flip.

Unabashed pride.

* * *

"May I have this dance?"

My eyes jerk from where I had been watching others sway on the dance floor situated in the center of the large ballroom to find Hendy watching me carefully.

"Are you sure you…feel up to it?"

He leans in closer, and that wicked grin sends shivers down my spine. "Why not give the tongues a reason to wag?" He winks and offers with self-deprecating humor, "A true *Beauty and the Beast* scenario, right?"

As if he senses my reprimand when my lips part, he interrupts me.

"Clue: Dance with a beautiful woman who's not only smart as hell but also voted the best chiropractor in Fernandina Beach?"

His *Jeopardy* phrased response brings a smile to my face while I shake my head. "I don't know the answer to that one."

Hendy leans in closer, his voice low and gravelly. "What is what I'd be more than honored to do?"

Rising from his chair, he holds a hand out to me, and I stand, allowing him to lead me to the dance floor. Even with the added height offered by my heels, the top of my head barely reaches his cheek.

His large hand resting at my side, mere inches above my hip, along with his light, easy grasp of my other hand are completely acceptable. Nothing is inappropriate about his touch, yet...I feel as though it's heated and my body is on high alert. The large span of his hand sends warmth radiating through me.

Everything—such intense awareness—that I should not be feeling about anyone aside from Dylan.

"Hey." My eyes fly up to Hendy, finding him watching me, his expression tender. "You okay?"

Nodding, I offer, "I'm fine," before tearing my eyes away, knowing he'll be able to see beneath it.

My gaze is unfocused as we sway, the song coming to an end before the DJ leads into a new one. Chris de Burgh's "Lady in Red."

My hair ruffles slightly from Hendy's chuckle at my temple. "This song is fitting."

Lifting my gaze to his, I see something flash in his eyes. "Really?"

His eyebrows raised, he curves his lips up at the corners. "With the way you look tonight? Hell, yes."

Immediately self-conscious, I glance down at my dress before meeting his gaze again. "You don't think it's too much?"

Hendy doesn't immediately answer as his eyes travel

from my toes all the way up to my hair before blowing out a heavy breath, his gaze focusing on something over my head, his jaw tight.

"Too much? No. To be blunt, it makes it damn difficult to remember you belong to someone else."

Swallowing hard, I let out a tiny breath before speaking, attempting to change the path of the conversation. "Clue: Grateful and proud that you're my plus one tonight."

His gaze flickers over my face, corners of his lips tipping up. "Answer: Who is Presley Cole?"

When I nod, he dips his head, his lips so close to my ear that when he speaks, his hot breath washes over me. "I'll never forget the way you look tonight. My very own, albeit temporary, 'Lady in Red.'"

Hendy doesn't back away for me to see his eyes, to gauge his expression, but stays here, swaying with me until the song ends and transitions to one that's faster paced. Only then do we part to make our way back to the table, and as I walk to my seat, I know one thing with certainty—I'll never forget this night. This night—one which could very well have turned out vastly different but was saved—has transformed into one of the most memorable evenings of my life.

Because of Hendy.

CHAPTER FIFTEEN

Hendy

The way the woman looked at me after we'd rescued her from Somali pirates on a night mission we'd been responsible for—when I'd carried her to the landing zone of the chopper—will never fade. She'd looked at me like I was some invincible, all-powerful hero.

Or my memory of a small Iraqi boy caught in the cross-fire when it was discovered his parents had been offering up intel on ISIS leaders nearby. We'd been sent to enter a small home to do a quick "snatch and grab" of one of the lead militants, and we stumbled upon them as they were about to behead the child. The moment we'd taken the ass-hole out, I'd sheltered the boy from other potential threats in the home until we'd secured the place. When I'd checked him over to ensure he was unharmed, the look on his face had been one of awe.

I'd insisted on opening Presley's car door when the va-let drove up to the resort's entrance, ensuring she was in safely. And I can't lie and say I didn't do my best to memo-rize everything about her before I said goodnight and shut that car door—to ensure I'll remember the way she looked tonight. For years to come.

But not only that, the expression on her face all evening was one that made me feel…normal. Like the old Hendy— the one women lusted over; the face women always wanted to caress and kiss.

Not the face people stared at. Not the face women would rather not touch with a ten-foot pole, let alone their lips.

Presley had looked at me much like that woman and child we'd rescued.

She had looked at me like I was *her* very own hero. But not only that, she looked at me—and treated me—like I was a regular man.

Shutting off the engine of my truck as soon as I pull into the driveway, I subconsciously run a hand down the left side of my face, my fingers grazing over the indentations in the flesh. Blowing out a long breath, I lean my head against the headrest, and my eyes fall closed. I can't help but wonder if I'll find anyone who can accept this version of me.

Someone who will be able to see past the numerous unattractive physical imperfections. Someone who could love the man I am now.

But I'm not sure that's even possible.

Glancing over at the rearview mirror, I find myself fantasizing for a moment at the sight I see—that the left side of my face is the same as the right, with only a few extremely faint scars. That I'm the same Hendy who used to have to turn away admirers. That I'm the same man who had women hanging all over him as soon as we were stateside between deployments. That I'm still the man women would refer to as "handsome" or "hot."

That I'm not a man impossible to love.

CHAPTER SIXTEEN

Presley

Thursday is normally the night Dylan comes over for dinner. It's supposed to be a designated time we both set aside in our busy schedules for each other. It says a lot that he rescheduled it for today—Friday—instead. I can't deny that I find myself questioning a whole hell of a lot about our relationship lately. I can't figure out why the two of us are together when it doesn't feel like we're *together.*

And I'd be lying if I said Hendy doesn't have anything to do with my uncertainty.

Being around Hendy, a man who's been through so much, has reinforced the fact that life is far too brief—that one should be happy. And the fact I haven't felt that fierce pull of attraction to Dylan the way I do when I'm near Hendy seems like a huge, red flag waving warnings at me.

"I want to talk. About us."

I expect Dylan to flash a worried look from where he sits across from me at the dinner table. Instead, with an unconcerned expression, he patiently waits for me to continue.

Folding my hands on the table and ignoring the plate

of food before me, I lean in. "I'm really not sure how to say this, but I…I'm finding myself wondering about things. About us. Why we're together. Why we're…" I trail off, losing a bit of steam, my voice faltering. "Why we're *still* together."

With a sigh that's off-putting and ripe with impatience, Dylan tips his head to the side, eyes growing squinty. "Just spit it out, Presley."

Rising from my chair, I begin to pace back and forth. "We've dated for years. And back then, we met because we had a class together and became friends. Now, though… is *this* all we're ever going to have? Boring dinners? Boring conversations? Boring work functions? Sex that's…" *Boring*. It's unspoken, but he's got to pick up on it. I mean, *come on*.

Pausing my pacing to let my eyes fall on him, I add, "Not to mention the important events you don't even bother to attend." His gaze hardens imperceptibly, but I push on, pacing again. "What I'm trying to say is what if I were to meet someone I felt attracted to? Someone fun and still so full of life even though…" I trail off, realizing I've said too much. What I've inadvertently admitted to.

And the fact that he's not spoken.

Turning to face him, I'm taken aback at the fact he doesn't appear upset after I've basically confessed to being attracted to someone else.

That I've confessed this to the man I'm engaged to marry.

"Presley." He releases a bored sigh which sets me on edge as he continues to eat.

"Why are we together, Dylan? It used to make sense. But now?" I wave a hand, gesturing between us. "Why are we still together?"

"Because of your par—" He freezes, and his eyes slowly, warily rise to meet mine. "I mean because I love you." His attempt to backpedal is far too obvious.

My eyes narrow on him dangerously. "Because of my parents? Because they're what? Well-known? Is that it?" My voice escalates as my anger soars.

Leaning back in his chair, he folds his hands together, eyeing me in an unnerving way. "Look, Presley. Your parents—your last name—gets people's attention. The firm appreciates that. And it sets me on the track for making partner sooner. Which means a better life for us."

He picks up his fork, waving it nonchalantly before stabbing a piece of steak. "And of course, we're going to be attracted to other people. I really thought we were on the same page." Shaking his head, he lets out a tight chuckle. "We've been together for *years*. If you need to take care of things, all I ask is you do it with discretion."

Surely, he isn't saying what I think he's saying.

He can't be.

Gaping at him for a beat before shaking it off, I pose my own million-dollar question. "Wait a minute. So, you're saying that you've been 'discreet' all these years?"

And I've been loyal to you the entire time—like a damn idiot.

He chuckles again, the sound grating on my nerves because absolutely *nothing* is humorous about this conversation. "Presley." His tone is similar to what one might use on a small child.

Condescending.

And suddenly, I see Dylan in a new light.

The always impeccably dressed accountant who has never once shown excitement about any of my achievements.

When I'd decided to open my own practice and wanted his thoughts and ideas; when I'd wanted to share my success in gaining a following of patients in such a brief amount of time; and when, over dinner, I'd wanted to tell him interesting or funny stories about patients over dinner—he'd redirect the conversation to himself and his own career.

I've been doing this for ten years.

"I've been taking care of my needs for a while. When you were swamped in med school, when you were getting acclimated to working in your first practice, and when you were prepping your new place."

I've been taking care of my needs for a while.

Wrapping my fingers around the top of the wooden dining room chair, as if to steady myself, I stare at him. "Taking care of your needs," I repeat slowly.

Attention back on his meal, he cuts another piece of steak. "Presley. Come on. You surely did the same when you were away at med school."

"I didn't." My words come out clipped as I continue to stare at him. As he chews, his eyes meet mine, and I see surprise edge into his expression. He clearly thought I'd been sleeping around as well.

Swallowing while taking a sip of wine, he stutters with what sounds like disbelief. "Y-you mean you…weren't?"

"No." *And I'm considering stabbing you with that steak knife.*

In the freaking junk. The same junk that's apparently making the rounds.

My eyes lower to my hands, still clenching the chair. My diamond engagement ring sparkles in the light, mocking me.

Moving over to where he sits, I grab the fork from his

grasp as my other hand lifts his plate from the table.

"Hey—"

Grabbing the steak knife and dropping it onto the plate, I move quickly to the kitchen and dump the food into the trash.

"Presley! What the hell are you doing?" He's incensed, and I'm faced with the dawning realization that he's never gotten this heated or been this passionate about me before. But the prospect of losing the clout he believes my name offers him and *food* will incite this kind of emotion.

Swinging around to face him, I point at the door. "Please leave."

He stares incredulously. "What the hell is wrong with you?"

Twisting the engagement ring off my finger, I thrust it at him, and caught off guard, he clumsily grasps at it.

"Take this." Disgust drips from my tone. "Not like it means anything, right? To honor? To cherish? Exactly how were you planning to do that while you were sticking your dick in other women?"

"Pres—"

"Don't." I cut him off abruptly. "Don't say another word."

He finally appears to recognize where this is going. "That's it? You're going to have a tantrum over something like this?" His sneer has me strongly considering grabbing that steak knife from the plate and hurling it at him.

Strongly considering it.

I walk over to the door with a much calmer demeanor than I could ever imagine possible, unlocking it, and swing it open. "Bye, Dylan."

The moment I slam the door closed behind him,

shutting out his muttering that I'll be calling him once I come to my senses, I lean back against it, flooded with emotions. Anger. Hurt.

One of them stands out, though, and it's telling.

Relief. Like somehow, deep down I knew all along something wasn't quite right. That Dylan and I weren't right for one another.

Letting out a long breath, I let my eyes fall closed with my head against the door. Vaguely, I register the sound of Dylan's protests fading, which means he's making his way to his car.

And I see one image in my mind. The person I wish I could call, the person I know would comfort me if he were to take me in his arms right now.

Hendy.

Instead, I pick up the phone and call someone else.

CHAPTER SEVENTEEN

Hendy

"What is The Renaissance period?" I say to the television, nearly to the final round of *Jeopardy*.

Lowering my gaze to my girl, Izzy, my new, specially trained service dog, I pet her soft head. She's a beauty, too—a unique mixed breed of Labrador Retriever and Boxer—with dark fur the color of chocolate and a white patch on her chest and the top of her nose.

I finally finished going through the lessons with a foundation located in Ponte Vedra Beach, which places rescue dogs in threat of being euthanized with veterans in need. The dogs go through intensive training, and I've been receiving instructions and attending classes as well. I'd been able to bring her home the other day, and it's like the entire place became brighter with her around.

Not to mention, she's already proven her worth when she'd noticed my anxiety the other night. My mind had drifted into the throes of a nightmare from the past, but with her wet nose pressed against my cheek and her low whimpering echoed in my ears, she roused me from my sleep.

"What do you think, girl? Should he bet it all on the Daily Double?" I murmur, referring to the one contestant on television.

"How much money do you have so far?" Kane's coming home a bit late after training at a work site down in south Jacksonville, setting his keys down on the kitchen counter.

"Only about twenty grand."

"Damn. Losing your mojo, darlin'?" I hear the smile in his tone.

"Nope. Just stumped me in the boy band category."

Kane walks around to settle his large frame onto the oversized leather sectional with a chuckle. "You mean to tell me you don't know your Backstreet Boys from *NSYNC?" He tsks at me.

"Yeah, can't tell one from the other. But as you can see, it's not exactly 'Tearin' up my Heart' that I didn't know many answers in that category."

Kane throws his head back in a laugh. "And all that money went 'Bye, Bye, Bye,' huh?" Looking over at Izzy, he holds out his hands. "Baby girl got no love for Uncle Kane?"

She raises her head to look over at him as if to scoff and say, "I'm good right here with my guy," before lowering her head for me to continue petting it and closing her eyes in doggy bliss.

Grinning back, my lips part to answer the next clue Alex Trebek announces, but my cell phone vibrating on the coffee table next to where my feet are propped interrupts me. Dropping my heels to the floor, I lean forward to grab my phone and see I have a new text message.

Lucia: Code rojo. She's going to that microbrewery on 3rd Street. And it's not going to be good. I'm stuck in Saint Augustine at a quinceañera for my

niece, and with traffic, it'll take me a while before I could get up there and rescue her. Do you think you could check on her, por favor?

I'm still trying to figure out what the hell Lucia's trying to tell me when her next text message makes me grow still.

Lucia: She broke things off with Dylan.

Holy *fuck*. I don't even know how to process this new development. There are warring emotions; I'm thrilled she's single for selfish reasons, obviously, but I'm also sad for her. Because I'm sure she's hurting. And the idea of Presley hurting—of her being in pain in any way—guts me.

Which is why my fingers fly over the keys, my response quick, as I rush to my bedroom to change.

I'm on my way.

* * *

She wasn't hard to find. At all. If there would've been an alert to be on the lookout for a woman itching to break free and drown her sorrows, Presley would be the poster child.

I pause just inside the door of the microbrewery, adjusting the brim of my ball cap lower over my eyes. I make it two steps toward the bar before I'm stopped by a brunette. Her hand on my arm causes me to instantly tense.

Looking down at her, I see she's got curves for days, massive tits, and the perfected I-practice-this-in-the-mirror pouty lips.

"Hey, handsome," she practically purrs. The cynical part of me realizes she only sees the right side of my face.

She's attractive, sure, and she'd likely be fine in bed. I would have tapped that ass without hesitation before. I would've eaten up the usual attention women have given me for most of my life. I sound like a dick, I know. But when a guy's over six feet tall with a mug like the one I used to have, it's one of those things. I didn't choose my looks or my stature. That was the luck of the draw—genetics. And I absolutely milked it for all it was worth.

Now, though, things are different. *I'm* different. This— this type of chick—just doesn't do anything for me. I'd be lying if I said it has nothing to do with the woman currently attempting to drink away her sorrows at the bar.

As politely as possible, I excuse myself from the brunette, allowing her a quick view of my entire face, but for once, the flash of dismay in her eyes doesn't have such a lasting effect on me. I'm more intent on making my way to where Presley sits at the end of the bar with two empty shot glasses in front of her.

Leaning in, I whisper in her ear, "Clue: Fastest way to get alcohol poisoning."

She jerks in surprise, nearly falling off the barstool, and my hands fly to her shoulders to steady her.

"Hendy! What are you doing here?" Her eyes narrow with teasing suspicion. "Are you stalking me?"

"The secret's out." I pause before crossing my eyes. "Does my stalker look give me away?"

Presley lets out a peal of laughter. "Oh, you're funny tonight." Turning toward the bartender standing a few feet away, she raises her voice—far louder than necessary. "Ryan!" She tosses a thumb in my direction. "Watch out for this guy. He'll make you laugh *so* hard."

Then she turns to me and hugs me; the unabashed way she throws her arms around my neck and embraces me is a testament to how much alcohol's in her system. Because as nice as this is, this isn't the Presley I've come to know.

Gently backing away from her and pulling her arms from around me, I peer at her closely. "How much have you had to drink?"

Her shoulders instantly slump, scowling as if I've reprimanded her. "Not enough."

Tugging the available barstool beside her closer to her and sliding onto it, I lean an arm across the back of hers. "What's going on? This"—I wave with my other hand, gesturing to her shot glasses—"doesn't seem like you."

A flicker of hurt crosses her face before she appears to stiffen. "Maybe I'm turning over a new leaf. Maybe I—" She abruptly stops, head whipping toward me, eyeing me suspiciously. "Wait a minute. How did you know I was here?"

I might as well be honest. "Lucia."

"Traitor," she mumbles under her breath.

"Are you going to tell me what's going on?"

She doesn't immediately answer; reaching for her drink, she's grasping it like it's a lifeline.

"Clue: Number one reason a woman drinks herself into oblivion." I wait patiently for her to give me the answer.

"Answer: What is a dirtbag fiancé who confesses to cheating on her repeatedly?"

Oh, *fuck* no. My fists clench so tightly it's a wonder my knuckles don't splinter into shards.

"And I decided I should celebrate my emancipation with drinks." Nodding as if to affirm her words, she adds, "Lots of drinks. To help me forget all the years I've wasted on him."

Shit. Running a hand over my face, I let out a slow exhale. "So you're planning on getting shitty tonight, huh?"

"Yep." She takes a long swig of her drink before setting it down on the lacquered wooden bar top. I snag the glass for a taste. As I take a sip, I nearly choke on it.

Long Island Iced Tea. A strong one, at that. I've known hardcore SEALs who turned into major shit shows from that cocktail alone. And here's Presley, who's not even half their size or muscle mass, downing them. Which means it's safe to say, I know what I'll be doing this evening.

I'll be holding back her hair.

* * *

"I love you, Ryan! Do you know how much?" Presley flings out both arms, nearly putting out my eye and simultaneously knocking the guy who's taken the seat beside her in the face. "This much!"

Presley Cole is an affectionate drunk. The only saving grace is I managed to get Ryan, the bartender, to start watering down her drinks about an hour ago.

Swaying in her seat, her head comes to rest on my shoulder. "Hendy?"

"Presley?"

Tipping her head up, she speaks, her breath washing against my neck. "Why are you here?"

Peering down at her, I furrow my brows. "What do you mean?"

Leaning away, she focuses her gaze on me, and for a moment, she doesn't appear quite as intoxicated. "Why are you here? With me right now?"

"Because Lucia sent me a text." My words are automatic, and I notice the immediate slump in her body as if the answer disappoints her.

"Then you're just here out of duty." Her tone is dull, and she speaks this not as a question but a statement.

And I make the decision right then to lay it on the line.

"No." Her eyes snap up to mine. "I'm not here out of duty. At least," I admit, "not completely." Pausing, I search her expression, and detecting a trace of hope in her eyes, I press on. "I'm here because there's no place I'd rather be."

Her face brightens, and the smile she gives me is breathtaking—literally robbing me of air. "Even if I'm sloppy drunk?"

With a laugh, I nod. "Even if you're sloppy drunk."

Suddenly serious, she lets out a long, dramatic sigh. "Hey."

"Hey," I answer slowly, wondering where the conversation's going next.

"You know that Sir Mix-a-lot guy who sang the song about big butts? Well, I have two beefs with him."

I run a hand down my face, trying my damnedest to hide my grin. "Do tell. What might those be?"

She ticks off one finger. "First off, guys getting hard-ons from a big butt? That surpasses creepy. Not to mention it's beyond gross." Ticking off another finger, she adds with the kind of emphasis only an extremely intoxicated person can get away with, "Second, what kind of asshat lists women's measurements like that? Thirty-six, twenty-four, thirty-six? And a woman who's only five-foot-three? Give me a break." Shaking her head with a look of disgust, she takes a swig of her drink before muttering, "I barely resist the urge to cover my ears when that song comes on."

Gesturing at herself, she says, "Look, I'm five-foot-seven, and on a really good day with a really great bra, I'm a solid B cup. Throw that song in the mix, and I find myself wanting to shake my fist in the air"—she raises a fist in demonstration—"and yell, 'Hey, universe! Yes, you! You can SUCK IT!'"

It takes all my effort not to burst out laughing at her dramatic yet obviously heartfelt speech as I roll my lips inward.

She lets out a long sigh and stares down at her drink. "But I refrain from doing so because the daughter of two renowned cardiologists should never behave in such a way. Or so I'm told."

"Well, I think that song's overrated."

Her head whips around, eyes wide with surprise. "You do?"

Nodding sagely, I lean toward her, lowering my voice. "Big butts are overrated in my opinion."

Her eyes flicker from my own then down to my lips, lingering there briefly. "Hendy, I—" She breaks off, and I recognize the look; the sudden paleness, the perspiration beading on her forehead.

Nearly toppling off the barstool, Presley darts for the nearby exit. Quickly tossing down money for her tab and grabbing her small purse and some napkins, I rush out after her. Finding her around the darkened corner of the building, I see she's bent over a row of bushes.

Tucking her purse beneath one arm, I slide my hands into her hair, pulling it back more firmly out of the way as she empties her stomach.

"Oh, God in heaven. What in the hell was I thinking?"

There's more heaving. Then she mumbles, "Dylan's an asshole." More heaving, followed by an additional plea to God.

Finally, once she's emptied her stomach and braced her hands on her knees, she slowly straightens. Pulling the two napkins I'd snagged at the bar from my back pocket, I hand them to her.

"You okay? Or are you ready for another rager?" I can't resist teasing her.

"Ha-ha." She rolls her eyes at me before groaning. "Can I maybe get swallowed up by these bushes? Please?"

"I'm going to let the fact that you just mentioned *bushes* and *swallowed* in the same sentence go." I grin and offer her a stick of gum from the small pack in my pocket before handing over her purse.

"Oh, thank you," she says with a sigh and unwraps the gum and pops it in her mouth. Finding a nearby trashcan, she tosses her napkins and gum wrapper in it before whipping back to me in alarm. "Oh, my gosh! I have to pay my tab! He probably thought I was—"

"Already taken care of."

Her mouth snaps shut as she stares at me for a beat. "You took care of it?"

Before I can answer her, I'm interrupted.

"Hey, man. Aren't you that Navy SEAL who was supposedly dead?"

CHAPTER EIGHTEEN

Presley

It's as if I can see every single one of Hendy's muscles tighten in response to the guy's question; his entire body draws up to appear even more imposing. It's a Friday night, and I'm clearly not the only one who's been drinking more than their allotted amount of alcohol. The guy sways on his feet, and one of his friends steps up beside him.

"Yeah, you're that fucking dude, aren't you?" The drunk guy's index finger jabs the air, pointing at Hendy, and I watch as a shuttered expression comes over him.

"You need to watch your mouth around the lady." Hendy's fingers cinch around my wrist, and he casually tugs me closer to him, shifting in front of me as if to protect me from a threat.

"Fuck that shit." The drunk guy's face twists into an ugly sneer. "What're you gonna do? You got fucking tortured by terrorists, right? And then you got a medal for it?"

Hendy says nothing, merely stares at the guy, and I watch, my eyes darting back and forth between them. The drunk guy's friend wises up and yanks on his arm.

"Hey, man. Leave him alone. Come on." He walks away, but it seems the drunk guy has other ideas.

"What are you going to do? Huh, scarface?" He taunts Hendy, who remains utterly still, watching him with that unnervingly silent, deadly, and intimidating stare.

"You want to know what I'll do?" He waits for the drunk guy to nod before he releases his hold on me, spine straightening further, shoulders wide, his stance ready to engage. Closing the distance between himself and the drunk guy and leaving only about a foot between them, he speaks, and his voice is dark and deep with an underlying steel.

"Take the final step. Come here, and I'll show you what I do to assholes who don't know the first thing about respecting others."

Hell, I'm not even the person he's directing his words at, and I'm intimidated. Because this version of Hendy is scary without doing anything more than speaking. Not once has he raised his voice, and not once has he done anything physically threatening, like raise a fist. Yet anyone with half a brain—sober or drunk—can plainly see he means business with his stance and dark, dangerous tone.

Something must finally break through the guy's cloud of drunkenness because he backs away with his hands up in surrender, nervousness lining his features. "My bad, man. My bad," he mutters before turning and following the path his friend took a moment earlier.

Hendy doesn't move an inch, but his eyes track the guy's movements as he walks off. I'm amped up, though, like I got gypped out of some action. And since I've been drinking, I'm mouthier than usual.

Shoving myself around Hendy, I call out after the guy, gesturing with my arms and taunting, "That's right! You'd better walk away!" Swaying in front of Hendy, he grabs my waist to steady me. I drop my arms, muttering, "That's right. How do you like me now, huh?"

Hendy barks out a laugh, turning me to face him, appearing amused. "Let's get you home before you decide to channel your inner Mike Tyson." Tipping his head to the side, he asks, "Ready to go?"

I consider his question briefly. "Do I have to?"

He offers only a close-lipped smirk. "Yes, ma'am."

Releasing a sigh, I look away. "Fine." My head snaps up as a thought hits me. "You're coming home with me?"

His eyes scan my face. "Yes." There's a pause as he eyes me curiously. "Since I'm the one who will be driving tonight."

"Oh."

That slightly lopsided smile makes another appearance. "You sound disappointed." He raises his eyebrows. "Why, Presley Cole, are you trying to get in my drawers?"

"Ye—*No*." Shit. My lips are loose from drinking. Attempting to school my expression, I place my hands on my hips. "I'll have you know that wasn't my…" I trail off as a thought hits me. "Wait a minute." Peering closer at his khaki pants, I ask, "So you're saying you're wearing underwear?"

Oh, no. I just said that out loud. To Hendy.

My patient.

Simmer down, Presley. Simmer. Stop asking patients if they're wearing underwear. Even if they do happen to be super smart, have crazy sex appeal, and probably wear some of those boxer briefs that won't be able to hide a huge—

Slapping my hands over my face, I groan. "What is wrong with me?"

"You're drunk." Hendy's hands cup my shoulders, and he steers me in another direction. "Let's head to my truck."

Dropping my hands with a sigh, I whisper, "Okay," as he takes my hand in his and guides me along the sidewalk. I'm trying my hardest to resist the sway that comes with the amount of liquor still in my system and concentrate on walking as straight as possible. But it's even more challenging because he's so distracting; the feel of his calloused fingertips grazing my skin sends a tantalizing awareness through me.

As we make our way to where he parked his truck on one of the nearby side streets in the downtown area, I observe women we pass who cast him inviting glances. He doesn't appear to notice, or if he does, he's ignoring it. I can't pretend I don't feel a sense of pride that I'm the one whose hand he's holding, the one he's escorting to his vehicle.

Of course, I'm also ignoring the fact he's doing this only because I drunkenly puked into some bushes, and that's the reason—the *only* reason—he's taking me home. But hey. If that's the way to get to hold the hand of a sexy former Navy SEAL who can nearly best me at *Jeopardy*, then I call that a win.

Pressing the key fob to unlock his vehicle, he opens the passenger door for me, turning and settling his hands at my waist. My startled eyes fly up to meet his, but he merely lifts me, placing me on the seat before reaching to fasten the seat belt across my chest.

"Wow." My tone is a mixture of bemusement and dry humor. "I can't say I've had someone do that for me—let alone a guy—since I was in the single digits."

He studies me briefly, reaching out to tuck some hair behind my ear with a quick wink. "Maybe you've been hanging around the wrong guys." With those words, he closes my door and crosses around the front to get in.

Fastening his own seat belt, he starts the truck and adjusts the air conditioning to battle the never-ending Florida humidity while I ponder his actions, his words.

This man has shown me more affection, more attention, and has been more caring toward me than someone I had been with for close to a decade. It makes me wonder if—

"Have you ever been in love?" As soon as my words are out, panic engulfs me because, yet again, I didn't mean to voice my thoughts. Before I can backtrack, to apologize, he answers.

"No."

I'm surprised at his response. "You answered that really quick." Leaning my head against the seat, I add, "And you sound so certain."

His look is intriguing, and I wish it weren't so dim in the cab of the truck. "Because I'm certain I've never been in love before. Because I've never…"

"Because you've never…?" I prompt.

Staring out the windshield, he exhales slowly. "I've never found anyone who made me want to commit. Anyone who had the qualities I could see myself appreciating for the long-term."

He falls silent for so long I think he's finished speaking when he begins again. "I've always thought of real love as finding the person you want to weather the storms of life with. The person who's so perfect for you, yet they couldn't be more imperfect." His lips curve up into a faint smile. "Someone who always ends up burning the toast but remembers exactly how I take my coffee and orders pepperoni pizza only to pick it off her pieces to give to me because it's my favorite and I always want extra.

"Someone who can forgive even when it's tough." Turning to meet my eyes, he softens his voice. "I think of real love like the kind that rolls up its sleeves and isn't afraid to get dirty, do some hard work, go through some tough shit because, after all the sweat and maybe some tears, too, I know the result is going to be worth it. That all the time spent and all the hard work went into making that love even better." Hendy shrugs. "I've just never found that with anyone."

Shifting slightly in his seat, he turns to look out the windshield again with a more subdued voice. "Some of my friends have found it, but I've never found someone who made me feel…" He trails off with a shrug.

Anything like I feel when I'm with you, I want him to say. Which is ridiculous. I shouldn't be feeling this. Not right now. I should be home licking my wounds, not fantasizing about the man next to me.

Instead, I want to lick him. *All* over.

"I'm so drunk," I whisper-groan more to myself than to him as my eyes fall closed.

"Let's get you home," Hendy says quietly, putting the truck in gear then pulling onto the street.

I decide to rest my eyes for a moment. It's probably safer to just chill out right now and try to keep my mouth shu—

"I Googled you. Hard."

CHAPTER NINETEEN

Hendy

"   *Googled you. Hard.*"

Presley's words have me teetering between laughing and an aroused-as-hell groan. Because the word *hard* coming from her lips is pure ecstasy and immediately sends blood rushing south to my cock.

Then the full force of her words hits me. My hands constrict on the steering wheel in an unforgivingly tight grip, and my muscles tense so much I fear they're nearly to the point of knotting.

She looked me up on the internet. That shouldn't surprise me, but it does. Until another emotion rapidly edges out that surprise.

Panic.

Panic that maybe she came across something that would end up tainting her view of me. Glancing briefly at her before returning my attention to the road, I hear her let out a soft groan beneath her breath.

"God, Presley. Just shut up already," she murmurs to herself.

This has my lips turning up a bit, but there's no denying my curiosity as to what information she dug up on me.

"Did you find anything interesting?"

Coming to a stop at the traffic light at Centre Street before we head onto Atlantic Avenue, I look over, trying to gauge her expression. Her head's turned to the side, relaxed against the seat, eyes soft, watching me.

"Like the fact that you're a badass? A modern-day Chuck Norris?" The corners of her mouth tilt up. "You could be one of those internet memes." Deepening her voice, she says, "*Chuck Norris didn't join the Navy! The Navy joined Chuck Norris!*" Laughing softly, she murmurs, "But yeah, I think I ended up even more impressed. You're a hero, Hendy."

A humorless laugh escapes me. I'm no hero. "Right." Turning onto South Fletcher Avenue to head home, I feel it.

Presley lays her palm over the hand I have resting on the middle console, and the comforting affection spreads warmth through my veins.

"Speaking of Googling hard," she begins with a strong hint of wicked mischief in her voice, "maybe you can show me just how har—"

"Presley Cole." My tone is one of warning even though I'm fighting a smile. Because tipsy Presley is more amusing than I would've expected. Certainly, she's naughtier than I ever imagined.

Which means it's taking every ounce of restraint not to pull off this road and tug her body over to straddle mine and show her exactly how hard I am.

"How do you do this?" she blurts out suddenly.

Confused, my brows furrow. "Do what?"

"How do you do this? It's like you have this effect on me whenever I'm around you where I always want more— more time with you, more talking, more fun. Just more…"

Every fiber in my body tenses at that moment because...shit. She's voicing what I've wished for all along. If only she hadn't been drinking tonight.

"It's like when you use one of those car wash vacuums, and you're going crazy trying to frantically get every possible square inch before your time's up"—she takes a quick breath, her words frantic, rushed—"and you're one quarter short of another vacuuming session and just when you're about to finish cleaning that last spot, in that crevice you only now discovered that seems to catch every god-forsaken crumb known to man, it shuts off. And you're mentally screaming, '*Nooooooo!*' but it's too late and then—"

"I'm pretty sure I get the idea." I struggle not to break into a huge smile at the way she's comparing a frantic need to get as much time with me as possible. She's so damn adorable like this. Partially flustered, honest, and that hint of desire I detect in her eyes... *Fuck.*

Being noble and doing the right thing might actually kill me tonight.

Pulling into her driveway, I park and turn off the ignition. Raising a hand, I slowly skim my thumb along her cheekbone. I watch her eyes flutter closed, her lips parting slightly as if my touch is something she wants to cherish, to bask in.

Leaning over the console, I softly brush my lips against her forehead. Backing away is fucking torture, but it's the look of disappointment in her eyes that nearly does me in. She clearly wants more than a peck on the forehead.

Exiting the truck, I walk around to open her door and help her down. Those eyes drift over my lips once more before meeting my gaze. "Clue: Person with the worst case of blue lady balls tonight."

My eyebrows nearly hit my hairline, and it appears as if she might have even surprised herself in voicing that one. "Answer: Who is Presley Cole?"

Pursing her lips, she carefully steps down from my truck before I close the door. Chuckling, I guide this still slightly unsteady beauty up the stairs, leading to the front door of the house.

"Sorry." Her tone is soft, faint. "I shouldn't have said that." Shaking her head, she mutters, "I should know better. No guy likes that kind of talk."

"That kind of talk, meaning…?" Watching her, I'm curious for her response.

Presley lets out a long sigh, eyes averted. "You know"—she waves a hand—"any talk that's remotely dirty."

I know I'm staring at her in disbelief. I can't help it. Because *what the hell?* "And you have this on authority that guys don't like dirty talk?"

"I do." She finally turns to look at me. "Among other things."

Among other things?

"And who told you this?" I'm still dumbfounded even though I'm sure I already know the answer.

"Dylan."

"And no other guy liked it?"

We've come to a stop at the top of the stairs and beneath the yellow outdoor light casting a soft glow over us. I can feel her embarrassment and see the flush spreading across her cheeks.

Turning her eyes away again, she mumbles, "Dylan's the only guy I've ever been with."

Oh, holy shit.

"I, uh," I stumble over the words, trying not to cause

her further embarrassment, "have it on good authority that most guys love dirty talk." With a pause, I can't restrain the slight smile that tugs my lips. "As far as other things, I can't speak for them. Because I, for one, am not into painful sex."

"But you'd, maybe, be okay with…" she trails off as if to get the nerve to finish with, "dirty talk and maybe some gentle bondage, though? Would most guys be okay doing that to a woman?"

Fuck. Me.

Right here. Please.

Fuck. *Lock it down, Hendy. Lock. It. Down.*

Exhaling a long breath, I clench and unclench my jaw because I'm dying to say a million and one things. Instead, I offer, "I think that's a safe bet."

Jesus. I sound like a simpleton.

Probably because all the damn blood has rushed from my brain to my dick, and thoughts are on rapid-fire through my brain along with images of me tying Presley up and having her scream my name.

Repeatedly.

Her head whips around to gaze at me. "Really?" Her voice is wispy, delicate sounding.

A simple nod in affirmation is all I offer while hoping she won't take notice of the hardening going on down below. Because the knowledge that Presley likes dirty talk and wants to be tied up is well beyond the realm of *hot*.

The knowledge that Presley has only been with one guy and clearly hasn't experienced much sexually is also hot. As. Fuck. Because the mere idea of teaching her—no, letting her use me to gain experience—is just…

Sign me the hell up for that.

"I mean"—she leans against the railing beside the front

door, handing me her keys—"it's not like I had guys banging down my door growing up." Her eyes close; her body looks relaxed, tipping her head back slightly.

"I was a nerd in school and having two different colored eyes made things pretty rough." Her lips quirk upward slightly. "The worst part was my Britney Spears obsession."

Watching as her eyes open, heavy-lidded, with the way she smiles at me, I know right now that this is another one of those moments. One I want to save in my memory bank for years to come.

Leaning against the door, I arch an eyebrow. "How obsessed are we talking here? Know all the words to every song, wear the little schoolgirl outfit from her first hit, and sing her songs all the time?"

Her lips twist. "Worse. That and owner of all her fragrances."

My brows furrow. "She had more than one perfume?"

"Yep. One of them was aptly named 'Curious.'"

We both laugh softly before falling silent. All of a sudden, her eyes widen, and her body straightens slightly.

"Wait a minute." She gets this tiny crease between her brows, and I'd give anything to press my lips to it. Tipping her head to the side, she asks, "How did you know where I live?"

Stepping closer, I rest my hands on the railing on either side of her and lean in. "Presley Cole. I may not be a SEAL anymore, but all that training doesn't just disappear. Plus," I pause, dipping my head, my lips close to her ear, "I had to make it a point to know where one of my favorite people lives." Backing away slightly, I slide her key into her lock.

And yeah. I'd be lying through my teeth if I said I didn't wish I were sliding something else inside. Of her.

CHAPTER TWENTY

Presley

M y eyes drift upward, coming to rest on his throat, and I'm mesmerized by his rapidly beating pulse. Without thinking, I raise on my toes, pressing my lips against that same pulse then nip at it gently.

Hendy instantly stills the moment my soft lips meet his skin, and his fingers fly to my hips, tightening, as my teeth graze his skin. I can't resist the urge to dart the tip of my tongue out to taste him.

"Presley." His voice is guttural. As he leans back, the eyes that meet mine are impossibly dark and hazy with heat. "You've been drinking tonight."

He's right; I can't argue with that. But I'd swear on everything this isn't alcohol fueled. It's something I'm acting on that's been churning deep inside me since…well, since the moment I met him.

The sound of an approaching car draws our attention to my driveway. And my stomach plummets.

What the hell is Dylan doing here?

Rushing out of his car, he hurries up the stairs, looking like a freaking mess. My eyes take in his hair, which certainly cannot be classified as gently mussed. He must have run his hands through it repeatedly. And his button-down shirt is untucked and wrinkled—something Dylan has always deemed unacceptable. He *abhors* wrinkles.

God, I can't even fathom how I stayed in a relationship with such a weirdo. Because geez, wrinkles happen.

"Presley! Where have you been?" He eyes Hendy as if he's just saved me from being mugged or something.

Hands on my hips, I narrow my eyes on him. "I've been out." I pause for emphasis. "Drinking." Then, for further impact, I whisper loud and dramatically, "At a *bar*."

Because wow, that's scandalous by Dylan's standards. And I don't miss Hendy's slight snicker.

"That's not like you." His eyes flicker over to Hendy again. "I was worried about you."

"Dylan." God, this is exhausting. "I was stone-cold sober earlier when I told you it was over. But now"—I shake my head—"I've drunk enough alcohol to probably put down a large animal." My head whips around, fixing a questioning look on Hendy. "A full-grown horse? Or you think something larger?"

"Larger," he answers without missing a beat, but I detect the corners of his lips lifting slightly. "Buffalo, probably."

I turn back to Dylan. "Right. And then I puked." As soon as I say the word *puke*, Dylan's lips curl up in disgust. "*Aaaaand*"—I draw the word out with emphasis, tossing a thumb in Hendy's direction—"he held my hair back for me."

"You"—he falters as if at a loss for words—"vomited? In public?"

Hendy snorts. Loudly.

Before I can respond to Dylan, he steps closer, grabbing my upper arm. "Look, you had your wild time. Now, you're going to come home with me, and we can talk this out."

When I try to tug my arm from his grasp, it only tightens painfully.

"Hey." Hendy's voice is deep, dark, and lethal sounding. I've never heard him sound like this—even earlier with that douchebag. This is different. There's more emotion behind it. And I can't help that tiny part of me that wonders if it's because of me—for me.

"Let her go. Now." When Dylan doesn't indicate he's planning to heed Hendy's order, his eyebrows rise and he takes a step closer. "Let her go, now, Ike."

Oooh. I can't help but giggle at Hendy referencing Ike Turner.

Towering over Dylan and practically dwarfing him in size, Hendy looks intimidating as hell. When Dylan relinquishes his hold, I let out a sigh, instantly rubbing my arm.

A large hand with fingers splayed wide lands on the center of Dylan's chest and presses against him to put more distance between us. "Now, you're going to get in your fucking Prius and get your ass out of here. You will not come back unless Presley invites you ba—"

"Which I won't." I can't help but interject.

Hendy doesn't miss a beat. "Nor will you contact her in any way. If she wants to talk to you—"

"Which I won't."

I get the feeling Hendy's trying not to laugh at me, but he continues. "Think it's pretty clear she wants you gone, man."

It might be pure desperation, but for whatever reason, Dylan resists and starts spouting off his mouth. "You want this"—he waves a hand toward Hendy—"over me? Have you lost your mind? His face looks like—"

Instantly, I'm the one in Dylan's face, angrier than I think I've ever been before in my life. Shoving at his chest, he falters against the back of the wooden railing I've pressed him into. "Don't. You. Dare," I practically snarl. "He has more integrity, more heart, more of anything and everything than you could ever have."

His face crumples. "But what am I going to tell my boss? The partners?"

I back away to stare at him incredulously. "That's what this is about? Your image at the firm?" Running a hand through my hair, I let out a loud grunt. Spinning around to face Hendy, I ask, "You know enough. You can help me hide his body, right?"

Without missing a beat, he darts his eyes over to Dylan as he whispers loudly, "I'd leave now, man." There's a millisecond pause. "While you can."

Still facing Hendy and noticing I haven't heard Dylan's retreating footsteps, I cross my arms and adopt a thoughtful tone. "We live right by the Atlantic Ocean. Bull sharks are known to come into shallow waters." I shrug. "Not totally unfathomable."

That's when I hear Dylan turn and make his way down the stairs to the driveway. I catch comments like "crazy" and "lost her mind." I only breathe a sigh of relief once he backs his car out of my driveway and heads off down the road.

Hendy and I stand in silence for a long moment before he finally speaks. "You do realize what I have to do now, right?"

Confused, I turn to look at him. "Um, cancel the prospect of ever owning a Prius as a vehicle?"

He throws his head back in a laugh—a real laugh—and I realize I haven't seen nor heard him laugh like this before. It's as if I just caught a true glimpse of how he used to be. The man who didn't feel the need to hide his face from others. The man who laughed—*really* laughed—often and readily.

"Presley Cole," he says, that lopsided smile so endearing, "there's no way in hell I'd ever consider owning a fucking Prius." His smile widens mischievously. "Those cars are for douchebags."

"Yeah," I sigh, turning back to gaze out at the road.

"But that wasn't what I was going to say." He pauses, waiting for me to meet his eyes, and the concern in them is evident. "I don't want to leave you here alone. I won't get any sleep worrying about you." Sliding his hands into the pockets of his jeans, he averts his gaze. "And I have someone waiting for me at home that I need to see."

CHAPTER TWENTY-ONE

Hendy

Driving the few miles it takes to get back to my place, I mull over tonight's events. Rescuing Presley at the bar, the run-in with both the asshole outside the bar and her ex, and her immediate defense of me. Most of all, I think of how much more she's allowed me to see of her, of her personality tonight. To say Presley Cole is multifaceted doesn't come close.

Exiting my truck and coming around to help her down, I hold her hand to guide her up the steps to my house. At least, I tell myself I'm holding on to ensure she safely ascends to the top. In reality, it's just an excuse to have her soft, delicate fingers on mine.

Unlocking the front door, I guide her inside and lock it behind us. As we enter the dimly lit entryway and slip off our flip-flops onto a nearby mat, I hope—damn near pray—she won't let go of my hand.

I've never felt this way before. Hell, I don't even think I've been much of a fan of handholding until now. Yet the way her palm feels against mine, how our fingers link—the way she holds me tightly, so securely, as though she, too, doesn't want to relinquish her hold feels so...*right*.

My ears strain as I catch a hint of the faintest whisper coming from Presley. "Please don't let go of my hand yet."

Smirking, I answer her. "I won't let go."

Ducking her head, she whispers. "Shit. I didn't—"

"Mean to say that out loud?" My lips stretch into a wide grin when her eyes fly up to find me watching her. Before I can comment further, I hear the now familiar sound of nails tapping against the hardwood floors. "Presley, I'd like you to meet my girl, Izzy."

Her eyebrows furrow as she glances down at our still joined hands then back up at me. "Your...girl?"

Releasing her hand, I lower myself to a knee. "Come here, girl. It's okay. She's friendly," I say in a subdued, soothing tone to Izzy as she comes into sight, approaching us tentatively. She nuzzles my neck as I pet her back, murmuring to her. "Did you miss me? Is Uncle Kane treating you right?"

"Are you lovebirds going to join me or are y'all planning on fornicating right there by the door?"

Rolling my eyes at Kane's question, I shoot back with a, "Quit embarrassing Presley, or she'll never put in a good word for you with Lucia."

"Aw, now." I can tell, simply by Kane's tone, that he's smiling as he speaks. "Them's fighting words." There's a pause. "You need me to head over to Doc's place tonight?"

My eyes quickly dart over to Presley before I scrub a hand over my face. Because shit. *Thanks, Windham, for basically asking if I'm going to get buck wild with Presley.*

While she's standing right here beside me.

Starting down the hallway leading to where Kane's watching television, Presley and Izzy follow. "Nope. I'm bunking on the couch tonight."

"No, you can't—"

I cut Presley's protest short when I turn and crowd her against the wall. Reaching out, I graze my index finger down her cheek. Leaning in close, I whisper, "I can." My eyes flit between her lips and eyes. "I want you to sleep in my bed tonight."

Her eyes remain on my lips as she whispers back, "With you in it, too?"

My face stretches into a naughty grin. "Not with me in it."

She blushes furiously upon realizing, once again, she's voiced her thoughts.

"But maybe at some point," I dip my head to dust my lips over her cheek, whispering huskily, "I'll join you."

Her eyes fly up to mine—wide—and her lips part in surprise.

I back away, grasping her hand again. "Let's get you situated for the night." Looking down at Izzy, I add, "Come on, girl. Let's get Presley set up, okay?"

As I lead Presley to my bedroom, I can't help but think this is the first time I've brought a woman home— let alone brought a woman back to my bedroom—in years.

Regardless of my attraction to her, she's been through a lot tonight, and I need to be respectful of that. Doesn't mean I can't fantasize—as long as I don't act on it—about making her scream my name, sliding deep inside that pussy I'm certain would be sweet as hell, gazing into her two different colored eyes while she comes all over my co—

Izzy's nose nudges my leg as I pull a T-shirt and boxers from my dresser for Presley to change into. When I look down at her, I instantly feel like I should apologize. It's like she's reprimanding me. *Dad, stop being a horny bastard around the nice lady.*

Damn it. With a resigned whisper, I pat Izzy on the head. "Thanks for keeping me in line, girl."

CHAPTER TWENTY-TWO

Presley

I'm the level-headed one—the doctor and lover of factoids. I've never been the whimsical girl who'd hoard her mother's old Harlequin romance novels and dream of a knight in shining armor. For the sex scenes, yes. Romance, not so much.

But right now, I swear romance is blanketing me—and I'm wondering if I've been missing out. If I let the no-nonsense part of me take over for far too long, and maybe that's why I allowed myself to stay with Dylan in a lifeless—and ultimately, loveless—relationship. Deep down, I think I knew it all along. I willingly sold myself short.

This, though, is something else entirely. Hendy, who's more than double my weight and just less than a foot taller than I am—a man who has a battered and scarred body—is a man who's slain real-life evildoers. This same man tenderly held my hand and willingly took care of me. Even after he'd watched me display my not-so-stellar—nor graceful—upchucking earlier and readily held back my hair.

And now, this night—which admittedly began with me being a freaking hot mess of epic proportions—is coming to an end. With that knowledge comes a stabbing pain in my chest, because I don't want it to end. I want this moment to last.

Watching him grab a T-shirt and a pair of boxers for me to change into, I hear him murmur something to Izzy before turning and handing me the clothes.

"The bathroom's right across the hall. Feel free to use whatever you need. Fresh towels are under the sink along with a pack of toothbrushes I just bought."

Holding the clothing to my chest, a sudden awkwardness settles over me. "Um." I falter, biting my lip and averting my eyes to settle on Izzy instead. "Thank you. For everything tonight." Mumbling, I add, "Sorry you had to witness all that."

Concentrating so intently on avoiding his eyes, I don't register his approach until he's standing right in front of me and a finger beneath my chin is tipping it up to meet his gaze.

"Hey," he says softly. "Don't apologize for anything. We all have moments like that."

I scoff. "Yeah. Except mine are more along the lines of a bad reality show," I add with a weak smile. "Thanks for rescuing me tonight. And for, kind of, slaying my dragon for me."

"Presley Cole." The way he says my name, the way it sounds rolling off his tongue is like a caress. "No need to thank me. I'd gladly rescue you any day of the week. And between you and me"—he tips his head to the side, a soft smile playing on his lips—"I'd call him more of an annoying cockroach that needed to be stepped on."

With a quick press of his lips to my forehead, he and Izzy leave the room, closing the door behind them. And I'm left standing here, still holding his clothes in my hand with a huge smile forming on my lips. Not only that, but something else is happening, too.

My heart feels like it's begun beating a little faster.

Something that never happened with Dylan.

* * *

I think I'm on the brink of confirming that it is, in fact, quite possible to get a contact orgasm from clothing alone.

But not just any clothing. I'm talking about Hendy's clothing—specifically the shirt he gave me to sleep in. This soft, cotton shirt engulfs my body while his unique scent clings to it. Burrowing beneath the plush covers on his bed, I can't withhold a soft sigh because although I'm comfortable and have brushed my teeth—thank God for that pack of new toothbrushes—something is missing.

Or someone.

Glancing over at the closed door of the bedroom, I wonder if he's already asleep on the couch. It hasn't been but a few minutes since he finally bid me good night and closed the door behind him. However, there's no denying my yearning to go to him. Merely to thank him again for coming out tonight.

Okay, so maybe I would like to take another look at him, too. Because Hendy in low-slung pajama pants and an old, worn T-shirt that stretches across his firm, broad chest is something I'd like to see again.

It's like something's happened, like he's somehow opened my very own Pandora's Box. Earlier when I'd mentioned dirty talk and the prospect of being tied up in bed, and he hadn't reared away as if I'd said something disgusting, it intrigued me. And I really want to know if those are things *he'd* be okay with.

Not just that, but that he'd be okay doing those things with *me*.

"God, Presley," I whisper to myself, flipping the covers up over my face. "Get your inner slut back on the leash."

And now, I'm whispering to myself beneath the covers of my patient's bed while wearing his T-shirt and boxers. My, how the mighty have fallen.

Except I don't have any regrets. In fact, I'm tempted to slip off my panties and touch myself while wearing Hendy's shirt. To imagine him here with me is easy with his scent surrounding me.

Just as I kick off the boxers beneath the covers and my daring fingers reach for my panties, I hear something. My hand freezes with my entire body covered, and I wait, wondering what sound I heard. Maybe it was Izzy.

The bedroom door cracks open. "Presley?" Hendy whispers.

My hands jerk, flipping the covers down. "Yes?" I sound guilty as hell, but maybe he won't notice. It's certainly dim enough in here with only tiny shards of moonlight peeking through the blinds.

"I brought this just in case." My eyes fall to the small wastebasket he sets beside the bed for me.

And if that doesn't drive home the fact that I've been a hot mess in front of him tonight, I'm not sure what would. Not sure I can call a guy bringing me a wastebasket in case I need to puke romantic.

Thoughtful, yes. Romantic, no.

"You okay?" he asks quietly.

I hesitate to answer because I am and…I'm not.

"Your bed is big enough." I pause. "For both of us…and

I trust you." I wince after the words spill from my lips. Even if there's truth to them, I hate the way they sound.

Needy. Pathetic.

I should know better—not only that, but I clearly need to handle myself better. This entire day has had me on a roller coaster ride of emotions. But I have to remember that although he's been kind and gracious enough to rescue me tonight, it doesn't mean he's interested.

"I don't really…" Hendy's words trail off. Running a hand down his face with a soft sigh, he says, "I sometimes have…dreams." There's a pregnant pause. "I, uh, don't want to hurt you by mistake. Not willing to risk it."

Turning his eyes to mine, even in the moonlit room, I detect the discomfort in his disclosure. But it's his next words which nearly shred my heart.

"I sometimes relive when they…tortured me."

CHAPTER TWENTY-THREE

Hendy

don't have a clue as to why I said that, why I admitted it. I certainly don't like to discuss it, even with Dr. Givens.

I mean I know Kane's heard me before. I've awoken a time or two with him standing nearby as if he was waiting, assessing whether to try to rouse me from my nightmare or to see if I would quickly pull myself out of it. Another time, I'd been so violent in my movements that I'd nearly injured him. Granted, it only happened once, but I'm still uneasy.

Even in the short time Izzy's been with me, she's managed to make a huge difference. But that doesn't mean I want to take a chance with Presley. God, the idea of accidentally hurting her in any way guts me.

Now that I've mentioned this to her, I feel like an idiot. I swear it practically screams pussy because here I am, a former Navy SEAL—arguably some of the most badass, toughest guys out there—who has nightmares about people hitting and cutting him.

Boo-*fucking*-hoo.

Presley shifts, sitting up in my bed, and the way her hair is slightly tousled, the fact that she's wearing my clothes… Shit. It'd be a lie if I said I wasn't dying to know if she's completely naked beneath it.

"Hendy…" She appears to be at a loss for words. "Have you been talking about this with Dr. Givens?"

Great. Just fucking great. "Yes." My answer comes out short, curt. Because the last thing I want is for her to have an image of me being a fucking pussy with nightmares. And driving a fucking Prius.

Ha. I had to add that in for shits and giggles.

There's a beat of silence before she responds. "Well, maybe you could, um, lie down with me for a minute." There's a pause. "Just to talk."

Just to talk. If she were any other woman, I'd know exactly what her game was, but she's not. Presley isn't anything like the women I'm used to. The ones who want me because of my now former job, my also former good looks, or the rumors they've heard about my dick.

Because it's big. And no, I'm not simply bragging.

I cock my head to the side, and I'm certain she can hear the teasing in my voice. "You just want to talk?"

Presley lets out a sigh. "Stop being a smartass. I just want to talk and wind down a bit."

With a smile, I quietly close the bedroom door with a soft click, and when I face the bed again, Presley's shifted over to make room for me.

The two steps it takes to make it over to the bed allow enough time for my mind to scream with warnings.

She's your doctor.

She just broke up with her fiancé.

You need to keep your dick in your pants.

Settling myself on the bed with one hand behind my head and my right hand resting on my chest, I find it challenging to keep from touching her. Not only because I'm more than double her size, but because, right now, I also want nothing more than to be able to look deeply into those eyes of hers while I fu—

"Do you miss it?"

Her voice draws me from my thoughts with a jolt. "Miss it?"

"You know"—she shifts to lie on her side, and I feel her gaze resting on me—"being out there." She pauses briefly. "With your guys."

I don't answer right away, and not only because I don't like talking about it, but also because normally, civilians don't understand. They don't get what it's like to be out there on the frontlines. To be the ones tasked with eliminating the enemy—to eliminate those who get their rocks off on hurting others, those who are innocent. We—me and my brothers-in-arms—are the ones who willingly signed up for that task. The ones who volunteered for the job because we believe in fighting the never-ending fight for freedom and protecting our fellow Americans.

What people don't get—what people don't notice—are our unseen scars. Because taking a life—no matter how shitty and evil an individual might be—is never easy. It's something that stays with you for the rest of your days, regardless of how many lives you might have saved by eliminating that one asshole.

"Of course." My voice is hoarse, and there's no masking the tinge of emotion in it because if someone gave me the chance to switch places with any of them, I'd do it in a fucking heartbeat. "They were some of my best friends who fiercely believed in the same ideals and wanted to make the world a better, safer, place." Swallowing hard, I add softly, "I miss them every damn day."

We lie here in silence, and I'm so lost in my thoughts that it startles me when I feel it. Her hand comes to rest on mine upon my chest. As much as I appreciate the gesture, I need to change the topic of conversation.

"Tell me more about your plans now that you're a single woman."

The hand on mine tenses just a fraction before she removes it, and I hear her head shift on the pillow to face away from me. Blowing out a heavy breath, she lets out a tiny, deprecating laugh at the end. "What am I *not* going to do is more like it."

"The sky's the limit, huh?"

"Pretty much." Her response is a near whisper as we lie in comfortable silence.

That's a fucking lie. I'm over here wishing—dying—for her to put her hand on mine again. To feel her touch.

The other part of me, bastard that he is, wants the same thing. Except in that scenario, her hand would be touching a part of me much lower.

"Hendy?"

Fuck. I'm such an asshole.

She turns to look at me, and once I meet her eyes, I notice she's worrying her bottom lip nervously. "Would you, maybe, help me…with something?"

"Help you with what?" *Do you need me to make sure my cock fits inside you? If so, sure. I'm on it.*

Sweet Jesus. My mother's rolling over in her grave right now. I just know it.

"Would you…" She takes a deep breath, shifting onto her side to face me fully before letting it out slowly. "Would you help me learn what guys normally like?"

She did not just ask me that.

"You don't need me for that, Pres." I hear the difference in my tone, the deepening of it, the slight raspiness. Because my dick is screaming, *Hell, yes!*

"But I…" She reaches out her other hand, placing it on my chest, and I'm frozen in place at the feel of her fingers on me, the way they move ever so slightly. Sure, she's touched me a dozen times before but never like this.

And all I can think about is those slim, soft fingers wrapped around my—

"I *do* need you for that. And I think you're the best person to teach me."

"Why me?" I ask suddenly.

A beat of silence passes before she answers, her eyes appearing to search mine for something. "Because you're you."

I can't hide my confusion. "I don't understand."

Nodding slowly, she lets out a tiny laugh. "You, Hendy. For one, you attract women by the herd wherever you go."

As my lips part to correct her that their attention isn't the good kind, but because of my scarred face, she interrupts me, briefly pressing a finger to my lips.

"Their attention is always on you because you have that *something*. But more than that"—her tone softens, becoming more subdued—"you've reminded me that life isn't guaranteed; that we need to live it to the fullest and have no regrets." Her gaze drops, shifting her focus to the bed covers as if embarrassed, and she adds, "I realize that now more than ever. And I know with certainty that I would've regretted marrying Dylan. Because he doesn't…didn't…"

My breath hitches as I wait for her to finish. When she makes no attempt to do so, I shamelessly prompt her. "Because he didn't…?"

Letting out a tiny sigh, she focuses the heavy weight of her gaze on me with barely banked lust. "Because he never made me feel the…heat, the yearning, the…" She drags her teeth against her bottom lip, nipping at it as if she's nervous. "Happiness." There's a pinching in my chest at her words, even as she continues. "He never made me feel like you do."

Her lips roll inward, pausing briefly before finishing barely on a whisper. "Because you make me feel *everything*."

CHAPTER TWENTY-FOUR

Presley

"**B**ecause you make me feel everything."

I said it. I really went ahead and said it. Tonight feels much like a transformational experience for me. Like a butterfly finally emerging from its cocoon after being trapped inside for so long.

And if I'm honest, I want to be the cocoon wrapped around Hendy. Like a succubus. And I realize how slutty and inappropriate that sounds. Not only is he my patient, but I also literally broke up with my fiancé mere hours ago. Yet here I am, basically hitting on this man.

But I spoke truthfully. Hendy's changed so much for me—my thinking, my perceptions. I've wasted so much of my time—of my life—already. I don't want to continue along that path. I want to *live.*

And Hendy is the one person who makes me feel so incredibly alive.

When he doesn't respond, I tear my eyes away, frantically trying to figure out how to save face.

Awkward doesn't begin to cover it.

As my lips part to brush off my words, his voice stops me, harsh, gravelly. "Wait."

My eyes fly to his, watching him warily.

He blows out a long breath, running a hand over his jaw. "Do you have any idea what it does to me when you say things like that?" With a groan, he stares up at the ceiling. "Damn it, Pres."

"What do you mean, what it does to—*ohhhh*." My words end on a wispy sigh, catching sight of the impressive tenting in his pajama pants. Sweet Jesus, this man is…*big*.

"Yeah," he says with a chuckle that turns into a groan. "Oh."

We fall silent for a moment until finally, I can't hold myself back anymore. And when I kick off the covers and swing my legs over to straddle his lap, it's as if he'd been anticipating my move, and his hands instantly go to my hips. My shirt rides up, the thin fabric of my thong doing nothing to dull the sensation of having his prodding hardness pressing against me through his cotton pants.

His eyes meet mine, fingertips flexing at my hips. Shards of moonlight filtering through the venetian blinds illuminate the room, and noting the tightness in his jaw, I raise my one hand to slide against it. The sound of the air conditioning kicking on, blowing cool air from the vents, does little to assuage the heat between us.

"You shouldn't clench your jaw like that," I whisper before slowly leaning forward to press my lips against his strong, square jawline. Relishing the faint rasp from the beginning of his whiskers, I can't resist darting out the tip of my tongue.

"It's hard not to." It sounds like he's speaking through gritted teeth.

My lips curve up at his words, and I can't resist teasing him. "That's not all that's—"

"Presley." The seriousness, the hint of urgency in his tone has me drawing back to meet his gaze. "Don't do this. Not like this." He swallows hard. "Please."

My stomach plummets, and my cheeks bloom with shameful heat. Trying to scramble off him, I rush my apology out. "I'm sorry. So sorry. I'm an id—"

His grip on my hips tighten, not allowing me off his lap. "Look at me."

Embarrassed, I slowly meet his gaze.

"Don't apologize." One hand reaches up, tenderly tucking some hair behind my ear. "It's taking every ounce of willpower—and then some—to resist fucking you six ways till Sunday right now."

My eyebrows furrow. "But—"

"But"—with a gentle smile, he speaks softly—"I can't." His warm breath washes against my lips. "As much as I want to bury myself so deep inside you, you'll feel me for days, as much as I'd like to take my time with you and learn every inch of your body…" His eyes are blazing with such intensity that my breath catches in my throat. "I can't do that. Not only because it's been mere hours after you've made a major life decision, but also because you and I both know you deserve more." His hand moves, his thumb tracing over my bottom lip in a sweet caress, his eyes following it. "More than me." His voice is a hoarse whisper, and I can feel the pain radiating from it.

As my lips part to speak, he interrupts and what he says next seals the deal—whether he realizes or wants to admit it.

"You deserve more than an ugly, scarred guy like me." His gaze drops as if he can't bring himself to look me in the eye.

His lips are so close to mine, and his words have elicited so many emotions that I can't take it anymore.

The moment my lips press against his, I relish their softness. I can tell he's restraining himself by the stiff way he continues to hold himself. Nipping at his lower lip, I gently tug at it, and that's the moment his large hand slides to cup the nape of my neck, fingers sifting through my hair. I think he's going to deepen the kiss but the gentle tugging of my hair—tugging me *away* from him—makes it clear that's not the case.

His gaze is searching, that crease between his brows pronounced. "You don't want this, Presley," he whispers, his hot breath washing against my lips.

Hendy thinks he's too scarred and that no one can care for him because of it. He doesn't believe anyone could love him…because he doesn't love himself. Doesn't love this version of himself. But he's wrong. I can see it; I can see past the roadblocks, past the marred skin, past his claims. Because a man who would risk his life for unnamed Americans, who would risk his life trying to save his "brothers," a man who would endure unfathomable torture for his country is a man who deserves more love than he realizes. He is more than able to be loved.

He just needs a reminder.

The thought pops into my mind immediately. *Yes, he needs a reminder.* He needs to realize he's loveable, regardless of the way he looks on the outside. He's so much more than meets the eye. My expression softens as my palm slides to the side of his cheek, and I gaze deeply into his eyes.

"You're wrong." Leaning closer, I kiss one corner of his lips. "I want this." I press a kiss to the other corner. "More than I think I've wanted anything before." This time, when my lips meet his, it's as though I've pushed him to his breaking point.

He makes a rough sound in the back of his throat; the hand still entwined in my hair steers me, angling my face to drive the kiss deeper. His tongue delves inside to slide against mine as the kiss turns frantic, devouring. I can't resist rocking over him, over his cock pressing hard against me, causing my panties to grow damp with my arousal.

Just as I moan against his lips, I'm abruptly lifted and placed back on my side of the bed. Our mingled heavy breathing fills the bedroom as we stare at one another for a beat before he lays back on his side of the bed, peering up at the ceiling.

"Pres." His voice is gravelly, and it's thrilling to think I had something to do with throwing him a bit off-balance. "You and I both know you drank quite a bit tonight. But not only that…" He trails off as I allow my eyes to take in his profile, watching as he swallows hard. "I don't want you to do something you will regret." Slowly, he turns his head on the pillow to look at me. "I don't want to be your regret in the morning."

Searching his face, I recognize his seriousness, and that he's totally stonewalling me.

Baby steps, Presley. Baby steps.

Inhaling deeply, I offer a small smile. "Bedtime story then?"

Slowly, he curves his lips up, and the corners of his eyes crinkle. "You've got yourself a deal."

Once I get situated beneath the covers, lying here on my side facing him, I close my eyes and listen to his deep, sexy voice.

"Once upon a time, there was a…"

CHAPTER TWENTY-FIVE

Hendy

Presley Cole might just bring me to my knees.

That's the main thought running through my mind as I watch her sleep in my bed, a faint smile playing on her lips. She's shifted and shoved the covers down a bit, offering me a view I'll definitely recall later. My shirt has ridden up on her, resting on her hips, and my fingers itch to raise it up even more.

Even worse is the urge—the desire—to slide my hand between her thighs, slip beneath her panties, and see if she's still wet. From when she'd rocked herself over me. Shit, the heat emanating from her pussy and the dampness I could feel nearly made me shoot my load then and there.

Fuck. Scrubbing a hand down my face, I will my hard-on to subside, but it's impossible. She was so damn hot when she was on top of me that it took every ounce of restraint I had not to flip her over on her back and slide my cock so deep inside her that she'd forget all about that ex-fiancé of hers, let alone she was engaged in the first place.

She's the only woman I've denied—the only woman I've held myself back from. The old Hendy wouldn't have hesitated to shove her back on the bed, tug aside those panties, and bury his cock inside her sweet pussy.

But I can't do that. Presley's got a heart of gold, and she sure as hell deserves better than a quick fuck from a beat-up former SEAL who looks like the stuff horror movies are made of.

Huffing out a sigh when sleep begins to tug at me, I quietly ease from the bed and carefully tuck the covers over Presley more securely. As I gaze down at her sleeping form, I feel an odd sensation roll over me. After leaning down to dust a soft kiss on her forehead, I turn and leave the room before I give in to the temptation to sleep there beside her.

That would be far too dangerous.

Slipping out of the bedroom, I find Izzy lying right outside, and I quietly close the door behind me. Izzy sticks close by as I pad across the cool hardwood floor to the door leading to the back deck facing the Atlantic Ocean and head outside. I settle into the comfortable cushions of one of the deck chairs, pat the large padded chaise beside me, and she jumps up, relaxing onto it.

A weary sigh blows past my lips while I stare up at the sky. Tonight is clear, appearing as though someone took handfuls of glitter and tossed them into the darkness.

At times like this, I'm bombarded with memories. Memories of one of my last conversations with Foster before he left the teams. He was ready to go but had been struggling with the decision.

"What about you? When do you think your time will be?" he asked me as we sat outside on base one night, the stars sparkling bright above us.

At first, I offered a casual shrug, but then realized I couldn't—wouldn't—bullshit one of my best friends.

"A few times, I wondered if it was already time. We all

know I don't have any family, and I'll be honest, the more I'm here, the more missions we go on, the more I think I'll find my time ending here." My throat grew thick at voicing that. *"I'm okay with it, though,"* I added softly. *"Because I know I won't be going out in anything less than a blaze of gunfire and glory."* I turned to him with a slight wry grin on my face, cocky even then.

Because I know I won't be going out in anything less than a blaze of gunfire and glory.

Hell if my words didn't come true a mere few years later.

Without warning, I'm instantly bombarded with the images from that fateful night. The night when I was certain I would, in fact, depart this world in a blaze of gunfire and glory.

Leaning my head back against the chair and allowing my eyes to fall closed, I swear I can see everything as if it were only yesterday, the memories so vivid.

A recon mission in the mountains of Afghanistan assigned to us, we had no choice but to fast-rope from the helicopter on the side of the mountain range due to the surrounding tree heights.

Shaw nudged me as we rode in that helo. Leaning toward me, he covered up the mic to his headset so the others wouldn't hear as he spoke in my ear. "You got a feeling?"

My eyes met his in the darkened interior, and I knew what he was asking. I'd often had that freaky sixth sense about things over the years. They were always spot-on, so when I got one of those feelings, I'd learned not to ignore them.

And tonight, my senses were screaming.

Covering my own mic, I answered him. "We need to be on it, man. This could turn into a colossal clusterfuck."

Shaw merely nodded, that crease between his brows the

only indication of his concern at my foreboding response. We had no idea we were walking right into a fucking ambush of epic proportions.

Fast-roping down, we made it what seemed to be only a handful of yards away from the helo before the RPG—rocket-propelled grenade—hit. The explosion had been so great we could immediately feel the scorching heat from it. The intense glare of the fiery crash, which had left only some rotor blades, caused me to flip up my night vision goggles.

Calling over our comms, I prayed I'd get a response from our pilots.

"Fuck!" I swore under my breath, scrambling with my guys to take cover. Which was a fucking joke since we were now in a damn valley.

Sitting ducks—illuminated by the massive bonfire. So much for us operating under the cover of darkness.

The ping of gunfire hitting the rocky terrain nearby was the next clue that my feeling was spot-on.

In the worst way possible.

Attempting to find a better spot to shield me from the flying bullets, at least for long enough to make the radio call for reinforcements, I watched as the others laid down cover fire.

"...repeat, requesting air support..."

I never got a chance to find out whether the call was heard amidst the crackly connection. I never got a chance to hear if anyone ever responded with the air support I requested. Because in the next moment, the world was fucking rocked off its axis.

The thing about an RPG is when it hits anywhere near you, it's utterly deafening. And then everything gets eerily quiet, and it's as if time slows. The impact of the RPG had thrown me back against the rocky earth, my head snapping back so abruptly it felt as though my brain literally rattled in my head. Amidst dust clouding from the explosion, I heard cussing in my comm. How that shit was still working was a miracle to me.

"Goddamn goatfuckers!" I heard Marty "McFly" McPherson groan.

Coughing to clear my throat of the nasty ass dust, I caught sight of Marty. And that would be the first time my heart would plummet to my stomach.

Though certainly not the last.

Crawling over to him, I reached for the tourniquets to help him prevent any more blood loss. Both of his arms had been blown off from around the elbow, and his right leg was shredded just below the knee. Always the smartass, he looked at me, as calm as ever, and said, "Hey, man. Give me a hand, will ya?"

I did what I could to try to get his tourniquets as tight as possible, telling him to hang tight. The explosion did us a small favor by blasting into the side of the mountain and creating a makeshift alcove which would help to keep Marty safe.

For now.

"Go."

My eyes flew to his in alarm.

He merely shook his head. "I don't need more help than this. I'm good, man. Go find the others."

Just then, another enormous explosion rocked the earth. Another fucking RPG hit.

Hand on his shoulder, I held his gaze. "We're getting the fuck out of here. In a few minutes." I hoped.

A smile tugged at the corners of his lips as if he heard my inner thoughts. But the look in his eyes at that moment would haunt me for years to come. Resignation. "See you in a few."

That would be the last time I saw Marty.

Making my way in search of the others while returning fire, I barely felt the impact of a few stray bullets hitting my body armor because my adrenaline was so high. I found Shaw Dempsey within a few feet of Danny Tyson. Shaw's legs were both blown off, and a pool of blood surrounded his body. Even though I saw the hole where the bullet had entered through the corner of his eye and exited clean out the back, I still confirmed he had no pulse.

Dragging Shaw and Danny, I situated them closer to the side of the mountain where an outcropping might—and I hoped to hell it would—provide some protection. I realized Danny's helmet had been blown off in the blast. As I was trying to staunch the blood pouring from a nasty wound near his temple before I assessed the rest of his injuries, I noted his flesh appeared as though someone had ripped it off from the hairline near his temple and back. He'd grabbed my wrist suddenly, drawing my attention.

"Fucking leg," he breathed out.

Shit. Looking down, I noticed a large shard of rock sticking out from his upper thigh; blood soaked his uniform pants.

Fuck, fuck, fuck!

"If we get a tourniquet on it quick enough, I might have about an hour to help you lay down fire."

I didn't meet his eyes, so intent on getting that tourniquet wrapped around his thigh. I didn't want him to see that I recognized his lie.

We both knew he was bullshitting me about having an hour because if his femoral artery was nicked bad enough—and I had the feeling that it was, judging from the amount of *blood soaking his pants and pooling beneath him—this tourniquet would only do so much.*

After I'd doctored Danny up as much as I could, I knew I had to find our pilots. Danny reached over to grab Shaw's extra ammo and sidearm for me. As I was readying to step back out in the gunfight, Danny's words carried over to me.

"See you later."

I knew what he was telling me. Without saying it, we both knew. This would be the last time we'd see one another. My brother was saying goodbye.

I nodded. "Later." Love you, man.

As I stepped into what I expected to be my final gunfight, my last attempt at fighting against evil, I was ready. My veins pulsed with the fury at these faceless bastards who so easily took the lives and well-being of some of the best guys I'd ever known. My vessels throbbed with heartache over losing guys who were my only remaining family.

But I was ready.

Ready to go out in a blaze of gunfire and glory.

Izzy nudges me, and I open my eyes, reaching out. "Hey, girl. I'm okay." I pet her, trying to communicate that I'm all right, that she doesn't have to worry about me. Her eyes watch me unnervingly.

With a heavy sigh, I lean my head back against the chair.

Because, much like Foster, she sees right through my bullshit, too.

CHAPTER TWENTY-SIX

Presley

I've never done the walk of shame before.

Lame, yes, I know, but when you've only been with one guy, and even *that* relationship wasn't exactly thrilling by anyone's standards, that's what happens.

There's something about waking up in a guy's shirt—which smells so freaking awesome—and having to put on your dress from the night before when you prepare to leave. It feels illicit. Exciting. Naughty.

Part of me wishes I could keep Hendy's shirt, but that would be more than a little weird. Tiptoeing across the hall to the bathroom with my clothing in hand, the door is ajar and I push it open, praying I make it undetected because my hair is a certifiable, ungodly mess. I breathe a small sigh of relief after closing myself in the bathroom and lean back against the door.

"Trying to escape from someone?"

I jerk, my eyes flying open to see Hendy standing outside the open shower door. He's getting dressed with one arm through a T-shirt and a towel securely wrapped around his waist. He eyes me with amusement. Clearly, in my haste to make it to the safety of the bathroom, I had thought the light had been left on, forgotten.

Not once did I check to see if a gorgeous, half-naked man was inside toweling off after his shower—drying his hard-muscled body wearing nothing but terry cloth, hiding that delicious cock I shamelessly tried to dry hump last night.

God, I sound like a horny teenager. I've never dry-humped anyone before—never even tried. Even the tiny snippet of what I experienced last night communicated how much I'd been missing. Because it had been über hot.

I'd also thrown caution to the wind, dismissing the fact he's my patient. I'd given in to my desires. Unprofessional, yes. But I don't regret it. Not only that, but I'm completely sober now, so that eliminates another one of Hendy's excuses from last night.

My arms tighten over the folded dress I'm holding against my chest as I take in the sight of the freshly showered man before me. It should be against the law for a man to be this gorgeous. His lightly bronzed skin is still slightly damp. A few droplets of water cling to his upper torso, scattered with scars, and it's right then that I wish I had the nerve to—

Wait a minute. That needs to change. Starting now. I've had a dull, lame existence up to this point. I've been a doormat—one seemingly specifically designed for Dylan. That needs to end, stat. It's time for Presley to get her groove back. Like in the movie, *How Stella Got Her Groove Back.* Except, in this case, I'm not sure I ever had a groove to begin with.

Nor do I have a hot Jamaican man interested in me. A Latino one, though, will definitely do. *Meow.*

I just meowed in my head. Oh, boy. Apparently, getting

my groove back has some serious side effects I'm not entirely sure I approve of. Regardless, I need to act. I am *not* letting this moment get past me.

Stepping forward, I let my dress and bra drop to the bathroom floor as I cross the distance until I'm in front of him. He's slid his other arm through the shirt, about to pull it down over those few beads of water clinging for dear life on his impressively broad chest where my eyes fixate. Part of me recognizes the fact he's turned a bit to ensure his right side is facing me. Because that's what he considers his "better view."

"Presley." My name sounds like a husky caress, falling from his lips.

Placing one hand to stop the shirt from dropping to completely cover up his torso, I lean forward, sipping a droplet of water just to the side of one nipple. His sharp intake of breath spurs me on, and my tongue darts out to trace over the same spot.

Tipping my head back to gaze up at him, I note his heavy gaze resting on me before my eyes are drawn to that thin trail of hair beginning at the bottom of his belly button and disappearing beneath the towel. My index finger circles his belly button, noting the contracting of his abdominal muscles before tracing it down over that trail leading to the promised land.

What kind of promises do you have for me? I think to myself naughtily.

Hendy lets out a choked laugh, drawing my surprised attention. Meeting his dark eyes, I see they are sparkling with humor as he raises his eyebrows at me.

"What kind of promises do I have for you?" he asks with that lopsided smile of his.

Hell. Again, I clearly need to work on keeping my internal thoughts from being voiced while around him. Before I can offer a response, a knock sounds on the door.

"Hey, sweet darlin'. You want some coffee?" Kane asks from outside the bathroom door.

My eyes dart to Hendy, silently questioning who Kane's talking to. His lips quirk slightly before he answers.

"Yes, sir," he answers, winking at me.

"I was actually asking the lovely doctor, but I'll take your order, too." I can hear the humor in Kane's voice. "How about you, darlin'?"

Blushing, I let my forehead rest against Hendy's chest. "Yes, please," I say weakly.

"Whenever you two lovebirds finish frolicking in there, I'll have it ready." Kane's voice trails off as he presumably heads back toward the kitchen.

Hendy's hand runs over my hair in a caress. "You've got to have the sexiest case of bed head I've ever seen." His voice is low, husky, sending shivers through me, and my nipples instantly perk up.

He's clearly trying to be kind because everyone knows there is no such thing as a good case of bed head. Especially for me. I always end up with what appears to be a cowlick or something crazy. Mumbling against his chest, I say, "Stop lying to me."

Leaning closer, his lips brushing against my temple as he speaks. "If I were lying, I sure as hell wouldn't be as hard as I am right now."

How? *How* am I supposed to maintain control around him when he says things like this? He's the only man who's made me feel this way, made me dismiss the proverbial line drawn between myself and my patient.

"You really shouldn't say things like that to me," I continue to mumble, still refusing to show my face, "when it's taking all my willpower to remain as un-slutty as possible."

A huff of warm breath washes over my face, and I realize he's laughing at me. "Presley Cole." The humor in his tone is apparent. "Don't you realize it's taking all *my* willpower not to guide your hand beneath this towel?" His lips dust against my skin in a soft caress as he speaks. "To show you how I want you to stroke me. To let you feel how much you turn me on."

One of his large hands glides over my shoulder, down my back, and over my ass, cupping me. "But even with all this, as fucking sweet as it is, I know what you really need this morning."

Leaning away, I raise my eyes to his dark ones, my gaze searching. "What I need?"

With a mischievous look, he leans in to whisper, "Coffee." His lips curve up into a devastatingly handsome smile that's so...*Hendy*. "You always need coffee after a night of drinking, Pres."

With a perfunctory kiss on my lips, he quickly pulls on his boxers beneath the towel before dropping it to don the pair of jeans sitting on the large vanity. Then comes the ball cap, and he pulls it down over his eyes. Playfully slapping my ass, he hangs up his towel then steps around me to exit the bathroom, closing the door behind him.

And I'm left standing dazed in the same spot. My fingertips touch my lips, and I swear I can still feel the heat from his kiss. Yet, it's one word that has a smile forming on my face.

Hendy called me Pres. He gave me a nickname. And everyone knows nicknames mean something. A term of endearment.

Which means I'm a tiny bit closer to showing him—proving to him—that he's much more than looks alone.

So much more.

* * *

"I hope like hell our boy here treated you with respect last night."

Kane says this as we're eating the breakfast he and Hendy insisted on making, declaring it their duty since I was their "overnight guest."

"He didn't try to pressure you into anything now, did he, darlin'?" Kane's mischievous sparkle in his eyes belies his concerned tone. "Because I always remind him, 'No means no.'"

"Jesus," Hendy mutters, running a hand over his face before shaking his head at his friend.

Grinning at Kane, I wink. "He was a perfect gentleman." Nodding as though he's proud and relieved to hear that, he takes a sip of coffee as I add, "It was me who was hell-bent on molesting him last night."

He chokes on his coffee while Hendy cough-laughs into his napkin. I merely dig into my scrambled eggs with a flourish.

"Ah, that does explain the"—his aquamarine eyes sparkle with amusement as he uses finger quotes—"'unusual noises' I heard at one point last night."

My chin drops down, concentrating on the food on my plate, and I can feel the flush of embarrassment spreading across my cheeks.

"Aw, now, darlin'. Don't be shy. I didn't hear you as much as I heard him."

Hendy's head jerks up from where he'd been spearing some scrambled eggs on his fork. "Excuse me?"

Kane has that wide, smug grin, and I can tell by that alone that he's up to no good.

"You know, when you were in the shower this morning." Taking a bite of toast, Kane winks at his roommate as my eyes volley back and forth between the two men.

Hendy merely flashes his roommate a death stare. And it dawns on me. *Ooooh.* Hendy had been doing…*that* in the shower.

"Especially liked your moaning, darlin'," Kane goes on. "Sounded a lot like this…" He sets down his fork and proceeds to make exaggerated sounds, running his hands over his face and hair as if attempting to impersonate the restaurant orgasm scene from the movie *When Harry Met Sally*.

"You're not right," Hendy mutters, but there's no bite to his words. His eyes crinkle at the corners as he shakes his head at Kane's theatrics.

Just then, Hendy pipes up to Kane. "Don't you know there ain't nothing wrong with a little bump and grind?" I snicker, immediately recognizing his reference to an old R. Kelly song.

"Even if it's solo?" Kane shoots back.

"Boys." My tone is a warning, but I'm really teasing. "I'm trying to eat here."

"Yes, ma'am," they answer in unison, and we eat in silence.

After a moment, I pick up on Hendy's faint humming, and it takes me a second to recognize what tune it is. Raising my eyes to meet his, I can't mask the smile forming on my face when he winks at me.

Returning to my breakfast, I join him in humming the song.

R. Kelly's "Bump and Grind."

CHAPTER TWENTY-SEVEN

Hendy

"Holy shit, woman. That feels incredible."

This is what I hear as soon as I make my way down the hallway, toting lunch for Presley. Lucia had let me in since they'd already locked the office doors for lunch. I'd been her first appointment of the morning, and Presley seemed like she'd been having a rough start even then, so I figured I'd surprise her with lunch.

"Ah, shit, Cole!"

By the sounds of it, I sure as hell have.

Some dude's groaning and yammering on about how good it feels—whatever *it* is that she's doing. Approaching the only room with a light on and door open, I hesitate, unsure of what I'm about to discover.

Instead, I find some massively tall guy on the adjustment table who looks like he doesn't have an ounce of fat in sight. His legs hang off the table farther than mine do so I'm guessing he's easily pushing over six-foot-six. He lets out a loud groan as Presley maneuvers him on his back and presses his bent leg up toward his chest.

"Quit whining like a damn baby, Becket." I see his leg inching closer to his chest. "If you did those exercises I told you to keep up with, you wouldn't be so tight."

The man grins mischievously. "But that's how the ladies like it. Nice and ti—"

"Don't go there, you perv." Presley cuts him off, but she has no bite in her tone, only amusement. She seems at ease with him.

With her concentration on the guy, a strand of hair's come loose from her ponytail, and my fingers itch to slide it back behind her ear. I recall how silky soft it felt the other night. That's not all I recall feeling the other night, of course, because the way she'd rocked her pussy against me had to have been the hottest fucking thin—

"Well, what do we have here?"

My eyes jerk away from Presley to find the guy peering up at me from where he still lies. Something about him seems familiar, but I can't place him.

"Presley Cole. Have you been holding out on me?"

"What?" She finally looks over at where I stand in the doorway, and I'd be lying if I said the smile she gives me doesn't make my heart beat a little faster. Because it isn't just a smile. Nope. It's one of those smiles that says, *I kissed you and rubbed my pussy all over your lap.*

Make no mistake; those smiles have got to be the best fucking kind.

"Hey, Hendy." There's an intimate quality to her tone, and I'm not the only one to take note of it.

"Hey, Hendy," he mimics, grinning wider as he appraises me. Right before getting swatted on the side of his head.

"Hey! I take enough hits on the field, woman."

Finally, it dawns on me where I recognize him. Becket Jones. I don't watch much pro football as I've always preferred college, but this guy plays for the local NFL team. If

I remember correctly, he got drafted after playing for the University of Florida.

"Well, then." Presley slowly lowers his leg, straightening it out. "You should've gotten some manners knocked into you. Lord knows you used to have them back in college."

Sitting up, Becket's gaze comes to rest on me, lifting his chin in a nod toward the bag of food in my hand. "You the new delivery guy?" His lips tip up at the corners. He's clearly fucking with me.

"Beck—"

I cut off Presley's warning of protest. "If you're asking if I'm the guy delivering a smack down to anyone harassing the lovely doctor, then yes."

Our eyes war for a moment before his face stretches into a wide smile and those perfectly white teeth nearly blind me. Without breaking eye contact with me as he speaks, he directs his words at Presley.

"I like him much better than Dyl-hole." His smile gets even wider. "Much better."

Swatting at Becket's shoulder, she admonishes, "That's enough. Time to go. You have to be up early tomorrow. Go home, lay low, and ice."

Rising to a standing position, he winks at Presley, slinging an arm around her neck and pulling her in for a bear hug. "You're a miracle worker, as always, Cole." Pressing a quick kiss to the top of her head, he releases her and grabs his keys from the chair in the corner of the room.

Stepping toward the doorway, Becket holds out a hand to me, and when I accept his handshake, he leans in. His voice is quiet and subdued as if he doesn't want Presley to hear, but the underlying steely currents are unmistakable. "Mess with her, and I'll crush you."

After a beat of silence passes, our eyes lock, and I smirk. "Thought you only threw the ball."

His eyebrows rise. "Ah, so you know who I am."

"Vaguely."

"Is that so." He says this not as a question but a challenging statement.

"Yep."

He pauses briefly, eyes cataloging me, catching on the left side of my face for far longer than I'd like, and I work hard to resist the urge to fidget.

"I know you from some—" He breaks off, eyes widening. "No fucking way."

"Way." Please don't let this guy ask the same asinine questions I normally get when someone recognizes me.

What was it like being held by them?

How many people have you killed?

Bet you get a lot of ass being a SEAL, huh?

None of those questions are okay. Well, maybe I would've been okay with the last one a while ago. But now things have changed. *I've* changed.

Instead, Becket surprises me.

One of his hands slaps against my chest. "You take good care of her; you got me?"

Pointedly eyeing his hand on my chest, I cock an eyebrow. "No can do." His features grow tight at my answer. "I'll take the *best* care of her." Then leaning in, my tone cocky, I add, "You got me?"

Instantly, it's like the ferocious mask is ripped from his face, and he's back to the jolly, happy man. Stepping around me with another playful slap to my shoulder, he glances over his shoulder at Presley.

"This one's all right, Cole."

"So relieved you approve," comes her dry response.

"I think I need to fan *my*self from all the testosterone here," Lucia sing-songs from where she's watching at the end of the hallway. With a playful pout, she crosses her arms. "*No*body ever gets crazy over me like that."

"Now, Lucia." Becket starts down the hallway toward her. "You should know I…"

Tuning out his words, I avert my gaze to Presley, who has her back to me. She's seated in a chair, still typing on the computer, entering notes for Becket.

"I wanted to, uh, surprise you with some lunch." *Fuck.* I sound like a pre-pubescent kid asking a chick out for the first time.

Jesus. I've got to get my shit together.

Clicking the mouse, the screen clears out, and she swivels around, peering up at me. "You brought me lunch? As a surprise?"

I can't quite put my finger on something in her tone. Disbelief, confusion, or possibly shock.

"Yes," I draw out the word slowly. Maybe that's not okay. Fuck me. I've never done this before.

And yeah, I realize I sound like a number one douche-bag. But it's the truth. The women have always come to me. I've never been the one to chase.

But something about her makes me want to do nice things for her. She's different. It isn't simply because she doesn't have any silicone fillers in her body, doesn't play games, doesn't act coy, doesn't do the pouty thing with her lips, or any shit like that. Presley Cole doesn't have "game."

Yet she has more game than she realizes. With her tall stature of about five-foot-seven, a slim waist, and breasts that might run on the smaller side, her legs and ass are killer. Legs so long they seem to go on forever, and an ass that's fucking perfection like someone sculpted it. An ass I've had my hands on, cupped while I pulled her down to grind against my cock.

With a silent groan, I blow out a long breath, willing my hard-on to let up. I'm trying to do something nice for the woman, and instead, here I am, getting a boner while holding our lunches.

Fucking stellar.

Folding her arms across her chest, she leans back in the desk chair, and her eyes track up my body, starting at my toes and lingering on my groin for a second longer than necessary. Her eyes flare with heat before rising to meet my gaze.

"Did you bring me dessert, too?"

And that's when my self-control disintegrates.

CHAPTER TWENTY-EIGHT

Presley

This is bad. Wrong. Inappropriate. He's my patient. I know this—fully recognize these facts.

It doesn't make me any less attracted to the man standing before me. The man who showed up to surprise me with lunch. While I know that might not seem like much to anyone else, it's a big deal for me. It seems like, more and more, Hendy's making me realize how little I had with Dylan. Because not once had he ever done something thoughtful like this for me.

It isn't only that, though. It's also the way his eyes drift over my entire body in a caress as if he's savoring it. The moment I notice the slight tenting in his jeans—jeans which appear so worn and soft, lovingly hugging his long, muscled legs—it instantly reminds me of the other night.

The night I basically humped him. In his bedroom.

Shit. The heat of embarrassment floods my cheeks. But I still can't say I regret it. It was hotter than hot. Especially when he told me a bedtime story about "a cool as hell, little northeastern Texas boy who *didn't* say darlin' every chance he got."

Yeah, his reference to Kane was pretty cute, as was his

story. Falling asleep listening to the comforting lull of his deep voice is something I know I won't soon forget.

While I recall those moments—one sexy and one sweet—and recognize I'm in my place of business, I can't help but wish right now could be a replay of that night. Except this time, we'd go all the way.

All the way. I think I nearly rolled my eyes so hard at my juvenile reference that they got stuck.

When my gaze meets Hendy's, he must sense the path of my thoughts because he sets the bag of takeout on the floor, kicks the door to the room closed, and stalks over to me. Leaning down, he braces his arms on either side of me, caging me in against my desk. His face is so close to mine that I detect his minty breath, and the heat in his eyes, slightly shadowed beneath his ball cap.

"You can't look at me like that." His voice is barely a whisper. "I'm trying to be good."

Tipping my head back, I find his lips are so close to mine. So close. "Stop trying to be good."

The smile he gives me is feral. "Oh, Pres. You don't want that." Tilting his head before lightly dusting his lips over mine, he whispers, "Otherwise, I'd have you on that chiropractic table, and there wouldn't be any adjustments happening."

My panties grow damp thinking about that—the images that flutter through my mind.

"Instead," he continues, his soft lips grazing along my cheekbone and over my earlobe, toying briefly with it, "I'd be so fucking deep inside you, thrusting into your sweet pussy, that you'd be the one needing your spine realigned afterward."

I said that my panties were growing damp—that's a lie.

They're soaked right now. To the point I think I might have to change them.

Because of this man before me, a man who has yet to touch me—really touch me—the way I want him to. Already, he's giving me what I want.

Yet he's not. Because I realize I want more. So much more.

My breathing is ragged, and I reach out to cup him and—oh, holy shit. He leans back slightly, my eyes flying up to meet his.

"Hendy," I breathe.

His eyes fall closed, and he presses against my hand, my fingers molding his hard flesh through the soft denim. Suddenly, he captures my wrist, stilling my movements.

He swallows hard, and his voice is deep, gravelly. "You have to stop."

"I'm concerned about something." My lips curve up slightly when I watch his eyebrows arch in question. "Because I'm not sure how that's going to fit." And I'm only half kidding. He feels *enormous*.

His lips part then close before he releases a pained chuckle. "Presley Cole. What am I going to do with you?"

I know what I'd like for him to do with me. And it's completely inappropriate for my workplace. Damn it. Being a responsible small business owner has a downside after all.

More than that, though, is the immediate thought—my response—following his question that startles me. Because without hesitation, my mind—and heart—had answered.

Love me.

* * *

"You and Becket met at UF?"

Hendy and I have just finished our lunch and are sitting at the small table in my office. Taking a sip of water, I nod. "Yes." I smile at the memory. "We were paired in Public Speaking 101 to do a presentation about whether God was a man or a woman." Shaking my head with a laugh, I add, "Of course, Becket chose the 'God is a woman' stance."

"Sounds like it was a hell of a speech."

"Oh, it was. He—"

"Excuse me." Lucia's voice draws our attention to where she's standing at the door. Pointing at Hendy, she says, "You, *mi*ster, have an appointment for a therapeutic massage with me in five *mi*nutes."

Hendy winks at her with a short nod. "Yes, ma'am."

Lucia turns to return down the hallway, and I can hear her mumbling something that sounds like, "*Dios*. A man like that brings you food; you ought to give him some *de*ssert."

Rising from the chair, I thank him for surprising me with lunch. "I appreciate you thinking of me." Taking our trash and placing it in the nearby bin, I don't realize he's moved swiftly until I straighten, finding him far closer than expected.

His hands reach out to frame my face delicately. "I always think of you." Pressing a kiss to my forehead, he whispers a goodbye before heading down the hall for his appointment with Lucia.

And again, he leaves me with words that seep into my heart. Like arid soil reacts to long-awaited rain, my heart soaks up his words like a soothing balm.

CHAPTER TWENTY-NINE

Hendy

"Well, ain't this just the cutest little setup."

My eyes flick up to see Kane canvassing the interior of our house with a smirk, his thick, muscular arms folded across his chest. "Seems to me someone's got sweet seduction on their mind, darlin'."

His eyes take in the sight of me wearing his favorite apron with the saying, *Chop it like it's hot.* "Sorry but that apron still looks better on me." Grinning wide, he raises his eyes to me. "Who's the lucky lady?"

That wide, shit-eating grin's killing me. Because he knows full well that I've only been interested in one woman from the start. The only woman on my mind nearly from day one, whom I've been getting closer to over the past few weeks. The only one who seems to see beneath the surface, who might actually see me for who I am.

The same woman I've been dying to bury my cock inside for far too long.

Shooting him a glare that's lacking in heat, I mutter, "You know who."

He laughs. "That I do, but I wanted to hear you admit who's been making you happy as a tick on a fat dog."

Pausing in placing the silverware on the table, I flash him an amused look. "You and your sayings, man."

Kane lifts a shoulder in a half-shrug. "South Texans are better with words." Flipping him the bird, I go back to setting the table, ignoring his dig at me being from northeastern Texas. Just because I was raised in a more urban environment doesn't mean I don't have a way with words.

Grin widening, he adds, "All that flowery shit goes a long way."

"Clearly." My tone is dry. "It's obviously worked wonders on Lucia."

"That woman…" He breaks off to shake his head, frustration etching his normally jovial features. "She's like Fort Knox to my charm."

"She's making you work for it, huh?" Just to give him shit, I furrow my brows. "You don't think you're barking up the wrong tree?"

With a look of frustration, he runs a hand down his face. "Hell, some days I'm not entirely sure, to be honest."

"Give it time, man." Moving over to the kitchen, I check on my chicken enchiladas in the oven. It's one of my favorite dishes my mother used to make.

"Am I invited to this little love picnic you two are planning to have?"

"When you say shit like 'love picnic,' that downgrades your cool factor." Tossing down the oven mitts on the counter, I level a stare on him.

"But don't you see, darlin'?" His grin widens. "We're the lone single guys—"

I throw up a hand. "Not true. Doc's still single."

Kane makes a face. "He's a former SEAL sniper. Like anyone's going to pass muster with him." Shaking his head, he goes on. "Found out he color coordinates his damn closet, and then the other day, he was *mentally* calculating the formula to find the momentum of a gun's recoil."

I wince. "Jesus."

At a loss for what to do with myself, I feel antsy as shit, having finished my preparations. Darting my eyes around the place, I scan, hoping to find something I'd somehow forgotten.

"Nervous, huh?"

My eyes clash with Kane's, and we don't speak for a moment, holding each other's stare, until finally...

"Weird Secret Confessions," we both speak in unison.

"Weird Secret Confessions" is something Kane started when I first moved in with him. He claimed that if we told each other one weird secret, it would help break the ice. Now, we do it when one of us is having a rough day or things aren't going smoothly.

"I'll go first." Kane runs a hand over his jaw, wearing a thoughtful expression. "For some reason, anytime I'm around a person who's blind, I feel the need to talk louder." He smirks at me with a shrug. "Backward as hell, but I always do it."

Shit. I'm scrambling for something decent. "I still hate when the different foods on my plate touch one another."

Kane gives me one of those looks. "You have *got* to be kidding me." With a short laugh, he says, "What are you? Ten?"

"Inches," I shoot back with a wide grin. He groans, realizing he'd left himself wide open for that reply.

"I blamed Izzy the other night for passing gas when it was me."

"Dude." He casts me a look. "Like I didn't know that."

Glancing down to where Izzy's lying a few feet away, lazily watching us, he smiles at her. "Sweet girl like you could never be gross like that, could you, darlin'?" He pauses, still using his sweet talk on my dog. "*Nooo.* Say no, Uncle Kane, I wouldn't do *that.*"

Of course, at that moment, Izzy makes some funny grumbling sound and hides her face in her paws.

"That's my girl, right there." I grin at Kane, proudly. "She knows who her daddy is."

"Now, Izzy." He pouts. "You're just gonna dismiss me like that?"

She raises her head and glances over at me as if to say, "Is this fool for real?" before walking over to the new doggy door we had installed for her. The door slides up, sensor-activated by the small microchip in her collar, allowing her to come and go from the house as she needs.

In this case, it's to get away from "Uncle Kane." I laugh to myself, glancing over at Kane with a smug smile.

"Women," he mutters, shaking his head.

Poor Kane. Don't think he's experienced a female he couldn't charm. With Lucia, and now Izzy, the guy probably thinks he's losing his mojo.

"Man. Not much lovin' these days, huh? Striking out with all the ladies lately?" I wink at Kane to add more fuel to the fire.

Crossing his arms, he has a mischievous glint to his stare. "Want me to stick around and help chaperone you and your lovely doctor?" My expression says it all because he tosses his head back with a laugh. "Then you need to watch your mouth, darlin'."

Walking down the hall to his bedroom, he disappears for a moment. Emerging with his hard guitar case, he scoops up his keys from atop the corner of the kitchen counter. His expression is more somber than I expect when he stops a few feet away from me.

"Heading out to catch a mid-week dinner over at Momma K's and then over Doc's to hang out. Might have a jam session with him." Eyeing me pointedly, he adds, "Which reminds me. It'd be nice if you came to a family dinner night, you know."

One Sunday a month, Momma K, Foster's mother, designates a family dinner night—one where everyone gathers at her house and she cooks a boatload of one of her Italian specialties. She's a wonderful woman, no doubt about it, but I can't manage the thought of attending one of those dinners.

I haven't seen her since I've been back, and as ashamed as I am to admit it, I can't bring myself to visit her. Maybe it's stupid and makes no sense, but I can go out in public and deal with the stares and gawking from strangers, but if I attended a dinner night at Momma K's and the group of friends—"family"—did that, it'd fucking destroy me.

"One of these days, it'd be nice if you tagged along." When I don't respond, he goes on with, "You need to decide to come out of hiding at some point." His words set me on edge because while I reluctantly admit their accuracy, I sure as hell don't appreciate the fact that someone recognizes I haven't shown up. That I'm hiding out.

The truth is I've become Mr. Avoidance to the fullest extent because I don't want to witness the look on their—or anyone else's—faces. Because I don't want to see anyone full of sympathy. Or worry. Or the worst one.

Pity.

"And don't get me started on the calls you've been

ignoring from Heath."

Fuck. I should have known Kane would pick up on that. Damn it.

I've been fielding calls from Heath Mitchum. Don't get me wrong; he's a great guy—I'm not debating that fact. The former SEAL had served and qualified for medical retirement eight years after being shot up—literally—so horribly in Iraq, he required a medivac and was resuscitated multiple times on the way to the nearest hospital.

Almost fifty surgeries later, many wouldn't know what he's been through by looking at him today. Sure, he has some obvious scarring, and his nose does appear a bit rougher looking than the average man, but considering he'd had to undergo numerous reconstructive surgeries to rebuild the side of his face, it is pretty damn impressive.

Heath wants me to be a spokesperson for his foundation—the very foundation which donated modified clothing to me while I recuperated in the hospital. While it would be employment, I would have to share my story.

Heath's organizing another speaking tour, and he's gathering a handful of his other spokespersons, other wounded veterans who will visit various cities all over the United States—including veteran's hospitals and rehabilitation centers—and sharing their experiences, sharing the importance of teamwork, of perseverance, and of never giving up when times are tough.

While that all sounds great, I don't know that I'm brave enough. Brave enough to open up and leave myself bare, completely exposed to others—to their opinions of that night, to their judgment.

As my lips part to spout off a cutting remark, the timer dings on the oven, alerting me to the fact that the enchiladas should be ready. Talk about saved by the bell.

Grabbing the oven mitts and busying myself with the careful removal of the hot casserole dish, I hear Kane mutter, "Yeah, that's what I thought."

Expecting him to head out the door, I set the dish on the stovetop to cool a bit. Once I turn to replace the oven mitts in one of the drawers, I find Kane still watching me.

"You got nothing?" He cocks an eyebrow at me.

I shake my head.

His aquamarine eyes peer at me. "Remember what I said. Own it. Like the phoenix." With a firm nod, he quietly exits the house, locking the door behind him.

With a sigh, I lean my forearms on the kitchen counter, staring sightlessly ahead. "Easier said than done," I murmur in the silence. "Easier said than done."

CHAPTER THIRTY

Presley

"Lucia, I am not wearing that!"

This has gone on for the better part of forty-five minutes. Lucia pushes some outfit on me, and I promptly veto it.

"But this is sexy." She pouts, gesturing to the fancy black dress she pulled from the recesses of my closet. "You can't go over there dressed like you just got off work." With a look of disgust at my closet, she mutters, "I swear most of the clothes in here belong to Mrs. *Doubt*fire."

With my hands on my hips, I give her a look. "I'm going over to watch the latest *Jeopardy* episode. It's not like we're going to a fancy ball."

Lucia smiles wide, winking suggestively. "Maybe you're going to be *deal*ing with more than one ball, eh?"

"Stop it." My warning does nothing but make her grin widen.

Reaching for my favorite pair of jeans, I pull them from my dresser drawer. "I'm going to wear these with a cute top, I think." Tapping my index finger to my lip in thought, I peruse my closet's offerings. Just as I'm about to reach for one, Lucia's arm darts out to snag a hanger holding a blue, satiny looking sleeveless top.

"This is the one." She holds it up to me. "It will bring out your eyes."

It is one of my favorites, so I concede. Sliding on my jeans and fastening them beneath my simple, knee-length robe, I slide it off, tossing it onto my bed, and gently pull my top down over my black lace bra.

Smoothing it down, I glance at Lucia. "What do you think?"

Her lips make a moue as she inspects me. "What do I think? I think, chica, that you will be the *di*nner entree"— she waves a hand to encompass my outfit—"looking like that."

Scoffing, I walk over to the adjoining bathroom to finish my makeup. "What are you doing tonight?" I ask as I carefully apply a coat of mascara to my lashes.

"Dinner with the familia." Her tone sounds dull as she says this, and I instantly know what she's not saying.

He'll be there. The man she's expected to marry.

The thing about Lucia's family is that, yes, they're warm and welcoming and everything I wish I had in parents—in a family—but they are stuck behind the times. They still believe in arranging suitors for their daughter to eventually marry. Regardless of whether true love is present.

And in Lucia's case, true love is most definitely *not* present.

"I'll be expecting a full report tomorrow," she sing-songs, waving at me before leaving.

Laughing softly at her, I finish up before walking out and grabbing my keys and small purse from the end of my kitchen counter.

* * *

Just as I've pulled into Hendy's driveway, my cell phone rings. Displaying the name of the one person I've been dreading talking to.

My mother.

"Hel—"

"What is this about you and Dylan breaking off your engagement?" She doesn't even let me finish the greeting, just starts right in.

I knew I shouldn't have answered. I *knew* it. But *noooo*. I didn't listen to that internal voice nearly wailing in alarm, telling me I needed to send my mother's call to voice mail.

Damn it.

Before I can even form a response, she rushes on, and I'm starting to wonder how she gets all these words out without taking an audible breath.

"And what is this about you being seen downtown *holding hands* with another man, Presley?" The way she spits out the words "holding hands" makes it sound as if we were doing something X-rated in public or something. Then again, that's my mother and her strict, old school Southern Baptist upbringing. Thou shall not lie, steal, covet thy neighbor's wife, or dance in public with a man.

"Holding hands?" I gasp in faux disgust. "What? I would *never* do something like that. What kind of troglodyte do you take me for, Mother?"

Thank goodness no one had witnessed my lovely puking display. That much I'm grateful for. God only knows what my mother would have to say about *that*.

There's a brief pause then, "Are you using sarcasm again,

Presley?" I can practically see her turning up her nose at me as she speaks. "You know that isn't very ladylike."

Out of the corner of my eye, I see the front door to the house open, and Hendy stepping out. I give him a little wave to let him know I'm okay, and as my mother drones on and on about how I should rethink the choice to end my relationship with Dylan because he's "such a nice, respectable young man"—*gag*—I allow my eyes to take in the sight of the man waiting for me.

God, he's something else. So imposing, yet I know firsthand how tender and gentle he can be. Wearing a pair of dark khaki cargo shorts and a blue, short-sleeved collared polo with his usual ball cap pulled low, he stands at the top of the stairs. I notice a flash of movement near his legs and realize Izzy has come out to sit beside him. She tips her head to the side, looking at me as if to ask, "Why aren't you coming up?"

And that's what makes me snap out of it.

"Mom, I have to go. I have dinner plans. I'll talk to you later."

"Wait! What do you mean you have dinner plans? With that *man* you were with?" The way she says the word "man" makes it sound like I'm having dinner with Lucifer himself and considering having his babies in order to take over the world, spreading sin and evil everywhere.

Instead of a man words can't truly encompass because he's that amazing.

"Love you! Talk to you soon!" I rush my words out and hurriedly press the button to end the call. With a sigh of relief, I turn my phone's ringer to silent and slide it back into my small purse.

Getting out of my car, I press the button twice before

the alarm beeps and slip my keys inside my purse, walking up the steps to where Hendy and Izzy await.

"You can do this Presley. Easy." I mutter under my breath, attempting a quick pep talk. "Easy like Sunday morning."

CHAPTER THIRTY-ONE

Hendy

"Apparently, Lionel Ritchie's joining us tonight. Welcome."

Those uniquely beautiful colored eyes fly up to mine, appearing startled before recovering slightly. Finally reaching the top step, she draws to a stop before me. "You know Lionel Ritchie, huh?"

"Of course." I grin. "Now, did I fantasize about someone singing 'Suddenly' while creating a clay sculpture of my face?" Giving a quick shake of my head, I say, "Not so much."

She laughs, the sound of it wrapping around me. "Well, there go my plans for tonight."

She steps closer, and I catch her essence—the trademark scent of her shampoo or bodywash. It's nothing fruity or heavy on the fragrance; it's simple. Clean and fresh.

"May I come in?"

Shit. She's been standing here waiting on my dumb ass while I muse about her smell.

Her scent, for God's sake. Maybe it's a good thing I haven't been around women and haven't tried this whole hanging out thing because I clearly suck at it. Royally.

"I mean"—she tilts her head to the side, eyes shining with humor—"we could stay out here and bask in everything."

"Bask in everything?" I'm confused.

"It's been approximately four weeks, and we've been hanging out, watching *Jeopardy* together most nights."

"Yes," I draw out the word slowly, unsure of where she's going with this.

"Well, this sexual tension thing?" She pauses. "It's pretty top-notch."

"Really." I have to fight a smile. Hard.

"Oh, yes. In fact"—she lets out a dramatic sigh—"I'd say it's crackling tension. Like chestnuts roasting on an open fire. Or those fireworks people set off that go *pop!pop!pop!* rapid-fire or—"

"Pres," I interrupt with a small laugh, scrubbing a hand over my jaw. "I get it."

"Well, what are you planning to do about it?" She waves a hand in gesture. "Because after all this anticipation, we don't want it to be a letdown in any way."

With a laugh, I step aside. "How about we start by heading inside?" Gesturing with my hand, I wait for her to precede me, of course. I allow my eyes to drift over her form and land right on her ass. Good God Almighty. Those jeans... More accurately, *Presley* in those jeans—this image is going straight to my spank bank. I'm such a sick fuck. But sweet Jesus, her ass is so damn sexy, especially encased in that denim.

As if realizing I need to be put in check, Izzy nudges me gently. My eyes find her sweet ones, and I nod.

"Got it," I murmur softly, so Presley doesn't hear me. "Be a gentleman." Then I wave for her to enter the house,

171

and I enter last behind my girls.

My girls. The possessive feeling that floods through me at the thought of Presley as mine is more powerful than I could ever have imagined.

It's good to have dreams, I think sarcastically.

The only problem with dreams is that you always wake up. And you're left empty-handed.

* * *

"Those kids are so much more intelligent than I can imagine being back in the day."

We're sitting out on the back deck, side by side in chairs, basking in the relaxing sounds of the ocean waves of the Atlantic less than a hundred yards from us. Izzy's curled up beneath the large patio table off to the side as we discuss the *Jeopardy* Teen Tournament we just watched.

Turning my head slightly to look at her, trying to ensure that the main view she has of me is mostly the right side of my face, I study her for a moment. "You can't tell me you weren't super smart back in school."

Appearing so relaxed with her head leaning back on the chair cushion, she focuses her eyes ahead and offers a soft smile. "I was pretty smart for high school standards, but those kids tonight? They were pretty damn impressive." Shifting, she rests her eyes on me. "Plus, I'll be the first one to admit that I can't tell a Rembrandt from a Picasso or Botticelli."

I chuckle, watching as her smile widens, and I swear, right here and now, I'm the happiest I've been in a while. But there's always a catch…

Sobering, I have to voice my concerns. "Presley. I

should apologize. Because"—I let out a long sigh, averting my eyes—"you're my doctor, and even though I'm only seeing you for adjustments twice a week now, I—"

"Feel uncomfortable with the situation," she interjects gently.

Meeting her gaze, I shake my head. "No. I just don't want to put you in an…" I falter, trying to find the right way to phrase it.

"Awkward situation." Her expression is one of understanding. "I get it. I was actually going to bring it up because the last thing I want to do is make you feel that way." She holds up a hand. "Don't get me wrong. I really love spending time with you. I do. But it's also difficult because of"—she gestures between us—"this, um…" She trails off, a flush spreading across her cheeks.

The fact she feels the same pull of attraction as I do is comforting. But I get where she's going with this. No one wants to have a potentially awkward situation on their hands, especially between a doctor and their patient.

"I'm down to only having to see you one time a week for an adjustment now, right?"

She regards me carefully before answering slowly, "Right."

"Then I'll be every other week, and then you'll submit your assessment to the VA."

She nods, and we both fall silent for a beat.

"Do you want to call it a night? For me to leave?" she asks, her tone subdued, as if she's uncertain.

I let out a harsh laugh. "You want the truth?"

"Always."

"I don't want you to leave. But I want you to know, I'll continue to treat you professionally in the office regardless of whether you stay or go." Swallowing past the lump in my throat, I've never felt this nervousness before because I've never been in this position. Never having to work up the nerve to ask a woman to stay the night, I force my words out, hoping they sound nonchalant. "What I want is for you to stay."

Fuck. I totally choked.

"Is that all?" she asks slowly.

My mouth flattens into a thin line, and I know I've got to find my fucking balls and say it. My voice is gravelly, hoarse. "What I want is for you to say you'll stay the night." Reaching out to run the pad of my thumb along her bottom lip, I find myself mesmerized by the way her lips part. "What I really want to do is lift you up on that table, peel off those jeans, and see what you've got on under them."

At my words, her hot breath washes over my thumb at her lips. "Is that all?"

Shaking my head, I keep my eyes locked on hers. "I want a whole hell of a lot more than that. Then, I want to make you scream my name—"

Her lips form a mischievous smile when she interrupts me. "Which would be what? Hendy or Cristiano?"

Dipping my head closer, my lips barely a centimeter away from hers, I whisper, "You can scream my full name if you want. As long as you know who's making you come undone, that's all that matters."

Moving abruptly to straddle my lap, Presley gives me a dry look. "I know you're probably wondering what's going on beneath"—she gestures to her face—"this façade of mild indifference." Leaning in closer, she locks her eyes with mine and says in a husky tone, "But the truth is you seriously made my panties melt by saying that."

"Really?" I grin. "So, if I were to slide beneath your jeans right here…" My hand slips down to cup her over the soft, worn denim, and her lips part to release a tiny moan. I swear I can feel the heat emanating from her core.

"You want me to touch you here?" I ask, pressing gently.

"Yes." Presley's voice is nearly inaudible. And it's then that it hits me.

Drawing back from her, I exhale a long, calming breath.

"Why'd you stop?"

Disgusted with myself, I roughly run a hand over my hat, looking away. "Shit. I didn't even kiss you first before I started groping you."

"It's probably for the best anyway."

Fuck. The bottom of my stomach just dropped out. I've fucked up. I've never wanted a woman more than Presley, and I've gone and fu—

"*Because*"—her voice jerks me from my self-recriminations—"you know, since I'm not a tipsy mess like before; if you had kissed me—if you had *really* kissed sober Presley Cole—your mind would've been. Completely. Blown."

CHAPTER THIRTY-TWO

Presley

"**B**ecause you know, since I'm not a tipsy mess, if you had kissed me—if you had really kissed sober Presley Cole—your mind would've been. Completely. Blown."

I'm so full of shit, but I'm going with it. Too late to back out now. I've got to own it.

"*And*," I draw out the word dramatically, "you'd hear angels weep because of the beauty of it, and you would've found yourself wondering how you've managed to live on this earth all this time and not experience a kiss of this caliber." I shrug nonchalantly.

Like I'm not completely talking out of my ass.

But it's all worth it the moment I see it. That smile—the real, genuine one that's wide and so damn addictive, especially with the way the right side lifts slightly higher than the left. If I could be the one person to make him smile like that all the time, I think life would be just about perfect.

"Angels weeping, huh?" he asks, amusement obvious in his tone.

"Yep."

We sit here, eyeing each other for a moment before I

roll my eyes, sliding off his lap.

"Well, what are you waiting for? I'm ready to play doctor and wounded Navy SEAL." I prop a hand on one hip for emphasis of my playful exasperation.

Rising from his chair, he reminds me of how imposing he can look, but not only that, I realize what he's doing—he's still trying to situate himself with his left side facing away from me.

"You need to stop." I step toward him, placing my palms against his firm chest. Looking up into his dark eyes, I plead, "Don't hide from me."

His jaw tightens as he holds my gaze. "You know I don't like for you to have to see it." His voice is low, barely a husky whisper.

Slowly raising one hand, I watch him much like I would a skittish animal as my palm gets closer and closer to the left side of his face. His jaw works, and I don't realize I'm holding my breath until my hand finally cradles his cheek. My breath whooshes out as we stand here, and I don't dare move for a moment—so he can get used to my touch.

He clamps his eyes shut, his expression appearing pained as if my touch hurts him. But as we stand here, neither of us moving, I watch as his expression relaxes—an infinitesimal slackening in the tightness in his strong jaw, the pectorals beneath my palm not feeling quite so tense.

When I slide my other hand up from his chest, lifting to gently grasp the bill of his ball cap, I raise it barely a millimeter; his eyes fly open, and I freeze.

"I don't want you to hide from me." My voice is faint but pleading before I add, "Please?"

I can see his warring emotions, and the one that pierces me the most is the fear in his eyes. Fear that my reaction will differ—that I will recoil from being exposed to the full, unencumbered view of his face. Because although he's allowed me to see him without his ball cap at my awards banquet, he's always been careful to turn the left side of his face away from me.

Suddenly, I feel a presence. We both look down to find Izzy has left her comfortable spot to sit near Hendy's feet, ears perked, alert, sensing his unease.

"It's okay, girl." His large hand rests on her head, and she nuzzles him as if trying to show him she's there and wants to reassure him, to comfort him. She gives him a doggy kiss on the back of his hand before returning to her spot, lying on her stomach, and resting her chin on her paws to watch us.

Turning to me, Hendy presses his lips tight, drawing my attention to them, and I'm reminded of the fact that I've only kissed him once. That night in his bedroom after he'd rescued me from the bar.

"Clue." My eyes fly up at his low, subdued tone. "Running away, shrieking in horror."

I know what he's doing—what he's trying to do. But it's not happening. I refuse to let it.

"Answer: What is what this girl is *not* going to do?" I hold his gaze, begging for him to believe me.

To trust me.

He closes his eyes, inhaling a deep breath as if for extra fortification before he looks off toward the beach and says one word.

"Okay."

Gently, carefully, I lift the ball cap the remainder of the way off his head, dropping it softly onto the cushion of the chair.

As soon as the hat hits the chair cushion, his entire body tenses. Shoulders rising, he stiffens his spine, as if preparing himself for rejection. As if he thinks the night he'd bared his face for the night I received my award was a fluke—that there was a chance I'd cringe in horror at the sight of him now.

With extra care, I frame his face with my palms, my thumbs grazing his cheekbones, while I peer up at him.

"I see you. As you are."

He doesn't speak for a beat. "And what do you see?" His voice is gravelly, coarse.

"I see a man who tries to hide from me." My thumb sweeps across one of the deeper scars on his cheek. "A man who thinks he has to hide from everyone. A man who doesn't realize he's far more than his looks. Although"—my lips quirk up at the corners—"he's pretty hot if I do say so my—"

Strong fingers encircle my wrists. "Pres. Stop." At my confused look, he goes on. "You don't have to do this…or say this."

Cocking my head to the side, I narrow my eyes. "You think I'm just saying this?"

He rolls his lips inward before offering a half-shrug.

Rising to my tiptoes, I scowl at him. "Listen here. I'll have you know that you're more impressive than any man I've ever met or ever known. And not because of what you've accomplished or what you've been through in your Navy career. You are so freaking smart, love *Jeopardy*, have a smile that makes me want to jump your bones instantly, and you're handsome as hell. You have more integrity than most people can shake a stick at. And you have a pretty massive…" I trail off with a mischievous smile.

His lips finally curl up in the start of what I hope will be one of those lopsided smiles I've come to love as he raises an eyebrow. "A pretty massive…? Heart?"

"Would you believe me if I said heart?"

He shakes his head.

"Ego?"

Another shake, his smile growing wider.

I let out a long, dramatic sigh. "Fine. A pretty massive penis."

There it is. There's that smile. Wide, with those perfect teeth showing and without the ball cap, facing me full-on, I'm wowed.

With a soft, brief kiss, I lean back with a sigh. "God, I love your smile."

His eyes soften. "If it gets you to look at me like that, then I'll do it all the time."

"Promise?"

He dips his head, his hands rising to thread in my hair and bring his lips closer to mine. "Promise."

And then his lips take mine in a kiss I know I'll remember for years to come. Not only because it's a magnificent one—it *is*. But it's so much more than that.

It's a kiss from a man who might finally allow me to truly "see" him.

CHAPTER THIRTY-THREE

Hendy

This is it. I'm really going to do this.

Fuck. I've never been so nervous before in my life. Never. Because hell if this doesn't feel like I'm preparing to bare my soul to Presley.

Kissing her, I pour everything into it—how much I want her, how much it means that she doesn't recoil in horror when I allow her to see my face. It's a hungry, greedy kiss laden with emotion.

More than that, though, my kiss is also tinged with regret. Regret because although she's seen my scars, seen my battered body, she hasn't yet seen it all. She hasn't laid eyes on my naked body—at the worst, most marred sections below my waistline, flaring out across the back of both hips and my ass. And if I can't refrain from cringing at the sight of it, if I avoid looking at my own reflection in the bathroom mirror when I get out of the shower to dry off, then I can't expect her not to do the same.

She's only human, after all.

Her tongue slips past my lips, darting inside, sending a jolt through my whole body. My fingers tighten their grasp of her hair, the silky strands sliding over my hands, deepening the kiss.

Her hand slides around to cup my ass, and I break the kiss in surprise. "Copping a feel, huh?"

She grins wickedly. "A fine ass like this one? You bet." That same hand glides to my front, cupping where I strain my khakis.

With a choked sound, a faint smile plays on my lips. "Not holding anything back tonight, are you?"

"Nope." Presley looks pleased with herself, her eyes shimmering with amusement. So much that I feel the need to throw her off-balance. Both figuratively and literally.

Scooping her up in my arms, she lets out a surprised yelp, her arms looping around my neck. "Wow. You really know how to sweep a girl off her feet." The way her fingers play with the short strands of hair at the base of my neck sends small shivers through me.

Padding over to the door leading inside the house, I step over the threshold and close it softly behind us, knowing Izzy can come inside whenever she's ready. Making my way to my bedroom, I kick the door closed and lower Presley's feet to the floor. The subtle streams of moonlight slipping through the blinds on the windows is our only light as we stand here. And dread fills me as I know what she's going to ask next.

"Can we turn on the small light?"

Inwardly wincing at her question even though I'd anticipated it, I make the two steps to the small lamp sitting on top of my dresser in the far corner of my room. Silently, I thank Presley for not requesting the overhead light with the four bright bulbs.

Small mercy there.

Twisting the small knob, the subtle *click* sounding far

louder in the quiet room, I hesitate before turning to face her.

Her gaze is watchful as she reaches for the hem of her shirt. "I'm going to take this off." Slowly, she raises it up and over her head before letting it drop silently to the floor. "And I want you to do the same." The last word has a questioning lilt to it.

Stepping over to her, I reach for my shirt, tugging it from where it's tucked into my khaki shorts. "You aren't completely bare-chested, so I'm not certain how fair this is."

Tipping her head to the side, she eyes me while reaching around her back to unfasten her bra. The moment she slides the straps from her shoulders and down her arms before letting it join her shirt on the floor, my breath catches in my throat. And I can see it.

I see the nervousness, the insecurity she feels because of her smaller breasts. Yet here she is, being brave and baring herself to me.

"You're beautiful," I breathe.

Her lips twist, and before she even begins to say it, I know it's going to be a brush-off. "You don't ha—"

My fingers release their grasp of the hem of my shirt to cradle her face with my palms, and I gaze deep into her eyes. "You are beautiful, Presley Cole."

Her eyes flicker with something I can't decipher. "Really?" she whispers.

"Really," I whisper back.

Our eyes remain locked for a beat before her hands grip my shirt. "We still need to get you out of this."

Inhaling a deep, calming breath, I allow her to push up my shirt, helping her tug it over my head and drop it to the floor. Standing before her, I hold myself stock-still as her hands smooth over my shoulders before pressing a kiss to the middle of my chest.

And I swear I can feel that kiss all the way to the core of my heart.

Just when I think this petite woman has rocked my world more than anyone ever before, she goes and takes it one step further. She slips around to stand behind me, her soft palms sliding down from the top of each of my shoulders in a caress, all the way down to my hands, linking her fingers with mine. And that's when I feel it.

Her lips against my skin.

My breath hitches at the touch of her lips against the harsh indentations of my marred flesh. She works her way over my back, ensuring she's kissed every single scar, every spot of puckered flesh from where I was whipped like an animal or where they carved into my skin like a butcher.

Her hands reach around my front to unfasten my khaki shorts, shoving them down and leaving me bare. I hold myself still as she takes in the sight of the scars continuing down my back to the marred areas extending from the base of my spine and spreading along my hips. With a barely noticeable pause, Presley dusts her lips across my flesh in a whisper of a caress, and my body jerks in response as if each nerve ending is hypersensitive. Each time she presses a kiss to an area—ones I can barely tolerate acknowledging—emotion wells up within me.

And each time her lips find another scar, I feel something I haven't felt since I lost my friends in that damn desert that fateful night.

My throat grows tight, and I instantly close my eyes, feeling them burn. As if that weren't enough, Presley takes it a step further with her tender, softly spoken words.

"You're more than your scars." There's a pause as her lips find yet another. "So much more."

And that's the moment I lose control.

CHAPTER THIRTY-FOUR

Presley

It's as if something within him snapped. Turning abruptly, I'm almost thrown off-balance by his movement. Hendy's hands fly to my face as his lips crash down on mine in a passionate, almost punishing kiss, so full of intense emotion.

My lips are feverish against his; our tongues spar while my hands glide along his heated skin in my need to feel all of him against me.

And I still can't deny my earlier surprise at finding him bare beneath those khakis.

Breaking the kiss, my eyes dart down, taking in the sight of his large arousal, proudly jutting out as if begging for my touch.

Amused, I raise my eyebrows. "Didn't take you for a commando kind of guy."

"I'm just full of"—he breaks off with a groan when my fingers grasp his hard cock—"surprises."

Working him with my hand, I feel him harden further; my thumb brushes over the tip, and I'm instantly lifted and gently placed on the bed. He tugs my jeans down over my hips and off my legs, leaving me clad in only a plain black pair of boy-cut panties.

He looks down at me while I admire his broad chest, those firm pectoral muscles and hard abs tapering into that strong V-line, and I find myself mesmerized by the view.

"If I take those panties off you now…" Joining me on the bed, he rests his knees on either side of my legs and trails a finger down the center of my chest. Swallowing hard, his eyes flit back and forth between my eyes and panties. "My mouth will be all over you."

Furrowing my eyebrows, I give him an odd look. "You say that like it's a bad thing."

Those lips curve up at the corners wickedly. "I'd like to think it'll be a good thing. But you should know that's not all I'll do." His hands glide along my sides in a caress.

"Oh?" My tone is a bit breathless. "What else would you do?"

He unleashes one of those smiles on me again, and my entire body melts.

Leaning down so his bare chest brushes against mine, he whispers huskily against my lips. "Why don't you let me show you?"

"And that right there is how babies are made, folks," I whisper-sigh before I reach up to tug his head down, pressing my lips against his, and swallowing his chuckle before I deepen the kiss.

Allowing my other hand to pull him closer, to have him exactly where I want him between my legs, I feel his hard cock pressing against my core, and his mouth swallows my moan when he rocks against me.

Gasping as a surge of arousal floods me, I feel my panties growing more damp, and I'm certain he can feel it. I wrap my legs around him and work myself against him, loving the way his hard cock presses against my clit.

Hendy makes a rough sound in the back of his throat before tearing his lips from mine. Our ragged, labored breathing is the only sound in the silence of his bedroom. Rearing back, he makes quick work of ridding me of my panties. Tossing them aside without a backward glance, he grasps my ankles with his large hands to spread my legs open farther. He lowers his face, thrusting his tongue deep inside me.

"Oh, sweet Jesus!"

His brief laughter rumbles through me, making my toes curl while I grip the covers on his bed and arch my body. To say he's tasting me would be a vast understatement.

Hendy is *devouring* me. And like that decadent dream I had of him, he's drawing moans from my lips and making me writhe against his mouth.

When he shifts, his lips latch onto my clit, and his tongue intermittently flicks it while he thrusts not one but two thick, long fingers deep inside me, and it pushes me over the edge. My body tenses, arching, before a powerful orgasm hits me, my muscles contracting and releasing around his fingers. He continues to gently work his fingers in and out of me as I come down from the high, tiny shudders wracking my body.

Opening my eyes, I find him watching me, and his gaze holds a unique intensity. Withdrawing his fingers from me, he parts his lips as he sucks them clean, holding my gaze the entire time. When he shifts off the bed, reaching toward the small nightstand, I clear my throat.

"Well. That was super fun, thanks."

His head whips around to look at me. And I bite my

lip, trying to stifle a smile as I meet eyes which are narrowing dangerously.

"Think you're leaving, do you?"

He gives my legs a swift tug, bringing me closer to where he now stands at the end of the bed. Grasping my wrist, he guides my hand to his cock, wrapping my fingers around his impressive girth.

"Maybe I'll stay," I whisper quickly, making him grin smugly.

While he backs away briefly to grab a condom, I move farther back on the bed, watching him slide on protection. Hendy climbs onto the bed, lowering himself between my legs. He braces himself above me on his forearms, and I notice he's subconsciously turning his face again—turning that left side away from me.

"Hey." I wait for his eyes to meet mine before raising my hands and cupping his face tenderly. "Let me see you." I pause. "All of you." There's a long beat before he gives a nearly imperceptible nod.

As the tip of his cock presses against my entrance, his expression has a touch of chagrin. "I'm praying I won't embarrass myself," he says, his eyes sparkling with a mixture of amusement and sheepishness. "But this is the first time I've been with a woman in"—he breaks off, his gaze averted briefly before returning to mine—"a long while."

Inching inside me, stretching me, allowing my body to acclimate to him, he holds my gaze, and I feel like he might finally be allowing me to see him—to see all of him.

Now, I realize I've underestimated myself. Sold myself short. It's become even more obvious that what I had with Dylan was nothing close to love. To what I *should* have felt.

I've also greatly underestimated Hendy. The man who

thinks no one can love him with the way he looks now. The man who thinks that because of his appearance, he's unworthy of love. But he's so incredibly wrong.

More than that, Hendy's underestimated me because he doesn't realize how mistaken he is. It's at this moment that I see the truth—the truth that sees beneath all appearances, that sees beneath the outer shell of a person, delving down to the core.

Because regardless of what he may think, how he or any others might view him, one fact remains.

I've started to fall in love with Cristiano "Hendy" Hendrixson.

CHAPTER THIRTY-FIVE

Hendy

D*on't fucking come yet. Don't. Fucking. Come. Yet. Regardless of how phenomenal she feels.*

I keep repeating this in my head, but hell, she feels so damn good. The way she clenches around me when I flick her nipple with my tongue or graze it with my teeth. But the real deal breaker is when she bends her knees, sliding her feet to plant them flat on the bed, working herself over me.

My hips thrust as deeply as I can, and I press my lips to the side of her neck, nipping at her before my tongue soothes the area. In response, she turns her head to press feverish kisses to the side of my face. And it hits me at that moment.

She's not just kissing my face. She's lovingly kissing it. The *left* side. Without any hesitation, whatsoever. And that's what sends me over the edge—those soft lips and the affection against my marred flesh.

"Pres," I groan against her neck, wildly thrusting in and out of her hot, wet pussy before reaching down to press my thumb against her clit and rub in circles. She lets out a loud gasp, and her inner muscles tighten around me as I continue to work her clit harder, my thrusts frenzied, and I pray she comes with me.

Just as my balls tighten near painfully, she lets out a soft cry before clenching around me rapid-fire. Pressing my lips to hers, I take her mouth in a passionate, wet kiss, thrusting three more times before my climax hits and I come hard.

Our harsh, ragged breathing fills the silent room before I realize my weight is likely crushing her. Shifting aside, I dispose of the condom in the nearby wastebasket before rolling back on the bed. Turning my head to look over at her, I bask in the sated look on her face.

Watching me, she pants slightly from exertion as a smug smile plays at her lips.

"That was pretty impressive, wasn't it?" She wiggles her eyebrows at me.

"Pretty impressive?"

"Yep." Her wide grin is full of mischief. "Considering I was the first person in a few years to"—she breaks off to sing-talk—"rock your world!"

Schooling my expression, I give her a stern look. "Who said you rocked my world?"

With a sigh full of exasperation, she rolls her eyes, reaching over to give a condescending pat to my chest. "Uh, your moans said it all, buddy boy."

Buddy boy. No way in hell can I restrain the laugh that bursts free, a smile tugging at my lips as I look over at her. Because I know the last time a woman made me smile and laugh in bed.

Never.

That's right. Never. I've never experienced anything like this. But Presley Cole…she's something else. She's so different from anyone I've ever been with. And not only physically. Sure, I used to prefer my women with more curves than she has, but I don't for one split second feel like I'm missing out. Presley brings so much more to the table than looks alone.

She's so damn smart, uniquely beautiful with those different colored eyes of hers, her sometimes goofy charm, and her slim physique. Not only that, but she also hasn't run off after really and truly *seeing* me.

I don't know how long this will last, but I know I'd be an idiot not to bask in this while she still finds me intriguing. I'm a rebound of sorts for her, something shiny and new.

I sure as hell don't look forward to the moment when my shine wears off.

* * *

"Don't touch me there!"

"Shhh!" Presley shushes me, her cheeks flushing with embarrassment from my joking exclamation at her hand cupping my ass. Especially since we'd both heard Kane come home from hanging out with Doc late last night.

We're in the shower, hands copping feels here and there, our hushed laughter often stifled by wet kisses.

I press her against the shower wall, kissing the side of her neck and whispering, "If I didn't think you were too sore, I'd take you up against this wall."

"I'm not—"

Leaning back, I cut off her protest with a look. "You are."

"Well"—she gives me a saucy smile as the warm water cascades over us—"that doesn't mean we can't have a little fun." Her fingers wrap around my cock, and I groan.

"Woman," I growl softly, pressing my lips to her ear. "You're going to be the death of me."

"I'm just saying…" One of her shoulders lifts in indifference. "I could go downtown." Presley wiggles her eyebrows at the suggestion.

"Pres."

She continues as if she didn't hear me, tapping an index finger to her lips in thought. "I mean, granted, I don't have experience like a lot of other women, but I think I could have this blowjob thing down pat. With the right amount of practice."

Pressing me against the shower wall, the thick steam from the water temperature surrounding us, she drops to her knees, looking up at me, those green and blue eyes mesmerizing.

"I'll do my best to heed the number one rule. Promise." Her smile is wicked, teasing.

"Rule number one?"

Her lips press against the tip, and her eyes shine with mischief. "Rule number one: no teeth."

A laugh bursts free before turning into a moan the moment her mouth slides over my cock, taking me as deep as she can.

And I can't deny that she makes good on her promise.

CHAPTER THIRTY-SIX

Presley

"This insect has four thousand muscles and transforms into something beautiful."

"What is the caterpillar?" Hendy and I both murmur in response.

Sitting in our usual spot at the bar in the microbrewery, we're watching *Jeopardy* while finishing up dinner and sipping beers.

Exchanging a quick smile, we turn back to the television, knowing Final *Jeopardy* is fast approaching.

"These so-called beans, pictured here, are not really beans but seeds of the plant."

"What is the coffee bean?" we answer in unison before Alex Trebek announces the commercial break before Final *Jeopardy* will begin.

As I turn to playfully nudge Hendy with my shoulder, an all-too-familiar voice calls my name.

Dylan.

Shifting around in my seat, I find him standing a few feet away, eyes accusing.

"Dylan." My tone is flat, unwelcoming.

"Presley, we need to talk." His eyes flick to where Hendy

sits beside me, and I feel Hendy shift as if to move and protect me.

Laying a hand on his forearm, I lean in and whisper, "I've got this." He meets my eyes, and I silently plead with him to let me handle it. With a nearly imperceptible nod, he leans back, but he's still imposing with the way he's sprawled on the barstool, shoulders wide. And I know the eyes mostly shadowed beneath that ball cap are astute, watching every single move Dylan makes.

Turning back to Dylan, I let out a sigh. "I don't have anything to say to you, Dylan. It's over."

"Presley, just listen." He must sense that his curt tone sets me on edge because he adds a more pleading, "Please," to the end. "The partners at work are upset about our broken engagement, and I've been doing a lot of thinking. And I realize what an idiot I've been." He pulls out a small, light blue jewelry box—one most anyone would recognize as from Tiffany's. Which means ostentatiousness and *really* freaking expensive.

When he lifts open the lid of the box, my suspicions are confirmed.

"Because," Dylan continues, "I should have gotten you what you deserve. What the future wife of a soon-to-be partner deserves."

Stunned, my eyes flit between the over-the-top ring to the expectant expression on my former fiancé's face. All the while, I sense the increasing tension radiating from the man by my side.

"Dylan, they're making you partner?" I ask slowly.

He appears to choose his words carefully. "No, but they will." His eyes study me intently. "Especially once they learn our engagement is back on."

Ah, so that's what this is all about.

Trying to rein in my exasperation, I take a deep fortifying breath. "Dylan, look. It's over." My tone is far more patient than I feel; that's for sure. "I'm not getting back together with you."

As if someone flipped a switch, his entire demeanor changes, eyes turning like ice, face stony. "Is it him?" His chin juts out, gesturing toward Hendy. "Are you still obsessed with scar face here?"

My entire body stiffens, anger pulsing through my veins. "Listen here, you—"

"I've got this." Hendy's whisper in my ear catches me off guard. Rising from his seat, he steps toward Dylan, towering over him.

"Do you not recall the little chat we had not that long ago?" Hendy takes another imposing step forward, dipping his head to murmur something I can't make out. Finally, sputtering, Dylan backs down and storms out of the bar.

Hendy's spine is stiff, shoulders broadened, and his stance ready. His eyes track Dylan's retreat as if needing the visual confirmation.

"Well." I let out a relieved sigh. "That was impressive."

Hendy turns slowly. "Think so?"

"Yeah, especially with whatever you said that made him scamper off like that."

He chuckles, shaking his head. "Ready to head out?"

"Definitely," I answer with another sigh.

After paying our bill, we exit with Hendy's hand holding mine, and I still can't get over the fact that this big, tough, former SEAL actually likes to hold hands. He's full of surprises.

"So"—I cock an eyebrow at him—"that was a

remarkable display back there."

He eyes me curiously. "What do you mean?"

"I mean you were nearly in full-fledged helicopter mom mode in the bar." Grinning, I can't resist teasing him more. "You remember those *Scooby Doo* cartoons? When they included Scrappy Doo? And he was all like, 'Let me at 'em! Let me at 'em!'?"

He slows to a stop, withdrawing his hand from mine and tugging my wrist, so I'm moved out of the path of others walking along the sidewalk in the downtown area. "Are you comparing me to an overeager, animated puppy?" Hendy eyes me from beneath the brim of his hat, his tone low and playfully dangerous.

"What if I am?"

The corners of his lips tilt upward, edging into a lopsided smirk. "You're going to pay for that, young lady."

Reaching around, I smack his ass playfully, grinning. "Ooh! Are you threatening me with a good time? Count me in."

Then I walk off with a skip in my step. Waiting, waiting, waiting …

A large, masculine hand grasps mine again. I glance at Hendy from the corner of my eye as we walk, approaching where he's parked his truck along the side street's curb.

"Seriously, though. You were pretty imposing back there."

He presses the button on his keys to unlock the vehicle. "Is that so?"

Turning abruptly, I crowd him, walking him back against the truck. "Yep. That was hot. The way you got all quiet and scary." I pause for emphasis and lower my voice. "And sexy."

He grins. "Really? Do tell. How hot was I back there?"

"Let me show you." Wrapping my hands around the back of his head, I tug him down, rising to my toes and tilting my head to press my lips against his. At the touch of his lips against mine, something ignites, and the kiss instantly turns hotter, tongues warring, his lips working over mine feverishly.

Drawing away, Hendy's unsteady breathing matches mine. "Any hotter, and we'll have to charge people to watch us."

A tiny, breathless laugh escapes my lips. "Maybe you should take me home."

Pressing a quick kiss to my forehead, he offers me a gentle smile, sending warmth running through me. "Agreed. Let's go."

* * *

As soon as we kick off our flip-flops in my house, I clasp my hands together with an expectant expression. "So. I have a proposal."

"I'm not really ready to get married yet, Pres." Hendy's dry response has me rolling my eyes with a laugh.

"Ha-ha. I actually wanted to see if you'd be up for trying something out with me…" I let my words trail off.

He raises his eyebrows. "Such as…?"

"Maybe, oh, I don't know"—I wave a hand around in what I'm certain is *not* coming off as nonchalance—"like tying me up in the bedroom?"

There's a beat of silence. Then another. Then another.

"You know what?" With an overly bright smile, I give a dismissive wave. "Never mi—"

"Okay."

"I'm sorry?" Surely, I didn't hear him correctly.

"Okay." His smile is devastating and almost…predatory?

"Oh."

A hoarse laugh erupts from him. "Wow. You sound thrilled."

"I'm just…surprised."

Stepping closer, he cages me in, bracing his hands on the wall on either side of me. "Pres. You offered to let me tie you up and have my wicked way with you." His lips graze the shell of my ear before his teeth nip my earlobe. "There's no way in hell I'd ever say no to that."

"Really?" My response is breathless.

Playfully tugging on my earlobe, he sends shivers down my spine before pressing kisses along the column of my neck; his hot breath washes against my skin. "Really."

The tip of his tongue darts out to taste me, pressing his body closer and letting me feel his arousal. "The thought of you, restrained on the bed…" His breath is ragged as he rocks against me. "Feel what it does to me." Another nudge from his delicious hardness. "Feel what you do to me."

My fingers encircle his wrist, guiding his hand down my body to slip beneath my sundress. Moving his hand between my thighs, I place it over my panties, my eyes heavy-lidded with lust and my voice husky. "Feel what you do to me."

Hendy pushes me over the edge at that moment as one of his fingers slides swiftly beneath the fabric and inside my wet heat. He pushes deep, and I can't withhold a gasp before he decides to slowly withdraw, only to thrust in deep again.

And that's when I decide I can't take any more.

CHAPTER THIRTY-SEVEN

Hendy

When Presley moved my hand to guide me to touch her, as soon as I cupped her, I swore the amount of heat radiating from her was singeing me. But nothing could have prepared me for when I slipped my finger inside her, and the snug way her muscles contracted around me.

Groaning against her neck, I push deep inside her, willing myself not to come in my fucking pants at the feel of her soaking my finger. Slowly withdrawing my finger from her pussy, only to thrust it deep, I listen as she lets out a low moan. But it's the pressing of her palms against my chest that draws me to a halt.

Her chest is rising and falling, and her breathing labored, those eyes of hers hazy with arousal. "You need to come with me." The corners of her lips tip up slightly. "Pun intended," she adds.

Taking my hand, she leads me down the hallway to her bedroom, and I find myself mesmerized by the way her soft, silky hair shifts slightly over her shoulders as she moves and at the way her tight ass looks in her sundress. Immediately, I think about cupping that same ass as I thrust deep inside her pussy.

Once we're ensconced in the dark bedroom, Presley reaches for the small lamp sitting on the bedside table. With a soft *click*, the bulb glows on what appears to be the lowest setting, and I'm grateful for that small mercy.

Spinning her around to face me, I grip her slim hips, walking her back to the bed. "Do you have something for me to tie you up with?"

Eyes wide, brimming with anticipation and maybe a little uncertainty, too, she nods. "In the drawer." Reaching for the small bedside table, she withdraws a long black strip of fabric. Before she can slide the drawer closed, I stop her.

"We'll be needing these." I lift out the strip of condoms and set them on the table before my eyes meet hers again.

She swallows hard. "All of them?"

A rough sounding laugh falls from my lips. Because there's thirty-six in a box. And since we already used some a few days ago, I'd say twenty or so are left.

Smiling down at her, my hand brushes back some stray hair from her face, and I dust a kiss on her lips. "Not all but maybe"—I hold her gaze with mine as the pad of my thumb toys with her luscious bottom lip—"quite a few."

"Oh, boy," she murmurs breathlessly.

My tone gets firmer. "Now, I need you naked on this bed." My hands skim down over her dress, reaching for the hem. Lifting it up and over her body to let it drop to the floor, I can't help the stutter of my breath.

Presley has surprised me yet again. In place of the usual pair of boy-short panties, she is wearing a lacy red thong with tiny, dainty ribbons on each hip. As my gaze drifts over her smooth stomach and upward, I discover the matching bra.

Gaze flying to hers, uncertainty etches her features. "I

know I'm not—"

I press my index finger to her lips, stopping her. "Don't." Because I know what she was going to say. She thinks she's lacking as if she's not so fucking gorgeous that it's killing me to refrain from tossing her back on this bed and fucking her without any fanfare at all and go into pure caveman mode.

She's so beautiful, and sure, her breasts easily fit right into my palms, but those rosy nipples beg for my lips, my tongue. Her ass is luscious, and those eyes of hers—those green and blue eyes that watch me with barely concealed lust—are irresistible. But that's not the biggest draw with Presley. It's her intelligence; her personality is what sends me over the edge.

And I'm man enough to admit the old Hendy might not have been able to see past the parade of surgically enhanced breasts, the centerfold-like figures, the barely-there IQs to recognize what Presley has to offer.

Simply everything.

Carefully peeling her thong down over her hips, I allow my hands to graze along her legs as I lower the thin fabric and help her step out of them. Rising again, she reaches behind her for the clasp to her bra, and once she undoes it, I help to slide the straps down her arms, casting it aside.

When she situates herself on her bed, her gaze tracks my movements. I can't resist the hesitation as my fingertips move to the brim of my ball cap, slowly lifting it off my head and setting it aside. Gripping the rear of my polo shirt collar, I tug it off, letting it drop to join her dress on the floor.

My hands shift to the waistband of my khaki shorts, and her eyes flicker downward, lips parting as if in anticipation. Unbuttoning and lowering the zipper, I shove my khakis down, kicking them off to the side. As soon as one of my knees hits the bed to climb onto it and join her, she stops me.

"Wait."

Her tone is soft as she shifts to her side, reaching for me. Trailing her fingertip down the length of my hardened cock, she follows the path of her finger with her eyes. When she reaches the tip, she glides her finger around the moisture there, and I have to stop her.

Encircling her wrist with my fingers, I draw her movement to a halt, her eyes flying up to mine.

"Lie back on the bed, Pres." I swallow hard, attempting to maintain some vestige of control. "I'll be calling the shots now."

Eyes locked with mine, she slowly resumes her prior position on the bed before raising her arms above her head.

With the long, black fabric in hand, I move onto the bed. Resting over her on my knees, I carefully bind her wrists together, leaving a line of slack before looping and wrapping the end of the fabric through the middle post of her headboard.

Peering down at her, I duck my head, brushing a soft kiss on her forehead before leaning back. "Tell me if you want me to stop. If you want me to untie you." Pressing a kiss to her lips, I whisper, "Okay?"

She gives a little nod. "Okay." There's a pause before her eyes turn mischievous. "What happens if I don't want you to stop?"

Letting out a husky laugh, I grin, dipping to press a kiss to her collarbone. "Oh, I can just about guarantee you won't want me to stop." I trail kisses lower.

"You sound a little full of yourse—" Her words break off in a gasp when my lips latch onto one nipple, sucking and flicking the hardened tip with my tongue. Presley arches into my touch, already struggling against her restraints.

My thumb and forefinger toy with her other nipple while I continue to love her with my mouth and tongue. Slipping downward, I leave a trail of kisses along her stomach until I'm soon cradled between her thighs.

I peer up the length of her body, my eyes traveling over the dips and curves and her now heaving chest. The way she looks as she's lying so beautifully naked and partially shadowed here and there from the dimly lit bedroom, baring herself to me, causes something to tighten in my chest.

"Ready to challenge my knot tying?" I nod toward where I've secured her to the bedpost, unable to resist a smug grin. My hands slide to widen her legs, and I lower my head, driving my tongue deep inside her—no pretense whatsoever, just me tasting her sweet pussy.

And God, does it taste good.

Fucking her with my tongue and lips, tasting her, I'm getting harder from the way she's writhing on the bed. Her gasps intermixed with moans of my name push me even closer to the precipice, and pre-come leaks at my tip. When she begins to pull her restraints taut, causing my grip on her thighs to tighten further, it nearly makes me come right then and there.

Reaching up, I tweak and toy with her clit with my thumb and forefinger. Instantly, more wetness coats my tongue. Pressing down on her clit and moving in circles, I can tell by her breathing she's close.

"Hendy," she says on a breathless moan.

Looking up, seeing her like this, at my mercy but so trusting, her eyes closed, breathing labored, nipples hardened peaks…I know this is one of those moments.

One I'll treasure because of the pure beauty of it.

CHAPTER THIRTY-EIGHT

Presley

"I'm…" I trail off, ending in a silent gasp as my inner muscles clench hard, body tensing before my release hits me. As I ride out my orgasm, my body moves of its own accord, pushing against Hendy's mouth and tongue.

And he takes it all. He lets me ride his tongue in shameless abandon until the waves pass and my body relaxes, slumping back onto the bed. Pressing kisses to my thighs and up along my torso, he brings himself to rest on his forearms above me.

"Hey." Hendy's lips graze mine.

"Hey."

"You okay?" His dark eyes are searching.

"I didn't ask you to stop." My whispered words belie the smugness laced in my tone.

Nuzzling my neck, he speaks softly. "Who said I was stopping?" I can feel him smile against my skin. "I'm only giving you a quick breather to regroup."

"I've regrouped."

My rapid response has him leaning back with a laugh, grinning down at me. "Want me to untie you or are you ready for more?"

My eyes are alit with humor. "Depends." I raise an eyebrow suggestively. "Think you're ready for what I've got planned if you untie me?"

"Don't threaten me with a good time." He grins, throwing my former words back at me.

Heat flares through me at what I plan to do to him. "Then maybe it's your turn to be tied up."

Hendy's entire body stills; his muscles rigid. And I realize how badly I've misstepped.

Shit, shit, shit!

"Hendy, I'm—"

"Don't," he commands quietly. "Don't." His eyes are understanding, but I can detect the slightly haunted edge they have now. "I know."

"I just like the idea of having you at my mercy," I whisper.

Hendy watches me, his eyes flickering from mine to my lips and then back before reaching above me to begin working at my restraints. I strain to hear his soft response, but when his words register, I'm assaulted with emotions.

"I'm always at your mercy."

As soon as I feel the give of my restraints, I lower my arms, cupping the sides of his face to hold his head in place. Gazing deeply into his eyes, I say softly, "Likewise." Drawing him down, I press my lips to his in a tender kiss. My breath feathers against his mouth as I whisper, "I'm always at your mercy. Regardless if I'm tied up."

Palms braced against his firm pectorals, I push gently, silently asking for him to shift onto his back. When he acquiesces, I move to lie on top of him, relishing in the feel of his hard-muscled body beneath mine.

And that's not all that's hard.

Grinning wickedly, I use my teeth to playfully tug at his bottom lip. God, that thing drives me crazy. He's got such incredible lips for a guy.

"I see you're ready for me, huh?"

"Seems so." I'm relieved to see the shadows have disappeared from his eyes.

"Think maybe I can"—I reach between us to grasp his firm hardness—"figure out something to do with this?" No way can I restrain my wide smile.

His hands go to my ass, and he lets out a long, satisfied sigh as his eyes fall closed. "As long as I can continue holding this ass, you can do whatever you want."

"Is that so?" Shit. I know he can hear the doubt in my tone—especially if *I* can hear it. Dylan always mentioned, in what I now realize were little digs here and there, about me not having enough meat on my bones, my body not being "lush" enough.

His eyes open, narrowing slightly. "That's definitely so." One corner of his lips tilts up, a wicked glint in his gaze. "Maybe you can come up here and let me taste you again, and I can have the best of both worlds. My mouth on your pussy, and your ass in my hands."

Sweet baby Jesus. I swear I had a mini orgasm from his words alone. But no, he's not going to distract me from my mission. No way.

Shifting down his body, I press a trail of kisses just below his belly button, following his goody trail down, down, down…

"Pres," he whispers, his fingers threading through my hair, and the moment my breath washes over his hard cock, they tighten their grasp.

"I plan to make you come as hard as I did." My tongue runs along his hardened length. "Maybe harder."

"Not sure if—" His taunting cuts off the moment the tip of my tongue darts out to lap up the moisture gathering at his tip. Sliding my mouth over him, I take him as deeply as I can. He's so thick and wide, and I can tell he's doing all he can to refrain from thrusting into my mouth and trying not to make me gag.

I work my mouth over him, one hand gripping him at the base of his cock. Creating a suction, I can feel the moment he's close.

"Pres," he utters on a breathless groan; his fingers tighten in my hair, almost painful in their grasp. "If you don't want—"

I hollow out my cheeks, cutting off his protest, and satisfaction rolls through me when he lets out another low moan. Because I know what he was trying to say. But I want him to come in my mouth. I want to taste him.

Hendy makes a rough sound in the back of his throat as his hips work. He comes in spurts, and I swallow it all—everything he gives me.

Once his body finally goes lax, I slide my mouth away, peering up at him only to catch his sated eyes watching me. Rolling my lips inward as if deep in thought, I tip my head to the side. "I'm pretty sure I made you come harder."

In a flash, his hands slip beneath my arms, lifting me up to rest atop his body, my face above his. His eyes alit with amusement. "You think so?"

"Oh, yes. And I also know what you're thinking." Bracing my weight with one hand on the bed beside him, my other hand reaches up to brush off imaginary dust from my shoulder as I let out a dramatic sigh. "Job well done,

Cole. Job. Well. Done."

A laugh bursts free from his mouth, erupting from deep within his chest, and that lopsided grin just...does something to me. But there's one thing he continues to do. Even now.

Whether it's subconscious or not, he's still trying to position himself, to tip his head, so the left side is away from me. The only time he doesn't is when he's distracted, which means I'll have to work on sidetracking him more. Maybe then he'll finally figure out I don't care about his scars. That he's the most incredible man I've ever met. That I'm falling deeper in love with him.

Shifting to roll a condom down his length, I slide down over him, taking him deep inside my body. I try to silently communicate all that, so maybe he'll realize—he'll understand—how I feel.

Maybe then he'll realize—regardless of the scars upon his flesh—that he's so much more.

Maybe then, he'll realize he's worth loving.

CHAPTER THIRTY-NINE

Presley

can't put my finger on it, but something about this woman just…doesn't *fit*.

"So, you're new to the area, Ms. Mathison?" I inquire as I prepare to adjust her spine for the first time. She's lying face down on the table, her dark hair confined to a long ponytail.

She brought in her X-rays from her former physician, saying she'd recently relocated here from Tampa, and Clara had confirmed Sheri Mathison had been under the care of a chiropractor there.

It still doesn't assuage that prickly feeling that something isn't adding up.

Once I finish with her adjustment, I smile and help her up to a sitting position.

"Thanks, Presley." Her smile is friendly enough, but her eyes throw me off. They seem like they're analyzing everything about me in the most unnerving way.

"No problem." I open the door of the room, gesturing for her to step out first, and we make our way down the hall to the receptionist desk. "I always call and check on my new patients after their initial adjustment, so if you see an unfamiliar number calling you, it's me."

"I look forward to it, Presley." She reaches out, shaking my hand, and it has to be the firmest handshake I've ever been on the receiving end of—from a female.

Saying goodbye with a smile, I turn and head back down the hall to see the next patient awaiting me.

And for the remainder of the day, I find myself reflecting on my encounter with Sheri Mathison.

* * *

My cell phone vibrates on my desk just as I sit down, planning to go over some notes on a new referral patient over my lunch break, and I can't help but smile at the name on the caller ID.

"Hey there."

"Can you help me? I'm looking for the hottest doctor on the island." His deep, husky voice is laced with humor.

"Hmm…" I pretend to think it over. "I believe she's at the office over on Citrona Avenue."

Laughter greets me, and the fact that I made Hendy laugh makes my day that much better, wiping away the odd feeling lingering from my earlier patient.

"Well, she's got this pair of gray pants on that drive me insane because they make her ass look so—"

"Ah-ah! Language, señor." I hear Lucia's voice in the background.

Wait a minute. Lucia's voice should not be in the background.

Noting the commotion coming from the hallway, I see a tall, familiar man step into the doorway of my office, and as he lowers his cell phone from his ear, he grins at me. The sight of the bag in his hands sends my empty stomach into a growling fit.

Raising his eyebrows, he says, "Whoa. Someone's starving."

Blowing out a long breath, I push my chair back from my desk and move over to the table where Hendy sets the bag of takeout, placing his keys and cell phone off to the side. "It's been a really strange day."

As we sit and he pulls the food, bottles of water, napkins, and plastic ware from the bag, he asks, "How so?"

"Well, I had a new patient who was—"

We're interrupted by the sound of his cell phone vibrating with an incoming call. I take notice of the name flashing on the caller ID before he silences it, ignoring the call.

Heath.

I nod toward his phone. "You can take that if you need to. I don't mind." Hendy's been ignoring this guy's calls, and I can't help but wonder why he doesn't want to talk to him.

Avoiding my eyes, he concentrates on opening the lid of the container holding his own salad with added blackened salmon atop it. "Nope. It's nothing important." His response is curt.

My lips part then close then part. And snap shut. I want to ask, but I'm not sure if I should. It's not like we ever stated anything as to our…whatever we have. I don't know if I even have the right to ask.

"Go ahead and say it." He lifts his head, eyes meeting mine. And damn it, he's again purposely angling his face, so I see the right side. Maybe it's subconscious, but it still unnerves me. And honestly, it hurts my feelings that he continues to do this with me.

Raising my eyebrows, I ask, "Say what?"

Cocking his head to the side, he gives me a look. "Say what you wanted to say a minute ago. When you opened and shut your mouth repeatedly."

"Repeatedly? No. Once, maybe."

"Twice."

"Fine. Twice," I say with narrowed eyes. "I was just wondering who this Heath guy is." Gesturing with my fork before I stab a large helping of my own salad, I add, "Maybe he's trying to sell you a timeshare in some random country no one's ever heard of."

His lips tilt up slightly. "He's a former SEAL. Wants me to get on board with his foundation."

I wait for him to expand, but there's nothing but silence. "*Aaaaaand?*"

"And I'm not in the position to do that."

"So you never plan on working ever again? At what? Age forty?" I'm picking at him, no doubt about it.

He gives me a sharp look at my sarcastic mention of his age. Or of the *incorrect* age. "Try early thirties."

I can't hide my smile. "Love how you're nonspecific about your age. Totally like a woman." Snickering, I add, "Next thing, you'll be celebrating your 'second twenty-first birthday.'" Raising a hand, I spread my fingers and wiggle them, making my voice high-pitched. "Woohoo!"

"Wow," he remarks drily. "Someone needs to crown the queen of sarcasm here today."

Recognizing I'm not getting anywhere with this line of conversation, I shift gears. "Did you know that some historians believe the legend of Minos suggests condom use in ancient societies dating back to 150 AD?"

"Well, hello subtle subject change." His eyes dance with amusement, and I note his expression isn't closed off like it had been mere minutes earlier. He takes a large bite of his salad.

"Or"—I lean in to lower my voice conspiratorially—"that the practice of gynecology dates all the way back to the 1800s?"

His chewing slows, giving me a look to which I offer a mischievous smile. "Ooh! I know! I can tell you all about how my gynecologist has these pictures of half-naked, muscular men tacked to the ceiling above the exam table, so patients have something to look at—"

"Do you like those pictures?"

My mouth snaps shut in surprise at his question and at the sharpness in his tone. Like he's…jealous of pictures?

Huh.

Studying him carefully, I answer slowly. "Well, they're not really my thing. My thing would be more like…" I trail off, and I can see I've hooked him.

"More like…?" he prods. Oh, yeah. He's hooked.

Letting out a whimsical sigh, I stare down at my salad. "More like a guy who's maybe six-foot-four and has crazy awesome muscles and skin the color of hot cocoa. But mostly," I glance around the room before leaning in close to whisper, "a guy who has a really huge—"

"Pres." No doubt about it. The corners of his lips are twitching in his attempt to restrain a smile.

"Brain." I finish with a roll of my eyes. "Geez. Get your mind out of the gutter." I take a bite of my salad and chew, my face a complete mask of innocence.

He shakes his head at me, continuing to eat his lunch. We sit in comfortable silence before I finally hear him mutter under his breath. Something that sounds an awful lot like, "Brain's not all I have that's huge."

CHAPTER FORTY

Hendy

After Presley and I had finished up lunch, I went back to work at TriShield Protection, whose office is located only a few streets over from her office. I'd been going over some last-minute things with Foster to prepare for his absence while he and Noelle are on their honeymoon.

Presley has some speaking engagement at a community college down in Jacksonville after work. She'll be addressing questions from students and won't be getting home until late tonight. Funny how in the short amount of time we've been spending together, I've found myself looking forward to seeing her after work and having more time with her on the weekends.

Not only that but Kane's due to get home later than normal, too, since he had to take care of an issue down at a site just south of Orange Park. Knowing how awful traffic is around that area, it isn't likely that I'll see him for a while.

Heading up the steps of the house, I unlock the door, and as soon as my right foot steps over the threshold, I sense someone's presence in the house.

My entire body is tense, rippling with the awareness.

Quietly closing the door, I casually set my keys on the entryway table beside the door, reaching beneath it to where we always keep a small handgun attached to the bottom underside.

But I don't make it that far.

"It's not there." The female voice, coming from down the hallway, draws my reach to a halt. "I've already secured all weapons."

Turning my head, I eye the large artificial floral arrangement sitting on a decorative built-in shelf a few feet away from where I stand. I have a small Beretta subcompact stashed there.

"I've secured *all* weapons, Mr. Hendrixson," she repeats.

Who the fuck am I dealing with?

Stepping forward, I approach the living room from the hallway, following the trail of her voice. My left hand moves to my side, fingers ready to reach for the large knife I have strapped to my right calf muscle beneath my khaki pants.

"Don't do it. I'm just here to talk."

Is she a fucking mind reader, too?

Approaching, stance ready and alert, I come upon a slender, dark-haired woman sitting at one of my dining room chairs. She's placed it against the wall to ensure herself an unencumbered view of all entrances and exits.

"Are you alone?" I ask.

"Yes."

Alarm rolls through me at the person who failed to greet me. "What'd you do to Izzy?"

"Relax, Mr. Hendrixson." Her lips offer the faintest of smiles. "She's on the deck, enjoying the large treat I brought her." Leveling me with a look, she adds, "She sensed I'm not here to cause harm."

That much remains to be seen.

"What do you want?"

"To talk."

"So talk." I eye her sharply, ensuring my peripheral vision tracks the remainder of the room from my position and the hallway at my back.

"You should sit for our talk."

My lips curve into a humorless smirk. "Maybe I'd rather stand."

Her eyes never leave mine. "I assure you that you'll want to sit for what I have to tell you." Her gaze flits briefly to the one armchair placed against the wall which would allow me a full view from the opposite side of the room. "That chair would ensure your full visibility."

Cautiously, I keep my eyes on her as I lower myself on the chair, noticing the woman has a binder lying on the table beside her.

Her eyes drift over me from head to toe and then back up, appraising me. But it isn't in typical fashion. No, this appraisal is one hundred percent clinical.

"You're looking much better, moving around more naturally, fluidly."

"Are you here to assess my health?" I cock an eyebrow sarcastically, but she doesn't answer my question.

"Tell me about your time in captivity, Mr. Hendrixson."

"It's Hendy." My tone is steely and hard, one which would make most people piss themselves—*had* made some people do so in the past—but it doesn't faze her one bit. "And I'm sure you can read all about it in the files you guys have on me."

She reeks of Uncle Sam. Of a spook. Some government shit.

Her lips curve slightly. "Ah, but I want to hear your personal story. What those reports might not have included."

"My guys and I were ambushed, got shot at, parts of us blown off, and then I was captured and tortured. Then healed. Tortured and healed." I hold her eyes, my gaze hard, cold. "Rinse and repeat," I grit out.

"That sounds pretty cut and dry."

"What do you want me to say? That it was a fucking dream vacation?" I make a derisive sound. "Do you think I don't wonder why the hell—"

"You were the only one to survive. Why they kept you alive," she finishes for me, and I notice the lack of inflection in her voice. She's not asking questions.

She's stating facts.

I lean back, fixing her with a hard stare. "It still doesn't make sense. Why me? Why take me? And why did they do everything the way they did?" I shake my head. "It's not their style." My lips press thin. "Because we all know they're known to mutilate the dead and torture those found alive. Before beheading them."

She remains quiet, regarding me carefully.

Leaning forward, I rest my forearms on my knees. "They'd carve and whip me only to finally send someone in to apply some medicinal salve and wait until a layer of skin had grown over the top of my wounds. Then it would start all over again."

"And then you were rescued and the entire village was destroyed to nothing but rubble," she finishes succinctly.

Steepling her fingers, she regards me. "Why do you think they demanded such a high ransom for you? Eight hundred million dollars is the most they ever demanded for a hostage." With a brief pause, she adds, "Not only that but why did they go to the trouble to spoof a call to Foster Kavanaugh, pretending to be the lawyer handling your will?"

I shrug. "Maybe they hit rock bottom with their funds. Who the hell knows?" Another shrug. "As for them contacting Fos, I have no fucking clue."

"What about the questions they asked you?"

My gaze narrows, wondering why she's changing gears and where she's going with this. "What do you mean?"

"They asked you for specific information, right?"

I don't immediately answer. "They asked me to tell them where the files were." My jaw clenches, recalling their shitty interpreter. Recalling the questions I'd been hammered with. The questions I hadn't told anyone because they hadn't made any sense.

The questions about my father.

She leans forward on her elbows. "They wanted information about your father."

My lips part to answer her before snapping shut. Because she hadn't asked a question. Instead, she'd phrased it as a statement.

As fact.

"My father died before I was born. My parents divorced while my mother was pregnant with me."

"Is that what you were told?"

What. The. Fuck.

My jaw clenches and unclenches in frustration. "Can you stop pussyfooting around and get to the point?"

"Your father worked for the government, and he had been undercover finding intel on some high-value targets associated with al-Qaeda." She pauses as if to wait for that to sink in. "Your mother changed her name and listed that on your birth certificate to ensure you would be a Hendrixson."

"What the hell are you talking about?"

"Your father was Latin American and had the dark hair and skin tone. He could easily pass for a Middle Easterner once he grew out his hair and dark beard. He was a shoo-in for that kind of work.

"Your mother gave him an ultimatum when she discovered she was pregnant with you. He chose his work—reluctantly so. But he loved you. Watched you grow up."

My heart is racing, my mind stuttering in shock. "What do you mean he watched me grow up?"

Rising slowly, she walks over to the windows overlooking the deck and distant view of the Atlantic Ocean. "As an operative, I understand, in ways most others can't fathom, what you went through in captivity. I think you deserve to know about your father. My loyalty to Paulo Cordeño is what brought me here."

She pauses and visibly swallows as if wrestling with emotion. "Your father initiated the plans which set your rescue mission into motion. He died shortly thereafter."

Time stills, my breath catching in my throat. Because that would mean my father had been alive all this time.

And for years—*years*—I'd been led to believe he was dead.

I scrub my hands over my face, breathing out, "*Fuck.*"

"Your father's last name was Cordeño. Your full birth name was Cristiano James Cordeño. Not Hendrixson. Your mother chose the last name of her maternal great-great-aunt who never married or had children. She was an only child and the last in the line of Hendrixsons. She knew the change wouldn't be obvious and wouldn't leave a clear trail."

My head snaps up, and I stare. "She knew all along he wasn't dead?" But I already know the answer before she turns to face me.

Her expression turns slightly sympathetic. "She was trying to protect you."

Shell-shocked, I'm trying to wrap my mind around this when a thought hits me, and I turn a sharp look on her. "My mother."

Her lips purse. "Mr. Hendrixson, her death—"

"Hendy," I correct her.

"Hendy," she says, "her death was legitimate."

That much is a relief.

"I was one of the individuals who worked alongside your father on his final mission."

"And by final, you mean…"

"He died trying to carry out that mission." She turns back, facing the window. "We were double-crossed, and he paid the ultimate price."

"I really hope to hell—"

"Yes." Her head whips around, and the iciness in her eyes makes me want to rear back. "I made sure of it. I'd only worked with him a short time before his death, but even in that short time, I'd come to care for him." Her tone softens slightly before adding, "Like a father." Her gaze turns steely again, jaw tense. "No way in hell was I going to let them live after causing the death of your father and compromising our entire team."

After a brief pause, she continues. "Your father was a good man. And he"—her lips quirk up ever so slightly as if she's drawing upon a fond memory—"loved trivia and random facts. He left me a clue which ultimately led me to discover this." She gestures to the binder on the dining room table. "It was hidden beneath the floorboards in his apartment. Turns out that he kept tabs on you over the years and documented much of it there."

Eyeing the binder with a mix of wariness and yearning, I turn to her. "Why didn't he say anything?"

"You know why."

Running my hands over my hair, I let out a grunt of frustration. "I know, but I can't expect to believe he never tried to get in touch with me."

There's a beat of silence as she studies me. Crossing her arms, she levels me with a look. "Do you remember your first new bike?"

My eyebrows furrow in confusion, wondering where she's going with this. "The one I got for Christmas?"

"The one your mother told you she couldn't afford."

Silence.

"He got it for you. He knew your mother couldn't afford it, but he still wanted you to have it. Couldn't bear the idea that his son was doing without because of the way things had turned out."

Staring at the floor, I mumble as I'm bombarded with new revelations. "He's the one who fixed Mom's car that year it was on its last leg."

She nods. "She refused a new car. Knew it would turn too many heads." Her lips curve up at the corners. "Cost him more to overhaul the entire car's engine than it would've to buy a new car. But he did it."

Waving, she gestures to the binder. "All this is in that binder. While I hadn't worked with your father long, after reading that, I feel like I know him even more. And one thing stands out—is more evident than anything else." Her gaze holds a fierce intensity. "He loved you. So much.

Regardless of your thoughts about anything else, he loved you and your mother."

Moving away from the windows, she crosses the room and stops at the hallway leading to the front door without turning. "Dr. Presley Cole is a lovely woman. Smart and generous. Very competent. You're lucky to have her in charge of your care."

I don't know how to respond so I remain silent for a beat.

"You going to stop popping up and watching me like a stalker?" I joke because I'd instantly recognized her from the two times before when I'd felt eyes on me. Then a thought dawns. "How the hell did you get in anyway?" There weren't any signs of forced entry. None. Nothing out of place.

Turning her head slightly, I can hear the tinge of a smile in her voice. "I learned from the best, Mr. Hendrixson." She pauses. "All your weapons and ammo are in your refrigerator. Now, if you'll excuse me, I have a job interview to prepare for with a friend of yours." Her steps are faint across the hardwood floors, nearing the front door.

"Wait," I rush out. "I never got your name."

She hesitates so long, I don't think she's going to answer me. "Sheridan Marx." The front door opens, and she adds, "And I'd consider Heath's offer if I were you."

The door closes quietly behind her, and I'm left sitting in the chair as if my entire world hasn't just been rocked from here to kingdom come.

Leaving me with only a single binder, certain to hold the mother of all mindfucks.

CHAPTER FORTY-ONE

Hendy

August 1ˢᵗ, Cristiano's birth:

I couldn't stay away. Not for this moment. I know I went against all regulations and protocol by sneaking into the nursery when the distracted lazy-ass nurses were gossiping about some hot doctor they wanted to sleep with.

He is so perfect. Alert—far more alert than any infant I've ever seen. I told him I loved him and that I was going to watch over him the best I could.

It was so damn hard to leave that nursery.

I skip a few pages and stop on another entry.

Ten years old, May:

I watched him rig a trap to try to catch the squirrel who had been the recurring culprit in chewing away at his tin-can telephone "wires." I don't think I've ever witnessed a ten-year-old take as much time to sketch out a design and construct it.

If only he'd put as much effort and time into his social studies homework assignments.

My lips curve up at this entry. It's true. That damn squirrel pissed me off. And I really hated those dumb assignments. Pretty sure it irritated the teacher when I continued to ace her tests, my love for factoids already firmly implanted in my DNA.

I flip through the binder, reading various entries; my eyes feel gritty, burning with the emotion they elicit, but I push on with a desperate need for more. For more evidence that my father loved me even if he wasn't in my life.

Fourteen years old, September:

He's still growing like a weed. Looks like he's going to get his height from me and possibly be even taller. He's got his mother's smile. That woman's smile could capture anyone's attention, so wide and infectious. Unfortunately, it appears the girls have already begun to fall under the spell of that and his charm. I really hope he practices safe sex. Or better yet, abstinence.

I flip some more pages, skipping ahead a bit. Noting the gaps in entries, I assume he was immersed in a job or mission or…whatever the hell it was he'd been doing.

Seventeen years old, May: *My son needs to be neutered. God help us. He's too much of a ladies' man already.*

I grin. Can't help it. It was the truth back then. And that had only been the beginning. As I turn the pages, he apparently realized that, too.

Twenty-four years old, September: *My son's SEAL team is stationed in Little Creek, Virginia, and he's quite popular with the ladies. Still. Known around these parts as a "man-whore," in fact. Not exactly what a father wants to hear. But he's been through the wringer quite a few times with the other guys.*

I think his buddy, Foster, is getting close to wanting out. I'd bet in about four years max. That kid has a head on his shoulders, investing more wisely than I'd expected. He's got his sights set on starting his own private security consulting firm, and I have no doubt he'll be successful. I'm certain Doc and Miller will follow eventually.

Rumors among the teams are that Cristiano—or Hendy as he's been nicknamed—has an uncanny sense of things when they're on a mission. A sense of impending danger. That he's saved his guys many times already.

He has no idea how proud I am of what he's doing for his country.

He has no idea how much I love him.

The ink is slightly smeared across the word "love," and I wonder if it was from a tear. But I guess it really doesn't matter. I'll never know since he's not around for me to ask.

With a handful of pages still to go, I'm not sure I can endure more. Scrubbing the heels of my hands against my eyes, I let out a groan. But just as I'm about to close the binder, something in the back catches my eye. Tucked behind the thick clear pocket in the rear of it is something thin, like paper. When I tug it free, I realize it's a well-worn photograph.

It's a photo of me getting pinned with my SEAL Trident. My mom had already passed away, the brain aneurysm taking her from me so fast—without a goodbye. One day, she was there, giving me yet another lecture on not getting any girl pregnant and to keep my head on straight, and the next, she was gone.

That day, at my Trident pinning ceremony, I recall thinking I could feel her presence.

Maybe I had felt my father's presence that day, too.

CHAPTER FORTY-TWO

Presley

"Wow," I breathe out, feeling as though my own world just got knocked off its axis. Shaking my head, I falter in finding the right words. "I don't even know what to say."

Hendy lets out a short, humorless chuckle. "Tell me about it."

He's just finished sharing his newfound knowledge of his father and his involvement in his life. We've spent much of this rainy, overcast Saturday sitting on my couch while going through his father's binder filled with memories, both written and photographs.

Resting my head on his lap, I kick my legs out on the rest of the couch. Izzy's snuggled happily on the area rug, napping. She had to inspect every room once they got here to ensure it passed muster, I guess. Once I gave her the baked treat I'd purchased for her, she was in heaven.

Hendy's hand goes to my hair, absently combing through the strands as he stares off, appearing lost in thought.

"I have to say, this Sheridan chick sounds pretty ba-dass," I'm teasing, trying to pull him from his funk. "Think if I train hard enough and started running on the beach with you instead of the treadmill, I could take her?"

His gaze meets mine, and I'm relieved to see his eyes are lighter, his lips tilting upward. "Totally." He winks.

Which means totally...*not.*

I scowl at him. "That wounds me. Deep."

His smile widens and turns a shade predatory. "Speaking of deep..."

"Seriously." I let out an exasperated sigh, trying to sound put off. "Give the guy some milkshake, and it's all downhill."

"Milkshake?" He looks amused.

"Yes." I nod. "Didn't you know my milkshake brings *all* the boys to the yard?" Sitting up, I playfully nudge his shoulder, as if I hadn't quoted the song "Milkshake" by Kelis. "Sheesh. Get with it."

All of a sudden, I'm tugged onto his lap. My legs straddle him, and my body presses against his hardened muscles. One hand firmly grips my hip, the other sliding to the nape of my neck.

"What do you mean"—angling his head, his hot, minty breath washes against my lips—"it brings *all* the boys? There should only be one, in particular, you're worried about."

My eyes lock with his, the heat blazing within the depths and making my breath hitch as I tease, "Well, you do happen to be the only one who has that special effect on me..."

His eyes narrow, trying to determine where I'm going with this. "Special effect?"

I nod. "You're the only one who causes my hands to be traitors."

One dark eyebrow arches in question. "Do tell."

"Well, it's like this." I glide my palms in a caress over his firm pectorals, maintaining eye contact. "It starts out all innocent and then *bam!*" I slip a palm between us, cupping him and letting out a sigh full of fake sadness. "And that happens. It's just…terrible. Damn traitorous hands effect."

With heavy-lidded eyes, he murmurs, "Just terrible."

He's hardening beneath my palm, and I can't resist the urge to trace the outline of his cock. Leaning in, I place my lips over his earlobe, toying with it before I whisper, "So terrible."

He lets out a groan before I'm flipped back onto the couch as he holds himself above me. The way he's lying, pressing right against my core, the thin fabric of my shorts fails to provide much of a barrier, and I can't resist arching up against him.

"You want that?" he whispers, his eyes dark with heat. "You want"—he pushes his hardening length against me—"that?"

"Yes." My hands move to his ball cap, and as I lift it from his head, he subtly turns his left side away.

Tossing the hat aside, I take his face in my hands. "Stop that." My tone is fierce. "Don't turn away from me."

His eyes flicker, and I watch the play of emotions on his face before he dips his head, pressing his lips to mine in a hungry, almost greedy kiss. And while I know he's partially doing this to distract me away from calling him out further on hiding his face from me, I fall victim to it. Because Hendy's kiss is unlike anything I've experienced; it's all-consuming. But the moment his hand moves to hold my head in place, angling his mouth to deepen the kiss further, his tongue sweeps inside to taste me, and I fall. Hard.

All the way.

My entire body feels like it's melting into him as if recognizing where it most wants to be.

As if my heart recognizes where it wants to call home.

CHAPTER FORTY-THREE

Hendy

I got roped into heading to Shenanigans, the multi-room bar in downtown Fernandina Beach, tonight for an event in the karaoke bar section with Foster and the others. It benefits the local charity foundation supporting wounded combat veterans and their transition to civilian life. A large sign posted next to the karaoke DJ's station explains how the event will work:

Have some karaoke fun while supporting our combat veterans!

- **Sing your song of choice for $1.00 or five songs for $4.00**
- **Spotlight someone else to sing your favorite song for $5.00 or have them sing five songs for $15.00**
- **If you want to sit back and enjoy the night, buy yourself immunity for $25.00**

Foster's been involved with this foundation, as he's big on hiring former military for his security consulting firm, and I commend him for doing so. God knows so many of us falter in the transition from military to civilian life.

Presley didn't hesitate to join me tonight, especially since tonight's also serving as Foster and Noelle's send-off.

They are leaving in the morning to get married and honeymoon in Barbados.

And judging by the way Presley's dressed, I'm going to have my work cut out for me in thwarting other guys' advances. She's wearing this slim-fitting, sleeveless black dress with large buttons down the front that barely hits mid-thigh. Her legs look like they go on for miles, and those simple wedge heels she's wearing accentuate them further. It's taking everything I have in me not to make up some excuse to skip out early, take her straight home, and—

"Wheweee! Is that look for me, darlin'? If so, I do believe you're burnin' me slap up."

Turning to find Kane watching me with the typical shit-eating grin, I sling an arm around his shoulders as my eyes return to watch Presley on the dance floor with the other guys' wives as well as Lucia while some girl sings—pretty well, I must admit—Cher's "Believe."

"If you could look *that* good in a dress like *that*, I wouldn't just be your roommate." I wink at him.

Kane lets out a long, dramatic sigh. "Well, hot damn. No way can I compete with that." We stand here, watching the women dance.

"Glad you made it out tonight." Kane's sober tone draws my attention. "It means a lot to us to have you here." He holds my gaze before turning back to the dance floor. "She's good for you."

My lips quirk up, watching Presley attempt the running man dance with Lucia. Good Lord, the woman isn't the least bit coordinated or graceful, but it's easy to see she's having a blast out there.

"She's amazing."

"You're pretty damn amazing, too, you know."

233

I flash him an odd look. "You making a play for me, Windham?" I expect his usual jovial smile and joking response. Instead, his aquamarine eyes pierce mine.

"Just want you to know only one person is holding you back." He slaps a hand on my shoulder. "You." His gaze returns to the dance floor, but I remain frozen, staring at him.

"But if you keep looking at me like that, I might make a play for you, darlin.'" And there he is. The Kane I've come to know.

Smirking, I let my arm drop from around his shoulders once I recognize the familiar song the karaoke DJ has cued for the next person to sing as Young MC's "Bust A Move."

"I think it's time to show my lovely lady I can move like Jagger."

"I think I'll join you." It's easy to see who's garnering Kane's attention with his gaze locked on Lucia.

Stepping onto the dance floor near Presley, I take her gently by the hips, drawing her to me. She tenses before recognizing my touch, relaxing against me as we move together. Spinning her around, I tug her close.

Dipping my head close to her ear to ensure she can hear me over the music, I say, "You look gorgeous tonight." Then I nip at her earlobe, adding, "It's driving me crazy. Those damn buttons."

Backing away, she peers up at me. A smile plays on her lips before she rises to her tiptoes and tilts her head to softly kiss me. My hand goes to the nape of her neck, holding her in place to deepen the kiss as my lips work over hers. I find myself wishing we weren't surrounded by people in a damn bar.

Wishing I had her at home, naked and thrusting my hard cock in and out of her tight, slick pussy.

"Break it up, you two!" Kane's loud voice has us drawing apart, and I stare down at Presley's lips, rosy and wet from our kiss. "Y'all just about made a baby right here on the dance floor."

Presley laughs, turning to Kane. "It wasn't that bad."

"Oh, but it was." This is from Lucia who's fanning herself. "I *nearly* orgasmed from watching you."

"Well, hot damn." Kane raises his eyebrows, adopting a teasing tone. "I reckon I'd pay to see such a thing."

Lucia gives Kane a saccharine-sweet smile. "Dreams are good, gringo."

Just then, the karaoke DJ announces a quick break and cues up some songs. When I hear "Cupid Shuffle," I tug Presley over to where others are already lining up on the dance floor.

"Wait!" She pulls against the hand I'm holding. "I don't know how to do this."

"Follow my lead. It's easy, I promise." Steering her in front of me, I place my lips to her ear. "It's all of four steps, each time. I'll guide you."

As I lead her through the dance, I realize I've missed this. Missed this part of what I used to do—who I used to be.

And I can't help but be grateful for the woman who's helping me find that part of myself again.

CHAPTER FORTY-FOUR

Presley

've never seen a man well over six feet tall, two-hundred-plus pounds of firm muscle, somehow manage to move so flawlessly. And know how to do the Cupid Shuffle. When he'd steered my back to his front, placing his lips to my ear so I could hear him over the music and whispered that he'd guide me through it, I think a tiny part of me melted into a puddle on that dance floor.

This is how I end up with a former Navy SEAL teaching me to do the Cupid Shuffle. Even with a few missteps or the time or two when I accidentally step on his toes, he doesn't fuss but merely grips my hips gently, redirecting me.

By the time the song is over, transitioning to a new one, I'm out of breath from laughing. I've been enjoying myself so much—and when I turn to face him, the way he looks down at me, the lightness in his eyes with a hint of something indecipherable, I know one thing is certain.

I haven't felt this happy—this lighthearted—in years.

Nearly the same moment I realize the new song the DJ's playing is a slow one, Marvin Gaye's "Let's Get It On," Hendy immediately snags my wrist, drawing me back to him.

"I do believe they're playing our song." His mouth turns up in amusement, eyes sparkling, but everything changes the moment he pulls me closer, dipping his head to my ear. When he sings along—his lips grazing the shell of my ear—it takes all my effort to withhold the shivers.

I'm painfully aware of the firmness of his pectorals beneath my palm. My other hand curls around part of his large bicep, allowing my fingertips to trace over the hard muscle beneath the sleeve of his polo.

His body tenses beneath my fingers, and my breath catches at the realization he's pressing hard against my stomach. That combined with the sexy, suggestive lyrics of the song has my nipples puckering into hardened peaks and my panties growing damp. The hands gripping my hips tighten slightly, one thumb grazing over my hipbone, and I can't help but wonder if he feels the thin strip of my thong beneath my dress. Wonder if he feels this same awareness.

When Hendy's muscles suddenly stiffen beneath my touch, my eyes instantly dart up, taking in the dark expression on his face. Following the direction of his gaze, I, too, stiffen when I see him.

Dylan.

God, can the guy not get a freaking clue?

Apparently not, because he approaches us, stepping away from the guys I recognize as some of his co-workers.

"Presley."

Hendy releases me to step forward.

"I'm starting to wonder if you have a memory issue." He folds his thick, muscular arms across his broad chest, looking more imposing than usual. "I'm Hendy, former Navy SEAL."

"Kane Windham, Green Beret." Kane steps up beside

Hendy, adopting the same pose. All signs of his usual light-hearted and fun personality is gone, and in its place is a mask of serious intensity—one I've not seen before.

Foster, who had been on the dance floor twirling his fiancée, steps up. "Foster Kavanaugh, also a former Navy SEAL."

"Which means, in ten thousand words or less"—Hendy leans in closer with a grin that speaks of pure intimidation, eyes cold—"we're experienced in kicking ass."

Foster stares down Dylan. "Remember that dude we took care of who messed with my sister?" he asks Hendy and Kane while maintaining a hard glare on Dylan.

"Yep." Kane immediately answers easily. "I reckon he's still eating soft foods. What with that jaw damage and all."

"And that guy who messed around on our friend Raine?" Foster prompts.

Hendy answers quickly. "That dude still walks with a limp, hunched over."

Dylan pales.

"So, the moral of the story is—" Kane starts.

"You'll end up the same way," Foster adds.

"If you come back and bother Presley." Hendy's the one to finish, fixing a lethally dark stare on Dylan.

"Capisce?" Foster grits out.

Dylan nods quickly—so quickly it appears his head's become loose and is threatening to topple off.

"Buh-bye now, darlin'." Kane waves him off, and Dylan doesn't hesitate before rushing away.

Once he's out of sight, the three of them exchange fist bumps, grinning smugly. I cross my arms, schooling my expression and waiting for Hendy to turn his attention back to me. Once he does, I watch as slight apprehension edges into his features, wondering if I'm upset with him. Crooking my index finger at him to come to me, he steps forward as Kane and Foster walk off to rejoin the others. Stepping closer to him, I lift on my toes to speak into his ear.

"You need to take me home now."

He leans away, eyes questioning. "Right now?"

"Right now."

He tips his head slightly. "Because you're…?"

Mad? That's what he's wondering. And he can't be further from the truth.

"Because I'm about to take advantage of you right here and now if you don't."

He doesn't say anything for a moment, and I watch as his entire face morphs into an enormous grin. Slipping a hand to the back of my head, he brings me close, angling his head to press his lips to mine in a perfunctory kiss. "Let's say goodnight to everyone."

Hendy hands off what appears to be a considerable amount of money to Foster, donating extra to the cause, and it only increases my admiration for him. After saying our goodbyes and giving our well wishes to the soon-to-be wedded couple, Hendy links his fingers with mine as we walk through the other sections of the multi-room bar and head toward the exit.

"Just so you know," I yell to be heard over the music from the live band playing in the room we're passing through, "I sometimes dance walk." I add some dorky movements to each step as I walk, and Hendy laughs, totally unbothered by my ridiculousness.

And I'm made aware, yet again, at how different Hendy is compared to Dylan. How he accepts me—my quirkiness—the way Dylan never did. The way my parents never have. The way they never will.

On the drive back to my house, I feel an overwhelming fluttering in the pit of my stomach, and I realize exactly what's happening. Realize that this is the moment—the moment I'll never forget.

It's the moment I've realized I'm officially head over heels, crazy in love with Cristiano Hendrixson.

Now all I have to do is hope he'll love me back.

CHAPTER FORTY-FIVE

Hendy

Two weeks later

I've already had my final allotted adjustment from Presley earlier this morning, and I picked up some sushi for our lunch to celebrate. The VA will assess her feedback and go from there.

Stopping in the doorway of her office, I watch her for a moment. She's pulled her light brown hair back into a no-nonsense ponytail, and she has that cute little crease between her brows as she concentrates on typing something on the computer.

"Hey, gorgeous."

My voice causes her to start, jumping in her chair, a hand flying to the center of her chest. "Hendy! You scared me." Her eyes dart to the screen before returning to me.

"I noticed." Giving her an odd look, I ask, "You okay?"

Letting out a long sigh, she nods. "Yes, today's schedule's been so heavy with patients and people who aren't feeling well or tweaked something in their necks." Rising from her chair, she gives me a weak-looking smile. "Glad to see you, though."

I close the distance, my hand sliding to the nape of her neck and tugging her in for a kiss. When she sighs against my mouth, I tug gently on her bottom lip. "Too bad we can't eat lunch and then have a dessert of our own," I whisper against her mouth.

"*Presley.*" Lucia's voice trailing down the hallway has us drawing apart. She appears in the doorway, flashing an apologetic look. "My newest client is interested in becoming a new *pa*tient, and Clara gave her the info packet, but if you have a moment, she had a quick question for you before she leaves?"

Presley's eyes dart to mine. "I'll be super quick. Promise."

"No problem." I give her a quick wink, and she heads off down the hall with Lucia.

Setting down the bag of takeout on her desk table, I turn to get Presley's large thermos of water from the far corner of her desk where she'd been working moments earlier. Reaching for it, I freeze as soon as I see what's on the screen.

Cristiano Hendrixson has experienced much relief through regular chiropractic adjustments, and aligning his spine has greatly affected his overall health. His mood has improved, and full mobility has returned. My main concern with this patient is not necessarily from a physical standpoint but one which is emotional and psychological.

Mr. Hendrixson does his best to hide his scars from others, especially the more severe ones located on the left side of his face.

My suggestions would be to have the patient undergo more intensive therapy sessions with a psychiatrist to assist him in fully moving past the "new" version of himself and

"Phew! Sorry it took me so—"

A feeling of betrayal rushes through my veins as I slowly meet her eyes. That feeling only gets worse when I witness her guilt. Her gaze darts back and forth between me and the computer screen while various emotions flit across her face before she steps toward me.

"Hendy, it—"

"Don't." I wave a hand, gesturing to the glowing screen of her computer. "You've said enough here." Stepping around her to head to the door, I feel the walls closing in on me and want to escape this damn office—to escape her—but the feel of her palm on my forearm stops me.

"Please don't be like this. You know I'm required to assess you in all areas and—"

I whip around to face her, my tone steely, lethally quiet. "And you what? Didn't think it would make any difference to mention that to me? That you"—I break off, nodding back toward her computer—"think that?"

"I have told you!" She tosses up her hands, frustration etching her features. "I told you from the start that this would be tricky. And you promised to understand. To understand I have to maintain professional standards. That I—"

"You sure maintained those well when you were sucking my dick."

The words fly out of my mouth before I can even register the devastating impact of them. Watching her head snap back as if I'd slapped her is proof of the effect of my words. But hurt and pride prevent me from apologizing.

The hurt vanishes from Presley's face as anger comes to the forefront, her lips pressing firm into a thin line as she advances on me. Poking her index finger on my chest in sharp jabs, she punctuates her words. I swear I feel each one deep within me, creating a brutally painful ache in my chest.

"You." *Jab.* "You hide from everyone!" *Jab, jab, jab.* "You hide from me!" She backs away, waving her hands and gesturing wildly. "You think I don't pick up on the fact that you turn your face away from me? Even after I've told you I think you're"—her voice cracks, and she looks away—"perfect the way you are."

Staring at the wall, her expression is so desolate it makes my chest feel impossibly tight. "I've told you so many times that I see you." Her head turns, and the moment her eyes meet mine, I feel like I've just been sucker punched as her eyes pin me with an impenetrable stare. "I've told you that I see you. I've begged you to let me see you—"

"And I did. I've taken my hat off—"

"You don't get it!" she cries out. Pain lines her features before she lets out a long, sad sigh, and shakes her head. "You just don't get it."

Stepping forward, she lays a palm on the center of my chest while her eyes avoid mine. Instead, her eyes focus on where she's touching me, where I can feel the heat of her hand beneath my shirt. She swallows hard before she speaks. "I fell in love with the man beneath all this." Her gaze rises, meeting mine, and they're glistening with unshed tears. "With the man who made me laugh, made me realize what had been missing from my life all along."

Slowly, she lets her hand drop, taking a resigned step back.

"But if you don't find a way to love the man you are now—to love yourself the way you are—then you'll never be able to truly love in return. And let's be honest here"—Presley lets out a humorless laugh that sounds more brittle than anything—"if I learned anything from my relationship with Dylan, it's that I deserve more."

She takes the few steps it takes to make it to the doorway, and though I refuse to track her movements with my eyes, I feel her stop at the threshold.

"You deserve better, too, you know. Even if it's not me."

With those softly spoken words, she disappears down the hallway.

CHAPTER FORTY-SIX

Presley

"Cucumbers are muy bueno." I hear a loud crunch from Lucia as she takes a bite out of a slice. "Not only for your swollen eyes but for your health."

"Why do I not have a partner?" I groan. "I need a partner. Then I would be able to shove my patients onto them on a day like today."

Lucia, upon seeing my face with tears trailing down my cheeks after I left Hendy in my office, hustled me straight into one of her massage rooms and told me to lie on the table. After ensuring she'd locked up after him, she placed some cucumber slices on my eyes and massaged my arms and upper neck.

She's also cussed up a storm in Spanish. And I'm pretty sure she called Hendy some bad names.

Once she's done her best to relax my muscles, attempting to ease the tension, I hear her take a seat in the chair in the corner as the lull of the relaxing music plays softly in the background.

"Want to discuss it now or later?"

"Definitely later," I mumble. "I need to keep it together

for the next round of patients." Thank goodness my schedule is packed solid for the next three hours. That will at least help pass the time quickly. Never have I been so glad it is Friday.

"Then I'm coming over tonight. And I'll bring extra *cu*cumbers."

Rising to a sitting position and catching the cucumber slices as they slide off my eyes, I offer a weak smile. "Deal."

* * *

"So, what are you going to do?"

Shrugging, I pull my knees up, wrapping my arms around them, my eyes downcast. "Not much I can do. I mean he's stuck." My sigh is heavy. "He's still hung up on his looks and can't seem to move past it. And if I can't help him with that, if I can't make him realize his looks aren't what matters…" I trail off when a knock sounds on the door.

My eyes fly to Lucia's in alarm, who instantly rises from her seat to stalk over, rigid spine proving she's ready to take on whoever is at the door. Oddly enough, when she looks through the peephole, her shoulders deflate a bit.

Opening it slightly, she speaks with a sharp tone. "What do you want?"

Expecting it to be Hendy, I'm caught off guard at the sound of Kane's familiar thick, Southern drawl. "Now, darlin'. Is that any way to greet a gentleman who's come bearing gifts?" I hear the familiar crinkling sound of plastic bags.

"*Pres*ley?" Lucia calls out in question.

"Come on in," I answer with a sigh.

I hear their hushed voices before Lucia reenters with Kane's broad form following shortly behind her. And I certainly don't miss the way his eyes canvass her form in appraisal.

Setting the bags on the kitchen counter, I watch as he pulls out two bottles of wine and holds them up in offering. "Chardonnay or Merlot?"

"Chardonnay, please."

Snuggling into my soft chenille blanket on the couch, I watch as he and Lucia work together, her showing him where the wine key and glasses are located. Once Kane pours the two glasses of wine, Lucia brings them over to set them carefully on coasters on the coffee table nearby where I'm seated. Kane then slides three large containers from the other bag, and I recognize the takeout packages from The Circle.

"Here's some shrimp and pasta." He holds up one container. "And these two are large spinach and cheese calzones." Setting them on the table alongside the wine with a bunch of napkins, he winks at me. "You, obviously, get first choice, darlin.'"

Choosing the pasta with shrimp, I move the container closer and remove the lid. "Word travels fast, huh?" Lucia hands me a fork, and I concentrate on digging into my dinner, absolutely famished since I'd lost my appetite earlier and didn't eat the lunch Hendy brought.

"And by word, if you mean this Colombian morsel of gorgeousness calling me, then yes."

My head whips up to stare at him before turning my eyes to Lucia who appears to be far too enthralled with her calzone. Returning my gaze to rest on Kane, I raise my eyebrows. "She called you?"

"Yes, ma'am." There's no mistaking the male pride, his chest puffing out ever so slightly. Lowering his voice conspiratorially, even though Lucia is sitting right beside us, he winks. "Thought it was time to call in the big guns."

Shaking my head with a tiny laugh, I stab a piece of shrimp with my fork and freeze at his next words.

"That's more like it. We need to see those pearly whites." There's a pause. "Plus, now that he's out of the picture, I get the two most beautiful ladies in Fernandina to myself."

"Ay, Dios mío," Lucia mutters, but there's no heat behind it.

"One thing's for certain, though." Kane's unusually serious tone, devoid of his normal use of darlin' and heavy Southern charm, draws both my and Lucia's attention. "You're the best damn thing to happen to him, Presley. If he doesn't—*can't*—see that, then it's his loss."

Nodding slowly, I fiddle with my fork, staring down at my dinner, my voice sounding small, hollow. "If only I could somehow believe that it's Hendy's loss."

Swallowing past the lump in my throat, I watch as a lone tear drops onto one of my shrimp, my vision blurring. "Because when he left me today, it felt like he took a part of me with him."

CHAPTER FORTY-SEVEN

Hendy

"I'm sorry to barge in on you like this, Momma K."

As I lean against her kitchen counter, Foster's mother shushes my apology, waving it off.

"Nonsense, sweetheart." The older woman's head disappears inside her refrigerator before withdrawing a large container I'd recognize anywhere. Prosciutto wrapped mozzarella. This sweet Italian woman cures everything with that stuff, I swear. "I figured you'd come around to see me when you were ready." Her dark eyes study me intently.

Reaching into the proffered container, I grab one prosciutto wrapped mozzarella. Lump forming in my throat, I avert my gaze, staring down at the cheese with the cured meat spiraling around it before I set it aside. My throat feels too tight, and likely, for the first time, Momma K's going to realize she can't fix this—can't fix *me*—with her offering of food.

"You've always been like another mom to me—to all of us. I should've come to see you earlier." I force the words out, heavy with regret, because they need to be voiced. This is long overdue.

"Hendy." Her tone is one filled with such sadness that

it has me raising my eyes to hers. "I know you had to take your time to deal with everything." Letting out a heavy sigh, Momma K steps toward me, reaching out to grasp one of my hands. "Especially after all you've been through. But you should know I'm always here for you, honey."

My eyes focus on her hand on mine, the older, slightly wrinkled skin a contrast to my own. But there's no mistaking the warmth of compassion in her touch.

"You probably know about…"

"About Dr. Presley?" I hear the smile in her voice as she moves away, checking on something in the oven.

"You heard about her?"

Turning around, Momma K rests against the counter, crossing her arms, and gives me one of *those* looks.

"Ah"—I let out a tight chuckle—"I forget how small Fernandina Beach is."

"Or that my other boys tell me everything." Her brown eyes sparkle with amusement.

I can't miss the fact that she says "other boys," implying I'm one of them. And that's the thing about Momma K; she takes everyone under her wing. Foster's sweet mother is that lady who insists everyone call her Momma K—not Mrs. Kavanaugh. She's the one who took it upon herself to send care packages to us when we were deployed along with Foster. Just because.

She's also the woman who insists on "family dinner nights" at least one Sunday a month. And those designated dinner nights include only three people who are blood-related: Momma K, Foster, and his sister, Laney. The other dozen or so are friends she's welcomed—with open arms.

And I'm the asshole who's been shunning it the entire time I've been here.

"She's a sweet young lady, your Pres—"

"I'm sorry," I interrupt abruptly. "I'm really sorry for everything. For not coming to see you. I just…" I falter, feeling the painful tightness in my chest as my eyes begin to burn. Gripping the brim of my ball cap, I tug it lower, my hands remaining atop my hat as I stare down at the kitchen floor. "I just…hate the way I…look." The last word comes out as a hoarse whisper.

As soon as her arms enfold me in her embrace, everything I've been dreading actually happens. Wrapping my arms around Momma K, I bow my head, my cheek pressed against her hair, and I cry.

For the first time since the night I lost my friends—my brothers—in that desert, I cry.

* * *

I let myself into the quiet house after my visit with Momma K, feeling emotionally drained. Upon closing and locking the door behind me, I hear the automatic doggy door slide up and the sound of Izzy's nails tapping on the hardwood floors. Coming to sit right before me as I slide off my flip-flops onto the mat by the door and set my keys on the small entryway table, I squat down to pet her soft fur.

"Hey, girl." She nuzzles me, her wet nose pressing against my cheek before she gives me one big doggy kiss. "I missed you, too." Izzy cocks her head to the side, and I swear it's like she's trying to figure out what's wrong with me.

"It's been one of those days." Rising, I walk over to drop onto the couch, bracing my forearms on my knees with my cell phone in hand. Izzy comes over and lies by my feet, placing her paws on them as if trying to comfort me.

Peering down at her, I twist my lips in a humorless grin. "You think I should call him, don't you?" As if she understands my question, she raises her head and tips it to the side like she's considering it. "That would mean you'd be traveling. Feel like road tripping with me?"

Raising up on all fours, she tentatively sets her chin on my knee, looking up at me with those soulful eyes that I swear can see everything. When she lets out a little grunt, I pet her head softly, a sigh breaking free. "I figured you'd say that."

Swiping my thumb at the screen of my cell phone until I find the number I'm searching for, I press the button, hearing the ringtone. And hell, if my heart isn't racing, and I don't feel the beginning of perspiration on my forehead. Especially when Heath answers.

"Hey, man! I've been hoping you'd call me back."

"Yeah, sorry about that." I blow out a heavy breath, forging on. "If you're still offering that position, I'd like to take you up on it."

"You're just in time. We're getting ready to kick off the tour starting with the West Coast. It'll mean traveling extensively for the next five and a half to six months. Think you could be ready to go and up here by tomorrow morning?"

Leaning back against the couch, I peer up at the ceiling for a moment before my eyes fall closed. Virginia Beach, where Heath's foundation headquarters are located, is about a nine-hour drive. Since Foster and Noelle returned from their honeymoon two days ago, I'm no longer needed at TriShield.

"I can be packed up and see you in the morning."

* * *

Preparing to leave the house, my truck already loaded, Izzy waits at the front door for me. I finally decide to send the text message.

I'm sorry for earlier. You deserve to be treated with the utmost respect, and I failed at that.

I know I can't be what you need the way I am now. I need to fix me.

My thumb hesitates over the keys before I finish with, **Clue: Man who'll miss you more than anything in the world while he's gone.**

I don't expect a response, so I silence my phone as I walk out with Izzy and lock up behind me.

CHAPTER FORTY-EIGHT

Presley

One month later

"Presley," Lucia's voice calls out as I prepare to go over some new patient files on my lunch break. "There's a big, burly man here to see you."

My head whips up, heart immediately beginning to race, because... Is it—

"Now, now, darlin'. Is that any way to speak to your future husband?"

My entire body deflates when I hear Kane's familiar Southern Texas drawl. No denying a part of me—okay, *all* of me—hoped it was Hendy who Lucia had been announcing.

Keep dreaming, Presley, I tell myself derisively. It's not exactly like the guy's been knocking down my door—or blowing up my phone—trying to get in touch with me. Hell, maybe I should feel lucky that he sent me those text messages before he left town.

I'm sorry for earlier. You deserve to be treated with the utmost respect, and I failed at that.

I know now that I can't be what you need the way I am now. I need to fix me.

Clue: Man who'll miss you more than anything in the world while he's gone.

The logical part of me understands and realizes the facts—Hendy may be healed physically, but he *isn't* healed emotionally. He has a major roadblock when it comes to accepting his appearance. And believing others could accept it, as well.

I'm not coping. Not coping well at all after being left behind by the man I truly fell in love with. The man I wish would realize I accept him the way he is—that I can love him.

Instead, I hide from the pain by burying myself in work.

And I've begun to run on the beach in the mornings, too. Because that's not pathetic in the least. Especially not when said person imagines running by the same man who used to run that same beach nearly every morning.

Nope. Not pathetic at all.

It *surpasses* pathetic.

"I've brought my favorite doctor some lunch." Kane lifts the large plastic takeout bag in gesture. "Want me to set your salad on the table here?"

Nodding slowly, I train my eyes on the bag, watching as he removes a large plastic container. "You got me a salad." My tone is flat, almost numb.

Kane stills before his eyes find mine. "Is this not okay?"

Attempting to shake it off, I roll my lips inward, attempting to stave off the emotions brimming at the surface. "It's fine. Great." The smile I fix on him feels as brittle as it is forced. "Thanks!"

Kane darts a look over to where Lucia remains propped against the doorjamb. "A little help here?" he murmurs.

"Don't ask me." She raises a hand as if to stop him. "I've never gone *lo*co over salad *be*fore."

"How did you…know to get that particular salad for me?" I ask quietly while simultaneously dreading and anticipating the answer.

"Because Hen—"

"Ahem!" Lucia's loud clearing of her throat does little to drown out Kane's response. At any other time, watching the two of them trade looks of warning as if trying to have a silent conversation would amuse me.

"Shit," he mutters beneath his breath before shifting gears. "Well, I figured you'd be hungry and…aw, shit." He lets the bag drop to the table with whatever else it holds and steps toward me, opening his arms.

"I'm sorry, darlin'. I was trying to—" He breaks off when I hurl myself at his chest, wrapping my arms around his large, muscular torso. "Help."

"I'm crying over a stupid salad." My voice is thick with emotion mixed with a tinge of deprecating humor as my tears dampen Kane's shirt. "I've reached a new level of low."

His chest rumbles slightly beneath my cheek, one hand smoothing down my hair while the other rubs my back soothingly. "Get it all out. You'll feel better." He pauses. "About the salad, of course," he tacks on, and if I had it in me to laugh, I would.

Kane smooths down my hair again. "My great-grandmother used to say that tears are like when God brings rain. They cleanse and make everything feel newer, fresher, and rejuvenated."

A weak smile tugs at my lips. "No offense, but I think she was full of it. Because I don't feel any of those things anytime I cry over him."

"Well, she did hit the bottle pretty hard…"

I can't resist a tiny snicker at his musing.

"Ah, that's more like it." The smile in his voice is evident, but then he sobers. "He misses you just as much," he says softly. "But I think you and I both knew it would've come to a head at some point. He needs to accept himself before he'll ever get it through that damn thick skull of his that anyone else could accept him the way he is."

I don't say anything as my tears slowly ebb. Finally, I ask what's been on my mind. "Has he talked to you about me?" Mustering up the courage, I lean back to peer up at him.

Those aquamarine eyes study me intently for a moment. "All the time." The edges of his lips curve up in the start of what I've come to know as his trademark grin. "Especially to make sure I'm not making any moves on you."

Shaking my head with a short humorless laugh, I look down at the floor.

"Hey." Raising my eyes back up, I meet his watchful gaze. "I guarantee he'll be back for you. Because right now, he's doing everything in his power to get himself right—to be the person you need him to be. The real question is do you love him enough to wait?"

As my lips part to answer, Lucia interrupts.

"He'd *bet*ter not make her wait long is what I say. None of this *Notebook* crap where so much times passes." She folds her arms across her chest, leveling a hard stare.

"Now, darlin'. I happen to like *The Notebook*." His head tips to the side. "Who doesn't want a letter written to them every day for a year?" He winks at her with a smirk. "I reckon I'd call that hardcore dedication."

Lucia rolls her eyes, but I can see she's trying hard not

to smile. "Ay, Dios mío. Why am I not surprised?" she mutters. Kane merely smiles wider in response.

As the two of them go back and forth, Kane's question replays in my mind.

The real question is do you love him enough to wait?

But I think he's wrong. I think the real question is whether I have it in me to risk waiting for him...only for him not to come back.

CHAPTER FORTY-NINE

Hendy

Three months later
Early September
San Diego, California

"Thanks so much for joining us tonight. I'm Cristiano Hendrixson, but most people call me Hendy. And this gorgeous lady here…" I pet Izzy's head briefly as she sits beside me on stage. I've come to learn she's a bit of an attention whore, loving being up here with me in the spotlight. "This is Izzy."

Straightening, I slip my hands into my pockets to resist the urge to fidget. "My story began when I was a young'un, and me and a buddy of mine snuck off to his basement to watch the war movie, *Apocalypse Now*. I wanted to be a Special Forces"—I use finger quotes—"'badass' from that moment on." Laughter at my naiveté fills the large auditorium, and I can't help but grin at my own foolishness.

"I know, I know. I'm cringing at how innocent I was back then, too. But the next day, I was doing pull-ups and everything else under the sun to get my ass in shape…"

Two weeks later
Carlsbad, New Mexico

"I graduated from the Naval Academy, thanks to my mother who always lectured me about the importance of getting an education and a degree under my belt." I glance upward, silently hoping Mom hears me where she's, well-deservedly, in heaven. Especially for putting up with me all those years.

"Afterward, I thought I was ready to become a Navy SEAL"—my tone is ripe with sarcasm—"because I mean how hard could it possibly be, right?" There's laughter amidst the crowd as I shake my head. "Well, in case you haven't noticed, in case you haven't gotten a good look at my face, it's clearly tougher than you think." I pause. "But from what I've been told, chicks dig scars."

This time, when the laughter comes again, my own joins with it.

Late October
Seattle, Washington

"After all the shit they did to me, not once did I regret signing up to serve my country. And man, considering the way the cavalry came storming in to rescue me and flattened that joint once we were out safely, nothing could ever compare to that feeling."

There's complete silence—you can literally hear a pin drop in the auditorium.

"Because men I'd never met risked their lives for me." Shaking my head, I add, "They didn't know me from Adam, but when they got word that a SEAL had gotten himself into some pretty bad shit, they came out, guns blazing. And regardless of what I'd thought—and I really always figured, hoped, my time would come to an end in a pile of brass—I don't think I could've felt more pride."

Swallowing past the lump in my throat, the same one I have to move past every time I retell this part of my story, I do my best to maintain composure. "I couldn't have felt more pride in my country, in the men who came to my rescue without a second thought..."

Mid-November
Kitsap, Washington
Naval Base

"Has it been tough as hell to go from that"—I gesture to the large projection screen behind me where a photo is displayed of me and some other guys I'd served with, taken long before that fateful night—"to this?" I wave a hand to encompass my face now. The face that's here for all to see. No ball cap in sight. And I'm certain the lights in this joint are picking up on every damn imperfection.

Traveling with the others on this tour and sharing our stories has helped me in ways I never imagined possible. Surrounded by these men—and woman—who are opening themselves up to complete strangers and sharing their experiences is empowering and cathartic. It's therapeutic in ways I could never have imagined.

Kara, the lone woman, is a former Army bomb technician who'd lost both arms when a bomb she was trying to dismantle had detonated. Leif, a former SEAL from the West Coast, has muscle missing from his right arm and along the outside of his right leg due to shrapnel from an explosion.

I could continue—there are six others, including Heath, who go out on the stage in whatever city or town we're in and share their personal accounts.

It's our final stop of the tour on the West Coast before it ends at Walter Reed Medical Center in Maryland. Then we get a much-needed break before we start again.

The outpouring of emails, letters, cards, and comments from those who stop to chat with us after we're finished each night has been awe-inspiring. What's more surprising is the number of women who attend these things and approach us guys.

"Chicks dig scars, man." Heath had told me that when several women had approached me on the first few nights of our tour. He'd noticed the shock, the surprise on my face.

The thing is I didn't pay them any attention because there was only one person who hasn't cared about my scars. The same person who hasn't given me attention *because* of them.

I finally managed to see what I needed to do. Not only did I have to accept how I looked on the outside, but I also had to figure out how to love—to appreciate—myself the way I am. Without that, there was no way anyone could love me...nor could I believe it possible.

Now that I've managed to come to terms with everything, it's time. Time to try to show Presley Cole she has my heart and hope like hell I can convince her I'm good enough for her.

That I'm a good enough man who's worthy of her love.

CHAPTER FIFTY

Presley

Early December

"What is a centipede?" I murmur softly beneath my breath.

"Sorry I'm late, chica." Lucia slides onto the barstool beside me at the microbrewery where I'm nursing a beer while watching *Jeopardy* on the mounted television. "My last client wanted to schedule for the next six months." Shaking her head, her long dark waves cascading past her shoulders. "Ay."

"No worries. Just glad you're here." I shrug casually as if it's no big deal.

Lucia gives me a knowing look then slaps a thin, wrapped rectangular present onto the bar top. Glancing around, she squints at me, accusingly. "Any *particular* reason we must sit here?"

My spine stiffens because I don't want to discuss it, nor do I want to admit I still sit at this particular end of the bar because…well, because this is where Hendy and I sat.

And I miss him. More than I'd like to admit. If I thought he'd hurt me plenty that day in my office, I was wrong.

Because he'd ended up skipping town and his disappearance only poured salt in the already open wounds.

It's my birthday, and I can't think of anything more pathetic than a woman who's still pining over a guy so much she insists on sitting in the same spot at a bar.

I keep wondering if maybe Hendy will send a text or something, but then I realize he has no way of knowing it's my birthday. It's not like I've mentioned it to him.

Taking a sip of my beer, I eye the present on the bar top. "It's thin." Picking it up and shaking it gently next to my ear, I smirk. "It's your recipe for Ajiaco, isn't it? And maybe your other recipes I keep begging for?" Ajiaco is a chicken, corn, and potato stew that is beyond delicious, and Lucia refuses to part with that recipe, among others.

She snorts dismissively. "I'd be disowned if I gave you those."

Ripping open the package, I pull out something wrapped in tissue paper. Flat, thin, and spiral-bound on one end, I realize it's a calendar of some sort.

But my breathing stutters when I see the title on the front.

The Official Fearless Tour Calendar

My hands shake, and my grip on each side of the calendar turns white-knuckled before Lucia lays her palm on my arm.

"Hey." Her tone is subdued, cautious. "You should see it for yourself." She pauses briefly. "How far he's come. And we both know much of that is because of you."

Inhaling a deep, calming breath, I flip it open to the first month's page. A handsome man by the name of Heath Mitchum, clad in American flag board shorts, smiles back at me. His body is riddled with healed wounds, and the right side of his torso, beginning beneath his underarm area down to his waistband is deformed, curving in and out.

However, his face draws my attention again because, in his eyes, I'd swear there's a hint of mischief. And that smile in and of itself is show-stopping in more ways than one; this man hasn't given up on life. Quite the opposite. He's someone who's ready for more of what life has in store for him. When I read the brief bio beneath his photo, I'm even more impressed, and tears begin to prick my eyes for all this man has endured.

I continue to page through the calendar, reading each bio and looking at each person's photo portraying their healed wounds. When I'm on the month of November and still haven't come across Hendy's designated month, there's so much nervousness in the pit of my stomach when my fingers hesitate to turn to the final page, to the month of December.

Nothing, however, could prepare me for what I see when I turn the page.

Hendy is posing, turned slightly, with the majority of the focus on his back and the left side of his face. Low-slung tan khakis emphasize his tapered waist. But that's not what catches my attention, not what makes my breath catch.

He's not wearing a ball cap. He's not hiding. There's no wide, seemingly carefree smile on his face as many of the others featured in the calendar, but the fact he's bared himself for this...

My fingers trace over his picture, over his body, his face, wishing he were here right now. So I could tell him how proud I am of him. Even if we're not together in any capacity, I want the best for him. I want him to be happy.

I can't lie and say I don't wish he could be happy with me. But if Hendy's taught me one thing, it's that nothing in life is guaranteed. That life is meant to be lived.

"And here's my present," Lucia interrupts me, setting an envelope on the bar top.

Frowning, I look at the envelope and then at her. "But I thought this..." I trail off in confusion, still holding the calendar.

She nudges my shoulder with hers. "That"—she gestures to the calendar—"was delivered to me a few days ago with this note." Withdrawing a small folded piece of paper from her purse, she hands it to me.

Accepting it from her, I internally scold myself for being so nervous about opening a piece of freaking paper.

Pres,

A certain someone let me know your birthday was coming up, and I wanted you to have this for many reasons. One being that I wouldn't be here, doing this right now if it weren't for you. (And the other chiropractors I've seen here and there while on the road haven't been nearly as great as you are.)

And I know how ironic it is that I'm traveling with these other individuals on "The Fearless Tour." Laughable, right? Especially since I've been anything but fearless in dealing with everything.

The second reason I wanted you to have this is to show you I'm making progress. Not just for you but for me, too. You were right that day, and I just didn't want to admit it. Instead

of manning up and choosing to deal with the obstacles in my life, choosing to handle them as I should in order to focus on the bigger picture, I hid from them. I'm not proud of that. I know better—hell, I learned better in BUD/S. Learned that hardships would come along the way and the key was not to let them overwhelm me. To handle diversity, to negotiate those obstacles in a manner that I would be proud of.

I didn't do that. Instead, I took it out on you. I hope you can forgive me somehow and be proud of the progress I've made so far.

You're still the most incredible woman I've ever met, and I am doing everything in my power to make you proud.

Until we meet again,

Hendy (and Izzy, too)

P.S. Clue: Jackass who still thinks you're the greatest thing since sliced bread.

My brows furrow as I flip the note over to the back, finding nothing else written down—no answer to the *Jeopardy*-like clue. Glancing at Lucia, I hold up the note. "That's it?"

Without answering, she withdraws a second note from her purse, handing it to me. Written on the same paper, I open it and find my lips curving up at the corners.

Lucia,

I know you're pissed at me—it wasn't tough to tell by all the text messages you sent me, half of which I had to use Google Translator for.

Kudos to all the creative cussing phrases, by the way. Anyway, I appreciate you letting me know Presley's birthday is coming up soon. If you could please give her this package and the other note, I'd appreciate it.

I'm working on being the best man I can be. If you end up giving that stuff to her, can you tell her that the answer to her clue is 'Who is Mr. December?'

And yeah, I realize you're rolling your eyes at me for that cheesy reference to the calendar, but hey, I'm a former SEAL, not Ernest Hemingway. Please take good care of her for me.

Hendy

P.S. Word is Kane's still striking out with you. Give the guy a chance, would you? I promise he's got his act together, far better than most.

"Wow," I breathe out, still staring at the note in my hands.

"I know." Lucia waves a hand, gesturing between the calendar and the envelope on the bar top. "Like my gift can compare to that?" She makes a dismissive sound.

Leaning my head on her shoulder, I let out a sigh. "If it's a spa day at the Omni, I'll be a happy camper."

"It's a spa day at the Omni." I can hear the smile in her voice.

After a beat of silence, I smile. "You're the bestest friend anyone could ask for. You know that, right?"

She pats me on the head. "No need to get all maudlin, now." There's a pause. "Did you notice what he said in his note?"

Raising my head to look at her, I tip my head to the side. "That he's working on himself?"

She studies me for a beat before answering softly. "He signed your note, 'Until we meet again.'" With an eyebrow raised, she flashes me a knowing look. "That means he's hoping you haven't yet closed that chapter."

Lucia nudges my shoulder with hers, her tone gentle. "You just have to decide if you're done reading or if you want to continue to see how the story ends."

CHAPTER FIFTY-ONE

Presley

Resting my chin on my hand, I slump in my desk chair, trying to stay focused on the new patient files in front of me. Hendy and I have exchanged some text messages over the past few months, and I'll admit, I held off from communicating with him at first—after he'd left. Because I was hurt, damn it.

But after his simple apologetic text message, I'd had time to digest everything. So, after a few weeks, I sent him a text message to say I hoped he was doing well and to tell Izzy hello from me. He responded back, thanking me, but it was along the lines of being too polite and stilted. Like we hadn't been anything more than acquaintances. As if we both were overly cautious with where the conversation might lead.

After he'd sent the note and the calendar for my birthday, however, I'd sent him a text message thanking him for thinking of me. His response had been simple but so sweet.

I always think of you, Pres. Always.

That was the turning point, ultimately, for us. I began to text him random *Jeopardy* clues here and there. Once I'd sent a **Hey. Clue: Thinks it's a brilliant idea to drink** prune smoothies.

He hadn't responded until much later that night, and as I was getting ready for bed, a text came in.

Sorry. Our flight was delayed on the tarmac because some lady went into early labor. They called for anyone who might be a medic or have any medic experience, so Heath and I ended up helping another nurse. That's why we're so late getting to the hotel and unpacked.

And answer: Who is Mrs. Sommers?

Someone needs to get that woman turned onto fruit smoothies, for God's sake. ☺

Another time, I'd sent him a picture I'd snapped really quick when Lucia wasn't looking. Kane had left her a note, along with a bouquet of sunflowers, saying her "sunny disposition" reminded him of those bright, cheerful flowers. She'd been holding the note, smiling wide as she read it once again.

Another night, he'd sent me some text messages that had brought tears to my eyes.

Tonight, a woman approached me after we'd finished speaking and told me she had gained such inspiration from all of us and thanked me. She told me I reminded her of her son who'd been killed in Iraq. She'd also mentioned the story of the phoenix rising from the ashes, saying she thought of me like that; that I was reborn, but only stronger now.

It made me think of something Kane had said to me a while back. He wanted me to "own it." To be proud of what I'd endured and survived. To take pride in my scars. And I didn't get it at the time. Maybe I

didn't want to get it. I wasn't ready.

But this woman tonight, not only had she lost her son, but she was a three-time cancer survivor. And here she was, complimenting *me*. **Turns out, they'd found another lump, and she was preparing to undergo treatment again. Her attitude inspired me. She'd asked me if I was close to my mother, and when I'd told her my mother had passed away a while back, she'd hugged me tight and told me that she knew my mother was proud of me. That** *she* **was proud of me, too.**

I responded afterward with a brief but to-the-point text.

I'm proud of you. And I know that woman is right. Your mother's proud of you. I'm certain of it.

Other nights, we'd exchanged silly text messages about a Final *Jeopardy* question that stumped us or, if we'd gotten it correct, gloated.

He'd written: **I had a beer AND got the right answer to Final *Jeopardy*. #winning**

I'd laughed and returned with: **#lifegoals #spoton**

But it was the last few text message exchanges that made my heart race. Because they had a different tone. More intimate.

For nearly three months, I've been without my ball cap (i.e. my "woobie"). Sure, I've had to be careful when I head out to go running in the sun, got to slather on more sunscreen over the left side of my face. But it's freeing. Sounds stupid, doesn't it? But I'm getting there, Pres. I'm trying. When I see you next, I want you to be proud. Maybe you'll even let

me take you out on a date.

I'd stared down at that text so long with my fingers hesitating over the keys, unsure of how to respond. He was clearly testing the waters, trying to gauge my interest. Finally, I'd typed: **Maybe even a date where we'd go out and I wouldn't end up puking in some bushes? Because that sounds super fancy.**

His response had been quick. **LOL**. Ah, memories were made that night, for sure.

Smiling, I wrote: **That's a nice way of saying I was a shitshow.**

But I wouldn't have changed any part of that, Pres, he'd written. **Even leaving things with us in a less than spectacular way, I still wouldn't go back and change any of it. And I'd hold your hair back for you any day of the week.**

That made me smile. **That's oddly romantic, Mr. Hendrixson.**

Smartass. I mean it. I wouldn't change any of it. Except for hurting you like I did. I'm sorry for that.

I hesitated but then decided to go for it. **Sorry enough to maybe even call me and talk like adults? Instead of texting back and forth like teenagers?**

Barely a second after I'd sent that text, my phone lit up with an incoming call from him.

"Hey." I heard the breathlessness in my voice, the excitement.

"Hey, Pres." God, the way he'd said my name, like a soft caress… My lips parted to say the words that begged to slip out, but I hesitated, letting out a sigh.

"Say it." He sounded like he was settling into bed, the sound of covers shifting. "Please. Whatever you were going to say just now."

"I was going to say that I…" I inhaled deeply, bracing to put myself out there. "I miss you."

He expelled a sigh. "Presley Cole." When he continued, I swore I could hear the smile in his voice. "I miss you like crazy."

My lips formed a wide smile. "You miss me for more than my awesome chiropractic adjustments?" I tease gently.

He chuckled softly. "I miss you for more than that." There was a brief pause. "I miss you for far more than your adjustments."

"Really? Do tell." I was fishing. I knew it, and he knew it, but luckily, he played along.

Letting out a long sigh that sounded tinged with sadness, he lowered his voice to a husky whisper. "I miss the way you'd nearly match me answer for answer at *Jeopardy*. I miss cooking for you and hanging out. I miss the way you'd make me laugh."

He paused, and his voice deepened to something low and seductive. "I miss the way you'd touch me, the way you'd look at me as if my appearance didn't matter. As if you…" Hendy trailed off, and for a long moment, I thought he wasn't going to finish until finally, he said, "As if you could see my potential; as if you thought I was good enough to love."

My chest tightened at his words, a lump developing in my throat. "I did," was all I could force out, so overcome with emotion.

There was no response for a long beat. "You did?" Then he quietly tacked on, "Past tense?"

"I do," I whispered softly, wishing with everything in me that I could see his face.

"I want to be good enough, Pres," he whispered back. "Good enough for you to love."

Ever since that conversation, we've continued texting, some calling, and exchanging a few silly selfies. He'd taken one of him and Izzy where he'd been indulging in an ice-cream cone. At the last minute, right when he'd pressed the button to take the picture, Izzy had stuck her tongue—her exceptionally long tongue, I might add—out for a taste, and the camera had caught it. I'd laughed out loud when I'd seen it along with Hendy's caption: **Clue: The man who refuses that much tongue action and throws his ice-cream cone away.**

I'd responded with a quick, teasing, **Never thought I'd see the day when you'd turn away tongue action from a lady.**

He'd responded with **LOL** and an emoticon of a smiley face with a tongue sticking out.

That was yesterday, and I haven't heard from him today. It's been a bit of a letdown after having so much back and forth communication with him, but I figure he must have gotten busy with something.

"I have a *de*livery for you."

Jerking in surprise, I glance over at the doorway to where Lucia stands. She waves a hand toward the hallway as if gesturing for someone to move into my office, and Kane steps into view.

"Hey." I smile up at Kane. Rising from my chair at my desk, I walk over to give him a quick hug.

"Hey, darlin'. I come bearing gifts." He's holding what appears to be a thick envelope, tapping it against his other palm.

"Gifts?" My brows furrow in confusion because my

birthday's already passed—nearly twelve days ago.

"Yes, ma'am." Kane grins. "A gift especially for you." He lifts one shoulder in a half-shrug. "I convinced him to stop being a pussy and just do this," he says as he hands me the envelope.

Cautiously accepting it, I slide it open and pull out what looks to be a folded piece of paper and some other items tucked in the folds. Opening it up, I find a typed letter.

Pres,

I've no doubt Kane will tell you, I've been a pussy about this. He's probably standing right next to you as you read this.

I break off to eye Kane who's, indeed, standing right beside me with his usual smirk.

Anyway, I wanted to give you something for your birthday instead of a lame calendar. I wanted to really give you something I thought you might appreciate and possibly end up enjoying.

I know it's a belated present, but I've included two airline gift cards to fly up to see the last night of our tour. Heath likes to end each tour at Walter Reed Medical Center since all of us have been there and know the men and women could use something to lift their spirits just as we needed it once. I've included two tickets to the tour because I figured you might not want to come alone. Maybe you can bring Lucia or whoever you want. I'd really love it if you could be there.

We'll be speaking three days in a row since they don't have a big enough space to gather all

the patients at once. I've got you tickets for the first night we're speaking there—Friday night—because I don't want you to be exhausted on the following Monday at work after traveling.

I'll understand completely if you don't want to come. I won't lie and say it won't hurt, but I'll understand, Pres. I've asked far too much of you, and I realize this. I just hoped that maybe you could come here and see for yourself how far I've come.

Happy Birthday, again, Pres. I miss you more than you can imagine.

Love,

Hendy

My slow, long exhale is the only sound in the room before Kane and Lucia finally speak.

"So darlin', what do you—"

"Are you going to—"

They both stop, exchanging a surprised look before turning back to me. My eyes flit back and forth between the two, and I focus on the letter and tickets in my hands, rolling my lips inward. Thinking.

Hell, who am I kidding? I'm not thinking about it. My mind was made up the instant I saw those tickets tucked inside the letter.

Raising my eyes to Lucia and Kane, I tip my head to the side. "Guess you'll have to do rock, paper, scissors to see who gets to come with me."

CHAPTER FIFTY-TWO

Hendy

December 20th
Walter Reed Medical Center

"You okay, man? You look like you're about to puke."

Turning, I meet Heath's concerned gaze. Choking out a forced laugh, I shake my head. "Just nervous." I run a hand down my face, adding, "Wondering if she'll show."

"Windham hasn't sent a text to update you?" Heath asks about Kane. I'd filled him in when I'd finally decided to send the letter and tickets.

"Nope." My lips twist. "Said it would"—I make finger quotes—"build anticipation."

Heath chuckles. "Sick bastard," he murmurs, but it lacks any heat. "Well"—he slaps a hand on my shoulder—"get yourself ready." He levels me a look. "And most importantly, be proud of yourself, man. Regardless of what happens with her." The hand on my shoulder gives a quick, comforting squeeze. "I've seen it with my own eyes, and I'm proud of you."

With those words, he walks off, leaving me to stare blankly at him while I drop down to sit on one of the nearby chairs. Someone steps up, walking closer to where I'm sitting while the others mingle off to the side. Izzy lies with her chin resting on my flip-flop clad feet. It might be December and pretty damn cold in Maryland, but I feel the need to wear them. Like the flip-flops are a little piece of Fernandina Beach with me. Like maybe a little piece of Presley is with me.

"Delivery for Mr. Hendrixson?" The delivery guy—in his late teens—glances around nervously, clearly intimidated by the looks of some of us, by our stature.

"Here." I raise my fingers at him, and he quickly steps over to me, handing me a large, oversized envelope that looks nearly three feet tall. Once I take it from him, I reach for some cash in my pocket to tip him, but he holds up a hand in protest.

"No need, sir. It's been taken care of. Have a great day." And like that, he's gone.

Casting an odd look at the envelope, I tear open the flap and pull out what's inside.

And there's no way I can resist the laughter that bursts free.

Because it's an enormous photo card of Foster, Kane, Doc, and everyone else standing below a banner that reads, *Kick ass, Hendy! We love you and are proud of you!* The smiles of everyone in the photo are so genuine that tears begin to prick my eyes. Each of them holds a small sign with a message on it.

Of course, Kane's holding one that says, *I love you more than they do.* And his expression is just as cocky, if not more so, than usual. But below that message, he'd added, *You rose from the ashes. Own it!*

Then I see Foster's sign, a smirk on his handsome face, and hell, if that doesn't make me laugh again. *I bet Heath twenty bucks you'd get teary-eyed at this. Love you, you pussy.*

Then beside him is his wife Noelle with a smirk of her own, holding a sign that says, *Don't worry. He's not getting any tonight for being snotty to you.*

Doc's expression is deadpan, but I can tell his green eyes crinkle with humor at the corners as he holds a sign that says, *Green Berets can't be trusted. You know I love your ass more.*

My eyes track over the rest of the faces and signs, going back and forth between laughter and fighting back the tears. But the moment I find Presley, my heart stops. Not only because I've missed the sight of her—I have—but because of the sign she holds.

Clue: Woman who is more proud than you can imagine and can't wait to see you. That right there sends me over the edge, and a lone tear trickles down my cheek.

"Well, fuck me. I owe Fos twenty dollars," Heath mutters off to the side.

And I don't even care. Because all this time, I'd thought I'd been doing the others a favor by staying away. So they wouldn't have to see my face. But I'd been missing the big picture.

Regardless of how much I tried to push them away, they hadn't budged. They gave me my room, sure, but not once had they given up on me. Not even when I'd given up on myself.

Looking down at this picture, it's evident more than ever. Even though these individuals aren't my blood relation, they're more family than I could have ever imagined.

I might have lost part of myself out there in that desert, but now, I finally realize what I've gained. I've gained a family—albeit a ragtag bunch.

A family who loves me unconditionally.

A family who didn't give up on me.

A family who believed—*believes*—I rose out of the ashes.

* * *

The applause and whistles are nearly deafening, and I notice the looks on many of the nurses' faces. Shock or even surprise to see that much of a reaction from some of these individuals who haven't shown much sign of life.

This is what it's about. Showing our fellow men and women that life's worth living. That they aren't worthless, that they aren't—nor haven't been—forgotten. To remind them of what they've overcome.

To remind them to be fearless and to live life with vigor.

My eyes have glossed over the crowd the entire time I was speaking in front of them, trying to pick Presley out, but it's difficult with the large number of individuals here tonight.

I thought for sure that, after that photo card, she was going to be here. While I know that something might have come up, I can't deny the fact that I'm bummed as hell at the prospect of her not being able to make it.

As the orderlies and nurses assist many of the patients back to their rooms, some stick around, wanting to shake our hands or say a few words of thanks. Once the crowd thins with barely a few stragglers in wheelchairs, I see a familiar burly form standing beside a petite woman.

My breath hitches as I take in the sight of Presley

standing beside Kane, watching as she draws near, her eyes trained on me. She's wearing a faded pair of jeans that perfectly fit her slim body and a long-sleeved, cotton shirt that accentuates her petite waist. Each step she takes brings her closer, causing my body to tense in anticipation.

She comes to a stop barely a foot away from me while Kane steps off to chat with Heath and the others. Those green and blue eyes regard me hesitantly. "I'm sorry we're late. Our flight was delayed because of the—"

Her words are cut off when I reach out my hand, slip my fingers into the front waistband of her jeans, and yank her to me, my mouth instantly on hers. Presley immediately arches against me, her hands moving to my face.

And I don't flinch the moment her hand cradles my left cheek. Instead, I imagine I can feel the heat—the love—in her touch.

"All right, all right. This is a public place, kids. Jesus." Heath's teasing remark breaks through my haze.

"I reckon I've not witnessed such a thorough tongue bath in some time," Kane adds as I break the kiss, resting my forehead on Presley's.

She huffs out a little laugh against my lips, her eyes still closed.

"Hey." I lean back slightly, my voice quiet, and wait for her eyes to meet mine. "I'm glad you're here. It means a lot to me."

Her eyes scan my features. "I'll always be here for you… if you let me."

My throat grows thick, and all I can manage is a nod. Dipping my head to brush my lips against hers again quickly, I reach for her hand. "Let me introduce you to the others. You'll love them."

CHAPTER FIFTY-THREE

Presley

December 24th

As soon as I slide onto the barstool—what I've come to refer to as my barstool—Ryan, the bartender, greets me with a water and the raspberry ale I usually order.

"Hey, Presley." He smiles, reaching for the remote to change the mounted television to *Jeopardy*. "Any appetizers?"

"Hmm." I tip my head to the side. "You know what? How about an order of the chipotle grilled shrimp, please?"

"You got it." He heads off to put in my order, and I sip my beer, watching the beginning of *Jeopardy*.

I've been stopping in here nearly every Thursday after work after Hendy left to join The Fearless Tour because nothing says 'loser' like a woman who continues to go to the same bar, sit in the same seat, and watch the same show as she did with the man she fell in love with.

The same man who was so different yet the same when I'd flown out to see him speak in Maryland. Different because he was confident; not hiding behind a ball cap, he

284

stood proudly before anyone and shared his experiences. He was the same in that he was still the Hendy I'd come to love—fun, sweet, thoughtful, and oh, so sexy.

That night, he'd taken me back to his hotel room after ditching the rest of his crew and Kane, who went out to dinner and bar hopping. We'd talked, and he'd confided in me about the woman, Katie, and her reaction to his face. How he'd let that and his own unacceptance lead his thoughts and his attitude. My heart ached to hear that story, for what it must have felt like, and I'd made sure to remind him how proud I was of him.

The way he'd made love to me throughout the night was different. His touch was more reverent as if he were memorizing, savoring me. He never once turned his face away from me, nor did he insist on leaving the lights off. There'd been two lamps near the desk area lit, and he'd allowed me to truly see him.

To see the man I love.

That was four days ago, and the tour was now officially over. I hadn't heard from him, but I chalked it up to the likelihood of it being hectic to wrap up their tour.

So…Christmas Eve is upon us, and here I am, sitting at the bar. Alone.

There's a word for that, I believe. It's called *pathetic*.

Ryan slides the small appetizer of shrimp in front of me with some extra napkins, and I thank him with a smile. Picking up a shrimp, I bite into it, discarding the tail to the far section of the plate. Answering the questions I know—or *think* I know the answers to—while I eat, soon the time for Final *Jeopardy* rolls around.

Taking a sip of water while pushing my now empty plate aside, I wait in anticipation for the Final *Jeopardy* clue:

"This insect can see in all directions at once."

"What is the dragonfly?" I answer.

Except that I'm not the only one to answer. Another voice joins mine.

A familiar one.

The one belonging to the man who owns my heart.

CHAPTER FIFTY-FOUR

Hendy

Hearing her give the answer to Final *Jeopardy*, I close my eyes, letting the soft lilt of her voice rush over me, and without thinking, I answer the question right along with her.

She slowly swivels around in her barstool, and my breath catches because although it's only been a few days since I saw her in Maryland, I don't know that I'll ever get over the fact that this beautiful woman accepts me the way I am.

Her eyes drift over me from head to toe, especially lingering on my face. As if she, too, is memorizing my features. As if she missed me as much as I missed her.

"Mind if I join you?"

Her gaze narrows on me, slightly amused. "Who is this Hendy who asks first instead of just doing?"

With a short laugh, I run a hand down my face, and she peers up at me, her eyes light up with mischief. "Well"—she leans in closer, lowering her voice—"I'll let you in on a secret."

"What's that?" I lower my voice to match hers.

"It's usually a sure thing when you're talking to the

same woman who let you tie her up and have your way with her."

This brings a smile to my lips.

"Oh, wow," she breathes out suddenly. "You smiled and jetted right past ruggedly handsome, with the added mysteriousness of those scars, and took it up to the highest level of breathtakingly handsome."

Huffing out a laugh, I shake my head. "You smooth talker, you."

We watch each other, and I get the feeling she's basking in the sight of me as much as I am of her.

"Walk me to my car?" She tips her head to the side in question.

"Absolutely."

She tosses down some money to cover her tab, and I help her slip down from the barstool. And it's at that moment it happens. When I grasp her delicate hand in my own, I feel it. Feel the overwhelming intensity, can almost hear the soft whisper of it.

Because with Presley's hand in mine, I feel like I've finally come home.

* * *

I haven't released her hand, and to be quite honest, I don't want to. Leisurely walking down the sidewalk in downtown Fernandina Beach, past the small locally owned shops and restaurants, we approach her parked car.

Presley reaches into her small purse to press the button on the key, unlocking it. Turning to face me, her car door at her back, she gazes at me with a tentative yet soft expression. "Did you really miss me?"

"More than anything in the world."

"So"—she rolls her lips inward—"here's the deal. I'm going to quote the Spice Girls and tell you what I want. What I really, *really* want."

There's no way I can restrain the smile forming on my lips. I truly never know what she's going to say from one moment to the next, and God, I'd missed that. "And what do you really, *really* want?"

Her expression sobers, her voice soft, wispy. "For you to be ready."

"Ready for what?"

"Ready for this." She launches herself at me, nearly catching me off guard. Wrapping her arms around my neck, one hand going to the back of my head, she guides my lips to hers.

Not even the slightest bit graceful, but I don't care because she's in my arms. I return the kiss, trying to pour everything into it. That I missed her like crazy.

That I love her more than life itself.

Breathless, she breaks the kiss, looking deeply into my eyes. "You were ready," she whispers with a tinge of wonder. "You caught me."

I nod, my throat tight with emotion, because I know what she's saying.

"I'm ready for you, Pres. And I promise I'll always be there to catch you." Leaning my forehead against hers, I allow my eyes to fall closed as I push on. "I'm ready for us. If you are."

There's a long pause. Long enough that it makes me nervous enough to back away to peer down at her. And, of course, she has a shit-eating grin on her face.

"Mr. Hendrixson." She tsks with a playful eye roll.

"Don't you know I was *born* ready?"

I choke out a laugh; my breath comes out in a whoosh of relief. "Presley Cole." I dust a soft kiss on her lips. "Never change." Pulling her close and wrapping her tight in my embrace, relishing in the fact she's in my arms, I whisper against her soft hair, "Never change."

CHAPTER FIFTY-FIVE

Hendy

Three weeks later
Sunday evening

"We're going somewhere special tonight, huh?" Presley eyes me curiously.

"Yep. Getting in a long overdue visit. Plus"—I wink at her—"I get to show off my girl."

She sighs happily in the passenger seat of my truck as I navigate through the streets of Fernandina Beach. Reaching over the console, I link her fingers through mine.

We've spent a lot of time catching up, talking, watching *Jeopardy,* and merely enjoying each other's presence. Making love. Often.

Well…I've been making love to her even though I haven't actually said the words. I have to admit I'm scared shitless. I know she cares for me, but I'm not sure if she still loves me…especially after everything I did. However, I have no qualms about doing whatever it takes to make her fall back in love with me. Whether it takes—weeks, months, or years—I'm not giving up.

Parking the truck alongside the curb of the older home,

I recognize Kane's truck, also parked at the curb because the driveway is overflowing with other cars.

"Whose house are we at?" Presley unbuckles her seat belt.

Exiting the vehicle and rounding the front to take her hand and help her out, I lock the truck, walking along the sidewalk leading to the driveway.

"A very special woman lives here. I know her as Momma K and"—I break off with a chuckle—"chances are, you'll know her as that, too." Smiling in the direction of the house as we walk up the driveway, I add, "She's like another mother to me—to many of us. She likes to take everyone under her wing. And tonight is the designated Sunday family dinner night."

"Wait a minute." Presley comes to a stop midway up the driveway. "Is this Mrs. Kavanaugh's house?"

I look at her oddly. "Yes," I answer slowly. "You know her?"

She gives a little laugh. "No, not really. But she's kind of a legend around here. She's like the unofficial-official nicest lady in Fernandina Beach, according to most."

Chuckling softly, I nod. "That's the truth."

We start walking up the remainder of the driveway but only make it two steps before she stops me again.

"Wait." The frantic note in her voice has me turning a worried look on her. "You're bringing me to meet your pseudo-mom. What does this mean?"

Tugging her closer, her body flush against mine, I cradle her face in my hands, dipping my head to meet her gaze intently. "Presley Cole. Don't you know yet?"

"Know what?" she answers with a whisper.

"That I love you more than life itself." I speak softly, my

lips brushing against hers with each word before I offer a tender smile. "I'm bringing you home to meet my family."

Her gorgeous eyes widen, the green and blue colors glistening with unshed tears. "Hendy." Her voice sounds tight, choked with emotion, and I hope to God it's not because she's going to tell me she can't possibly love me back.

"I…" She hesitates, and my stomach drops. Then she shoves at my shoulder with a hand, a wet laugh escaping her lips. "You ass! You tell me that now—that you love me—on someone's driveway?"

"Yeah, man. Not suave." Our heads whip around to see Foster standing in the doorway, his wife, Noelle, standing beside him.

His wife flicks him in the shoulder, giving him a look. "Seriously? This coming from a man who told me he loved me in the office. At *work*."

Foster raises an eyebrow, his typical cocky smirk on his lips. "And you loved every minute of it."

"Leave them alone." Noelle tugs him inside, and he gives her a playful swat on her ass.

"Only following because I enjoy the view."

"Whatever, Kavanaugh." Her dry response trails off as the two head inside the house.

Turning back to Presley, I nod my head toward the house. "Think you're ready for all that? Because that's a taste of what's to come with those yahoos."

She purses her lips, tipping her head to the side in thought. "I don't think just yet."

My face drops. "Oh. Well, I—"

"Because I haven't told you what I've wanted to say for a while."

My eyes flit over her face, trying to gauge her expression.

"Okay," I say slowly, hesitation lining my tone.

Placing a hand on the center of my chest, she raises her eyes to meet mine. "I love you, Cristiano Hendrixson. More than life itself." Cocking her head to the side, she gives me a playful wink. "And then some."

As my lips part to respond, she stops me with her next words, her tone serious and heartfelt.

"You're my very own phoenix, rising from the ashes." She swallows hard, and a tear escapes, trickling down one cheek. I wipe it gently with my thumb. "Reborn, even better than before." A few more tears fall.

"Pres." My voice is thick with emotion. "I love you so damn much," I whisper.

She lifts up, pressing her lips to mine in a kiss filled with promise. With love.

With hope.

Breaking the kiss, she wipes the tears from her cheeks and smiles up at me brightly. "Ready?"

Grasping her hand in mine, I smile down at the beautiful woman by my side. "Ready."

We walk up to the door to Momma K's house, slipping inside, and are bombarded with greetings from everyone. They instantly welcome Presley into the fold. And I finally understand.

Some have to experience great falls to fully realize their worth.

Some have to face immense challenges to prove themselves.

Some end up falling into the fires of hell, only to rise from the ashes, stronger and better than before. Realizing the gift of rebirth for what it is.

Realizing that, sometimes, love really does conquer all.

EPILOGUE

Presley

Nine months later

"You're serious?"

"Yes, I'm serious." I flash Hendy an amused look.

"I'm not entirely sure about this outfit," he says slowly, looking down at himself in his gladiator-like costume.

I toss him a look, wiggling my eyebrows suggestively. "You look hot, so how are you not okay with it?"

"Well, I do have this massive sword." He holds up the costume prop, waving it, cutting the air in dramatic swipes, a lopsided grin playing at his lips. "Even if it is made of cheap plastic and manufactured in a sweatshop somewhere where child labor is legal."

"Oh, stop." I roll my eyes, turning to head in the direction of the bathroom. "I need to put on my wig. Then I'll be ready to go."

As I'm fixing my Cleopatra wig, readying myself to attend the Halloween party with the rest of our friends downtown at Shenanigans, I hear Hendy call out to me.

"Pres? Can you bring my phone when you're done? I

think it's on the nightstand next to my side of the bed."

"Sure." Finished, I turn off the light, exiting the bathroom. Stepping over to the nightstand, I reach for his phone. And instantly freeze.

Right beside it is a small, black velvet jewelry box. Darting a glance behind me, I don't see Hendy in sight. Picking up the box, I carefully—tentatively—open it.

Only to find nothing inside except for a small folded piece of paper wedged into the crease where a ring would go.

Tugging the paper out, I open it to see a written message.

Turn around for yes.

Get naked and lie on the bed for no so I can change it to a yes.

Laughter escapes my lips, and I shake my head at what is so typical Hendy.

Feeling his presence, I turn halfway and eye him, attempting to school my expression. "I guess," I let out a long, resigned sigh, "I need to get naked and lie on the bed, then." Another sigh full of sham disappointment. "Bummer."

Grinning wide, he brings one hand up, finger and thumb showing me the ring. "Sure this won't convince you enough?"

"Hmm." I step closer, pursing my lips. "Not really." Gently pressing down on the hand holding the ring, I hold his gaze. "Clue: Person who doesn't care about a ring but wants to spend the rest of her life with you."

He furrows his brows in thought. "Who is…Izzy?"

Playfully slapping at his chest, I roll my eyes. "Hen—"

"Hey." He tugs me close, one hand sliding up to cup my cheek, and his thumb sweeps across it in a tender caress.

"Clue: Man who wants to make you his legally because he wants to do it right. Wants to give you everything you deserve." He swallows hard. "That and so much more."

His expression is tender, love radiating in his gaze. "I love you, Pres. I've never loved anyone the way I love you. As terrible as it was to go through what I did, I'd do it all over—I'd go through hell all over again. As long as it meant finding you." His thumb swipes at a stray tear on my cheek. "As long as it means I get to love you," he pauses, his gaze searching, "forever."

Studying him, I whisper slowly, "I'll marry you on one condition."

"Name it."

"We get to name our daughter Emilia, after your mother."

There's a pause, and I can tell I've caught him off guard before he answers slowly, "Okay."

"Okay?" I ask again, and he nods, appearing confused. "Good." He slides the ring on my finger, kissing me softly, and I whisper against his lips. "By the way, Emilia should be here in a few months."

He freezes. Then he glances down at my still flat stomach then back up at me. Lips parting, he falters. "You mean…"

Biting my lip to try to hide a smile, I nod. "I mean." I try to gauge his expression, hoping he's okay with this development.

"Holy shit." The widest grin takes over his face, his hands moving to my hips, squatting down, thumbs brushing alongside my hipbones. "A baby?" He utters the question softly and with such wonder.

"A baby."

He eyes me with mischief. "That explains your nipples being so tender." He shakes his head, probably recalling me telling him my menstrual cycle was out of whack and making my nipples crazy sensitive. "Liar," he murmurs softly, his tone playful. "When?"

"It's still early. Not for another seven months."

Looking at my stomach, he presses a soft kiss to it before glancing back up at me. "You don't think it's a boy?"

I smile. "No. It's just a feeling I get. I really think it'll be a girl."

"God help us if she's anything like me."

Tugging him up, he rises, and I press a tender kiss to his lips. "If she's like her father, she'll be one thing."

"And what's that?"

"Perfect." I pause for a beat. "But we'll have to consider a chastity belt."

He throws his head back in a husky laugh. "You may be right about that."

As we leave the house, heading to join the others at the party, I send up a prayer of thanks. Emilia and Paulo Cordeño, Hendy's parents, are looking down on us from heaven, and I want them to know how grateful I am for their one gift—the gift that has changed my life in ways I could never have imagined possible.

Their son, Cristiano "Hendy" Hendrixson.

My very own phoenix who rose from the ashes.

THE END

NOTE FROM THE AUTHOR

For those suffering from PTSD, please know that you are not alone. It's estimated that 22—twenty-two!—veterans take their own lives each day. <u>Please</u> don't make that same choice. You have options (the information below is from the National Center for PTSD website):

    -Call 911

    -Go to the nearest Emergency Room

    -Call the Suicide Prevention Lifeline 1-800-273-8255

    -Contact the Veterans Crisis Line: 1-800-273-8255, press 1 (text 838255)

There are numerous foundations/nonprofits who provide assistance to these men and women who have sacrificed so much for our country and its people. The Battle Buddy Foundation (www.tbbf.org), Combat Wounded Coalition for Wounded Wear (www.facebook.com/combatwoundedcoalition, www.combatwoundedcoalition.org) and Irreverent Warriors (/www.irreverentwarriors.com) are three I'm most familiar with and each do a stellar job at creating awareness as well as organizing activities/outings for our war veterans. My family and I have participated in events held by Combat Wounded Coalition for Wounded Wear and have met the founder, Lt. Jason Redman (Ret.), former US Navy SEAL, who is an incredible individual in his right.

Please know that there are individuals out there who can help you deal with the extraordinary strain of having both the visible and invisible scars of battle.

Dear Reader,

Thank you so much for taking the time to read this book! I'd love to hear what you thought about Presley and Hendy's story. If you would be so kind as to leave a review on the site where you purchased the book, it would be appreciated beyond words. And if you send me an email at rcboldtbooks@gmail.com with the link to your review, I'll send you a personal 'thank you'!

Please know that I truly appreciate you taking time from your busy schedule to read this book! If you'd like to stay up to date on my future releases, you can sign up for my mailing list (I'm the most anti-SPAMMY person ever—promise!) via this link: http://eepurl.com/cgftw5

ALSO BY RC BOLDT

Standalones:
Out of Love
CLAM JAM
BLUE BALLS (Coming August 2017!)

The Teach Me Series:
Wildest Dream (Book One)
Hard To Handle (Book Two)
Remember When (Book Three)
Laws of Attraction (Book Four)

Stay Connected to RC Boldt:

Facebook: https://goo.gl/iy2YzG

Website: www.rcboldtbooks.com

Twitter: https://goo.gl/cOs4hK

Instagram: https://goo.gl/TdDrBb

Facebook Readers Group
www.facebook.com/groups/BBBReaders

Intrigued by Noelle and Foster? Keep reading for a sneak
peek of *Out of Love*.

PROLOGUE

Foster Kavanaugh

"I just got these contracts signed." Noelle Davis, my office manager, puts two files down on my desk. "Tell me again why these people don't allow e-signing?" She huffs out a breath, blowing some stray blond hair off her face while I watch her return to her desk.

And, for the trillionth time, I resist the urge to brush aside her hair for her. Which pisses me the hell off. Because I know the facts:

1. Noelle is off limits as my employee.
2. You never shit where you eat.
3. Noelle is worth her weight in gold since she helps run our office more smoothly than it ever has.

There are probably more facts that will come to me later but right now—I can't think of them. Hell, right now I can barely think. All because this saucy blonde minx is bending over in the pencil skirt she's wearing. Taunting me.

And I know someone—or something, rather—that needs a reminder of those three facts I just listed. And he's currently pressing against my khaki pants as if trying to say, *Target is in range. Ready to attack.*

God, I'm a sick motherfucker.

Running a hand down my face, trying to stifle a groan, I turn my attention back to the updated program details I'm compiling. I run TriShield Protection, a private security consulting firm, here in Fernandina Beach, Florida. We contract out to a specific sector of private businesses along with international airports, training their employees to properly address and deal with any possible attacks, terrorist or otherwise. We also have a bunch of contracts with the local military bases.

After leaving the SEALs, I knew what I wanted to do. I had invested my money wisely and knew, with my credentials and commendations, I'd be a shoo-in for this business. I hired only former military for those carrying out the instructional support and assessments. One of these reasons was because we knew our shit. We knew what would work when faced with someone intent on causing harm to others. We weren't going to be the ones who said garbage like, "Well, according to these studies, it would behoove you to…"

Fuck, no. First of all, I hope to hell I never say the word behoove in my lifetime. But the point is, we aren't pencil pushers. We don't sit behind a desk all day and still think we have our finger on the pulse. We have all been out there, faced death on a near daily basis and know what that's like. We know what to do to stay alive; we all need to try and stay one step ahead of the enemy.

The second reason I hire only former military is because I recognize—fully—how difficult it is to go from having the non-stop brotherhood in the military to civilian life in one fell swoop. It's a transition which most civilians don't understand, as well as why those loud noises put you on alert, why you always sit facing the main entrance of a restaurant, or any establishment, with your back to the wall to best observe any potential threat.

People don't fucking get it.

Just because you leave war and incessant violence behind you—oceans away—doesn't mean it leaves you. It doesn't say, *Oh, Kavanaugh, you're leaving the military? Cool, bro. Sweet dreams at night. I know you'll forget all about shooting that ten-year-old kid aiming an RPG at your men, right?*

Cue the major eye-rolling on that delusional-as-shit comment.

So, here I am. Still trying to give back to my country, trying to keep people safe from assholes intent as hell on taking away our freedom, and still provide support to those in transition. Those like Miller Vaughn and Roman "Doc" Watts, both former SEALs, as well as Langley—"Lee"— Ford, former combat pararescue jumper and the only female hire aside from Noelle, and Kane Windham, former Green Beret.

Yeah, my crew's damn impressive, if I do say so myself. And things had been going smoothly—well, as smoothly as it could before I hired an office manager. The business grew far faster than I had anticipated. But it has been great, no major kinks along the way to deal with. All my employees got along well. Smooth sailing.

Until her. Until Noelle Davis.

Yeah, I just had to hire her. She had been the most qualified and competent applicant, had excellent references from her former job and had passed my "military-style harassment" test with flying colors. God knows I look forward to my daily dose of verbal sparring with her, even though I'm certain she tolerates me because I'm the one who signs off on her paycheck.

And, okay, the woman runs this place like a well-oiled machine. I have to admit that much.

But I should have known there'd be an issue.

I should have known she would be nothing but trouble. Even during the interview, I swear I knew. Like a fucking omen or something. I knew—and let's be honest, my buddy down below really knew—she was trouble.

Trouble. The kind of trouble you want to get yourself into. Pun intended. Also, the kind of trouble you knew you couldn't afford getting mixed up in.

I know what you're probably going to ask; *Then why the hell did you hire her, Foster?*

And I only have one really shitty answer for you.

Evidently I'm one sick, sadistic fucker.

Noelle Davis

"Annie Wilkes. I can't find the file on…" My boss spouts off his newest lovely nickname for me as he asks me for a file I've likely already placed on his desk.

Yeah, we call each other names. Which is just too freaking ridiculous, I know. But it's kind of our … *thing*. It's what we do. We fling jabs, insults, barbs back and forth all. The. Time. The crazy thing?

It started before day one.

"Are you planning on wearing clothing like that all the time, Marilyn?" The brazenness was evident in his tone as we went over my employment contract. As if I hadn't accurately understood what he meant earlier by the whole, "You'll be working around former military. Which means we dish out harassment in mass quantities."

That day I had been wearing a dress similar to the famed white dress Marilyn Monroe had worn in the, "Oops! Is that air blowing up my dress?" movie scene. Mine was yellow and I had paired it with a white button down cardigan. Trust me, it was suitable for the office, knee-length and not showing any bits of flesh in any scandalous manner. Nothing over the top. I was decidedly *not* attempting to be the sex symbol Ms. Marilyn had been.

"Not sure, Shrek," I had shot back without thinking. "Are you planning on being surly all the time?"

For a split second, I damned my mouth and my lack of filter. It had gotten me into trouble before, I'm not going to lie. People had referred to it as being "spunky." But, let's be real here. It's just a nice way of saying I have no filter and I give as good as I get.

However, it didn't seem to faze Foster. At all. Commence the spewing of banter back and forth. And the rest, as they say, was history.

I knew he had done a more thorough background check than most employers do simply because of the job itself. I would have access to a buttload of information—some of it classified, perhaps. So, he had to make sure I was on the up and up. And I was—*er*, am.

Kind of.

Okay, so I may have lied to him at the time of my interview. And I'm pretty certain he knew as soon as it spewed forth from my lips—as soon as I had answered his probing question, "What made you move from Destin to Fernandina Beach?"

I'm not proud of it, but I didn't want to get into it with who I hoped was to be my new boss. Instead, I had given the nonchalant answer of, "I needed a change of scenery, wanted a job where I had more responsibility, and really love the quiet beach town of Fernandina Beach." I also didn't tell Foster the entire truth because a part of me didn't want to jinx anything. Didn't want to tempt fate and have my past, what I was running from—no, *moving on* from—rear its ugly head.

And, let me tell you. Its head is ugly. Actually, more like fugly.

Now, my boss is currently referring to me as the evil woman, Annie Wilkes, from the movie *Misery*. I should also mention that my boss, alpha male galore, also happens to have a body so fine and well-honed, you could ping quarters off of him.

Anywhere. Seriously. A-ny-where. Those quarters would ping off of him and probably take out someone's eye.

And when the man smiles, one of those genuine smiles, and not the mischievous ones reserved for when he and I are trading insults, it's like Fourth of July-style fireworks have erupted. Beautiful. Wondrous. Enough to make even Mother Teresa's lady parts tingle.

I know, I know. Shame on me and my blasphemous thoughts.

As if that's not enough, he has a dog. A dog he adores. A dog he runs with along the beach at the crack of dawn. I only know this because I may have stumbled out onto my back deck of the tiny beach house I rent with coffee in hand to sit and bask in the peacefulness that is the Atlantic Ocean. And, trust me, I would've known that body, that stride, anywhere.

He runs without a shirt, by the way. Think tanned, toned, muscular goodness. Not to mention his short, close-cropped brown hair, and eyes the color of the finest whiskey. And that's all wrapped up in a man who appears to *barely* stand me.

I've clearly got some mad skills when it comes to having my boss *not* like me. But it's a good thing, I promise. Because my lady parts are on a strict lockdown. Think of the part from the first *Lord Of The Rings* movie where Gandalf bellows, "You shall not pass!" That's kind of what's going on for me.

Because I've already been ripped to shreds as it is. By the sole reason I left Destin. My emotions and my self-esteem had plummeted because of that "reason." I knew it would only be a matter of time before things escalated further. That was why I planned my getaway under the radar with only two people knowing my destination. Only two people helped me—the only ones I trusted.

So while I might have to internally scold my vagina for wanting to detach itself from my body and jump into Foster Kavanaugh's arms, I have my reasons for keeping everything else under wraps. Me and men? We're on a serious sabbatical.

I just have to continuously remind my nether regions that while my boss might exude addicting crack-like pheromones, I must resist. I can't afford to make another colossal mistake. Not to mention, I really enjoy my job and coworkers. And it's pretty clear my boss doesn't care for me and only keeps me around because I'm so freaking good at running this office.

So as long as I look and don't touch, it's all good, right?

Um, yeah. I clearly need to work on sounding more convincing.

ACKNOWLEDGMENTS

This book was quite a challenge to write and I shed many tears while doing so. Hendy will always have a special place in my heart.

To the two men whose experiences were interwoven to create Hendy's story, no amount of thank you's will suffice. Your sacrifices, your bravery, and your love for this country and its people is awe-inspiring. *JC*, I know you're giving them a run for their money in heaven, as we speak. I certainly hope I did your story justice in my own way. And *JR*, thank you for being so willing to share the details of your ambush.

My readers! The fact that I actually have readers is just … incredible!! Thank you for choosing to read these books. Without your support, your sweet emails and reviews, and you sharing my books with others, none of this would be possible. I am forever grateful.

My husband and my daughter, thanks for being freaking awesome beyond words.

My parents, for their continued support. And for my mother who has no qualms about telling others to read my books—even the ones with "questionable" titles. Also, FOR THE LOVE OF EVERYTHING THAT'S HOLY, just admit that I'm your favorite child, already. Geez.

Sarah, my Australian BFF. There's no way I could have made it this far without you or our WhatsApp texting, voice messages or phone dates. #LYLT

Amber G., I adore you and your gracious generosity! I'm so incredibly grateful for all of your help!!

Boldt's Beach Babes—you guys are the most stellar

individuals! I am beyond grateful for your support, excitement, and feedback when I share my ideas with you. I'm clearly biased but I think I have the best readers group!! Love you all!!

All the book bloggers out there who have been so wonderful to me! I could never manage to truly show my gratitude for all of your support. Please know that the time you take to read and review my books and/or do promo posts is appreciated beyond words.

My beta readers who spent their own time to comb through my book and help me refine it! You all are freaking stellar and I'm so grateful for your help!!

Kata C., for just being you (which is awesome, by the way). I love you, mi playa.

Lucy—Honestly, I don't know where to begin. It's a pleasure to have you in my life and I'm grateful for the laughter we've shared as well as the never-ending encouragement.

JB—You are a rock star with your eagle eyes and help with everything. Thank you for loving Hendy as much as I do!

Leddy—No words can manage to say how grateful I am for all of your help/insight. The next SS&B lunch date is on me.

Steph—You willingly took on Hendy and Presley and helped me so much! Massive thanks for your time and help with everything!

Brandi—Seriously. I don't know where to start. All I have to say is you are amazing and I adore you!

Linda—Thanks for taking a chance on me and actually putting out. Results, that is. But, really. You've changed everything for me and made me see the possibilities and for that I could never thank you enough.

To wine and coffee (don't judge me, people) for being there when I'm under duress because of deadlines. Without you both, this book wouldn't be possible.

ABOUT THE AUTHOR

RC Boldt is the wife of Mr. Boldt, a retired Navy Chief, mother of Little Miss Boldt, and former teacher of many students. She currently lives on the southeastern coast of North Carolina, enjoys long walks on the beach, running, reading, people watching, and singing karaoke. If you're in the mood for some killer homemade mojitos, can't recall the lyrics to a particular 80's song, or just need to hang around a nonconformist who will do almost anything for a laugh, she's your girl.

RC loves hearing from her readers at rcboldtbooks@gmail.com. You can also check out her website at www.rcboldtbooks.com or her Facebook page www.facebook.com/rcboldtauthor for the latest updates on upcoming book releases.

CPSIA information can be obtained
at www.ICGtesting.com
Printed in the USA
BVOW06s1029020617

485880BV00004B/21/P